THE SKIN BENEATH

THE SKIN BENEATH

NAIRNE HOLTZ

INSOMNIAC PRESS

Library and Archives Canada Cataloguing in Publication

Holtz, Nairne, 1967-   The skin beneath / Nairne Holtz.

ISBN 978-1-897178-39-3

    I. Title.
PS8615.O455S65 2007   C813'.6   C2007-901157-8

The publisher gratefully acknowledges the support of the Canada
Council, the Ontario Arts Council and the Department of Cana-
dian Heritage through the Book Publishing Industry Development
Program.

Printed and bound in Canada

Insomniac Press, 192 Spadina Avenue, Suite 403
Toronto, Ontario, Canada, M5T 2C2
www.insomniacpress.com

For Wendy

"No, facts is precisely what there is not, only interpretations."
— Friedrich Nietzsche, *The Will to Power*

"If you want to keep a secret, you must also hide it from yourself."
— George Orwell, *1984*

PART ONE
QUESTIONS

CHAPTER ONE

Sam unlocks the mailbox in the lobby of her building, takes out a single envelope, opens the back flap to discover a postcard inside. She reads the words on the postcard: "Your sister died while investigating a political conspiracy. Coincidence? How often do women kill themselves with a gun? Think about it."

Sam reads the words on the postcard a second, third, and fourth time with growing discomfort. Her life can't twist apart. It's the new millennium, the year of the future, the year of the anticlimax. Computers failed to crash, and the apocalypse hasn't happened. The postcard is a joke, a hoax. Or is it? When Chloe died, Sam discovered she had been living every day in denial—fully expecting one breath to follow another—perpetual motion for herself and for those she loved. But she learned grief awaits.

As far as Sam knows Chloe didn't shoot herself: she died of a drug overdose in a New York hotel room. But whoever sent Sam the postcard has another, unofficial version of Chloe's death. Getting the postcard is weird, but the allegation itself somehow isn't shocking, isn't inconsistent with her sister's character.

The unsigned words on the postcard are typed onto paper, cut out, and glued to the back. The method isn't as cinematic as clipping words and letters from a magazine, but the intention is the same—to leave no trace of the author. Sam's name and address on the envelope are also typed.

Sam flips the postcard over and regards the image: a naked black man hanging from a white cross. Across the top of the card is the phrase: "Makaveli the Don Killuminati." The artwork is colourful, a narrative realism Sam associates with cartoons and tattoos. She examines the tiny print and learns the image is taken from a Tupac Shakur album cover.

At work Sam googles the name "Tupac Shakur," then adds the search term "conspiracy." (For four years she has been employed as a temp, a job she expected to be temporary.) A quick scan of the first dozen of hundreds of websites informs her that Tupac is a hip hop legend who was murdered in the prime of his career, gunned down in Las Vegas on Friday the 13th of September, 1996. His killer has never been apprehended. Speculation about his death continues to spread like an underground fire—snuffed out on the surface but with heat still consuming the roots below. A website claims Tupac set himself up to die. As evidence, the author of the site points to Tupac's final music video, made a month before he died, which shows the gangster rapper being ushered into heaven, a foreshadowing of his death his fan deems too great a coincidence to be one. Another website claims his death is a disappearing act, and Tupac still walks the Earth, just like Elvis.

Sam spends her lunch hour sitting in a food court staring at the postcard. Chloe died in August of 1995, a year before Tupac Shakur, so it doesn't seem as if the alleged political conspiracy could have had anything to do with his murder. Is the image from the album cover intended to be symbolic? Perhaps someone is telling Sam her sister is a martyr. Who sent the letter? The envelope has no return address, but edged around the stamp is the word "Mexico."

CHAPTER TWO

When Sam was a little girl, she followed her older sister Chloe everywhere. Dogged her. Tagged along, unwanted. Shadow, Chloe would call her.

Chloe was wrong. Sam felt like a real person when she was with Chloe. Sam became a shadow, a slice of herself, when she wasn't with her sister—when Chloe wasn't there.

"Go away," Chloe would say, wrinkling her nose at Sam. When she refused to disappear, Chloe would heave a dramatic sigh before conceding, "Okay, Samantha, you can play with me. You can be the boy."

The boy fetched objects for the girl. The boy built the Blanket Camp. The boy didn't get to put on the denim halter dress worn for the game of Teenage Orphan Attending Her First Disco. Being the boy was punishment, but it never felt that way. Punishment was the time Chloe and Sam played hide-and-seek. Chloe explained the rules to Sam, but the words scattered in her head. Following Chloe's thoughts wasn't as easy as following Chloe because she was ten years old and Sam was four. They played indoors because it was raining. Water filmed along the windowpanes. Their father was cleaning the kitchen while listening to opera. Chloe and Sam went upstairs to his bedroom.

"Put your hands over your eyes," Chloe said.

Through gaps in her fingers, Sam stared at her sister's face, swimming in freckles. Peekaboo. I see you.

"You're not supposed to look," Chloe said.

Sam scissored her fingers shut. Counted down. Counted

to twenty, got mixed up and started over. She opened her eyes. Now I see you, now I don't. She surveyed the room, then checked under the bed and behind the door. She dashed over to the closet, creaked open the folding door. On the floor were Dad's many pairs of shoes: Wallabees, Top-Siders, loafers, and boots. Clutching the sleeve of a sweater, she pulled it to the right. She shifted suits and pants until she reached the back of the closet, where she saw a large black fur coat Mom used to wear. She must have left it behind. A red braid dangled against the dark fur. Sam grabbed the coat.

"Found you."

"You found me," Chloe agreed, as she stepped out of the closet. She didn't sound disappointed. She had wanted Sam to find her. "Okay." Chloe said, "My turn now."

One-two-three-four-five-six-seven-eight-nine-ten-eleven-twelve-thirteen-fourteen-fifteen-sixteen-seventeen-eighteen-nineteen-twenty. "Here I come, ready or not."

Anticipating discovery, Sam stood in the closet, draped in the fur coat where Chloe had been. Sam hadn't grasped the point of hide-and-seek; she thought she was supposed to use the same hiding place. Chloe's footsteps faded as she left the room. Sam waited. Scratched her arms. Wherever the fur came into contact with her body, she itched. At nursery school someone read a story about a girl who covered herself in animal skins and became a wolf who ate people. Her family moved from their village, leaving no forwarding address. The girl tried to hunt them down. She asked people where her family had gone, and when they could or would not help her, she ate them. The emptiness in her belly was filled, but not the emptiness in her heart. Bad girls came to bad ends. If Sam wasn't good, her family would leave. Her mother already had. Sam's heart beat harder, maracas shaking in her chest. She crouched down to get away from the coat, but it slid from the hanger and crashed on top of her. She thrashed the coat out of her way and ran out of the closet.

Sam found her sister downstairs reading a book on the couch. Chloe looked up. She tried for nonchalance, but her eyes glinted with guilt. Sam began to sob. Chloe dropped her book and gathered Sam in her arms.

Sam cried, "I thought you'd never find me. I thought you left me."

Chloe said, "Don't you know I'd never leave you?"

But of course she did.

CHAPTER THREE

Because she has decided to talk to her father about the postcard, Sam doesn't go home after work. Instead she takes the subway north to the part of the city where she grew up, a quiet commuter suburb now awash in traffic, condo construction, and gaudy electronic billboards. She walks the ten blocks from the subway to her father's house. Spring has arrived, bringing a cloying fragrance of lilacs and magnolia blossoms. Yuppie parents drag their kids up and down the street in wagons, as if they are crippled emperors. Sam lived here in a stately, brown, brick house but currently resides in a one-room flat above a store on the west side of the city, close to the University of Toronto, where her father teaches art history, and where she takes various courses but never manages to finish a degree. The west side is home to the birds of the night, the pierced and tattooed set, filmmakers, musicians, or people like Sam who just dress like an artist.

Sam's father opens the door of his house. Kenneth O'Connor is wearing a bow tie—it's his shtick, something to liven up his customary pressed khakis and pale cotton shirts. Sam hasn't seen her father in several months, and his copper hair seems more woven with steel. She's a younger version of her father with the same reddish hair, freckles, square jaw, and thin frame. When her father's colleagues meet her, they think she's his son, not his daughter. Sam passes for a guy until a closer inspection, until someone notices her small breasts and puts them together with her height, which at barely 5'5" is shorter than most men.

"Sam. How unexpected. Tell me, have you had supper?"

"I'm not hungry." Sam *is* peckish, but her father always forgets she doesn't eat meat. Whenever she reminds him, he challenges her vegetarianism. Conservation of non-renewable sources of energy, reduction in the risk of heart disease, the cruelty of factory farming—she scatters reasons like seeds. Although the truth is Sam can't bring herself to chew and swallow a creature who can look her in the eye.

"Would you like something to drink?"

As she takes her shoes off in the foyer, Sam shakes her head, then follows her father into his living room where he reduces the volume on the trill of Baroque issuing from his compact disc player. The room is styled in Danish modern, and Sam sits on one end of a rectangular teak sofa.

Dad picks up a striped bowl from a trolley displaying attenuated vases. "Steven found this at a flea market when he was at a conference last week in the Midwest. Some of the German immigrants who settled in the States brought over Danish ceramics, and he paid five dollars for it."

"Is it Saxbo?" Sam's father and his boyfriend, Steven, collect Scandinavian art pottery and are obsessed with works produced by the Saxbo studio.

He sets the bowl down. "The days of getting Saxbo at a garage sale are gone forever. This is a Rörstrand, but we've always found them pleasing."

"Where's Steven?" Sam doesn't really care. She's glad he isn't around, but she asks about him as a way to stretch beyond the mundane conversations she usually has with her father revolving around his and Steven's consumer choices: what downtown restaurant they tried, where they went for a weekend getaway, and what new pottery they bought.

"He's at the gym." Sam's father sits down in the Swan, a chair with two brown side panels flowing upward in the shape of tucked-in wings.

"That's weird," Sam says. Steven is nothing like the guys

she sees in the gay ghetto with their buff bodies and shaved heads, which make them look as if they just got out of the Armed Forces. Steven teaches at a private boys' school and reminds Sam of a heavily inbred crown prince. He's interested in heraldry and wears ascots.

Dad raises an eyebrow at her. "As much as I wish you would, it isn't like you to drop by. Do you need money?"

Sam crosses her arms. "Have I ever asked you for money? Well...since the winter I was twenty and got laid off? And you gave me a whole fifty dollars." Except when it comes to his personal possessions, her father isn't the type to dole out cash.

"Why Sam, I had no idea you retained such bitterness over that incident." A puckish smile forms on his lips. He doesn't think there is anything wrong with how he behaved. He wrote the original tough-love manual.

"I want to talk about Chloe. Did she shoot herself?" Sam is using the family guerrilla tactics Chloe was known for: the verbal Scud, accuracy questionable.

Her father's smile vanishes, his forehead wrinkles. In his pinched skin, Sam glimpses his geriatric future. "Why are you asking?"

What sort of answer is that? Why isn't he telling her the question is ridiculous? For the first time in her life, Sam raises her voice at him. "You lied! You lied to me! You told me she overdosed. And that it was most likely an accident."

"There were drugs in her system, Percodan." His fingers frame his mouth, signalling his reluctance to give her information. "But yes, she died of a self-inflicted gun wound to the chest. I didn't tell you at the time because I didn't want to add to your distress. In fact, I don't remember mentioning it to anyone besides Steven. How did you find out?"

"Someone sent me an anonymous note." From an ample front pocket on baggy, black cargo pants, Sam withdraws the envelope and postcard and hands them to her father. The only fresh conclusion she has drawn is the person who wrote the postcard was not particularly close to Chloe. The postcard is addressed to "Samantha," not "Sam." When she started school, Sam dropped the long version of her name. But the anonymous author is in possession of a fact she didn't know: a gun caused her sister's death.

As he reads the postcard, Sam's father frowns even more. When he finishes reading, he tucks the card into the envelope and gives it back to her, holding just the edge, as if the envelope contains powdered anthrax spores. Sam waits for him to speak, but he is silent. He leans forward to pluck a discoloured petal from a bouquet of white tulips on the coffee table. The flowers are arranged in the vase with synchronized precision, a corsage of soldiers. Her father is so unlike her sister in taste and temperament. Chloe's favourite flowers were wild roses, the petals of which she cast around her bedroom. She listened to punk, loved *The X-Files*, and read books about political assassinations.

Sam meets her father's gaze. "We both know Chloe was a conspiracy freak."

"Please don't tell me you're going to try to turn what happened to your sister into a conspiracy theory." He sinks back into the chair, closing his eyes. Chloe made Sam and her father watch Oliver Stone movies with her. Sam's father disliked the movies, particularly the Kennedy one. He rejects all conspiracy theory as the simplistic fantasies of crackpots and thought even Oliver Stone could have done better.

Once again, Sam raises her voice. She doesn't yell but comes close. "Don't do this. Don't just dismiss it."

"I understand. You're trying to construct meaning from that which is senseless." He bites off the word "senseless." He is so fastidious in the way he talks about Chloe; direct discussion of her death has become taboo. His discretion keeps his and Sam's emotions in a chokehold. Since they have never openly mourned, their heartache has never abated. Policies of containment are always corrupt.

"Dad, listen. Whoever wrote this…" —Sam pauses to wave the letter—"…was right. Women rarely use guns to commit suicide."

He opens his eyes with reluctance, as if Sam is shining a light into them. Lines like crinkled tissue form in the corners of his eyes, making him look tired. "What is it you want from me?"

Her father never surrenders, never lets anyone else be in charge. Sam has won but doesn't feel triumphant—she feels uneasy at having power over him. "To be able to ask you questions. To have you answer me."

Her father keeps secrets, rarely tells anecdotes, and offers no memories of his life. Chloe pestered him, once asking him how old he had been when he had sex for the first time. He ordered her to her room. To Sam, he says, "What would you like to know?"

"Did the police say she killed herself?"

"She didn't leave a suicide note, so the official police report ruling was death by misadventure."

Sam leans forward on the couch. "Then, theoretically, it's possible someone could have killed her?"

"There weren't any indications of murder. The fingerprints on the gun were hers."

"How could she have gotten a gun?"

"Is that a rhetorical question?" Annoyance sweeps across his face. "I have no idea how she got a revolver anymore than I know what she was doing in New York or…" He stops.

Say it, Sam thinks, say it. You don't know why she would have taken her own life. But the words don't come, the words are clenched in a fist. He may not want to know but she does. She wants to know everything. There are so many questions to which she doesn't have answers that she can't even say whether or not the postcard is a hoax. About a year and a half before she died, Chloe impulsively moved to Montreal. During that time Sam wasn't especially close to her sister, was even somewhat angry with her. Sam has no idea what Chloe was up to in Montreal, where her fascination with conspiracy theories could have led her. Sam only dimly understands the reason for her next question. "Do you remember the name of the pub where Chloe worked in Montreal?"

He shakes his head, then pauses. A flicker of recognition crosses his face. He likes to solve problems, crossword puzzles mostly. "I had to sort out her taxes. She never bothered to file any. According to her T4 slips, she was employed at Le Lapin Blanc."

The White Rabbit, where Chloe, like Alice, fell down a hole.

"Sam, this isn't about Chloe. This is about you."

"That's not true." Irritation pinpricks her. Will he always deflect discussion of Chloe?

Her father's response is to walk over to the couch and put his hand on Sam's shoulder, which makes her realize she's wrong. He's not avoiding the topic of Chloe; he's concerned for Sam. The dry warmth of his fingers is reassuring, but she shifts her shoulder out of his reach. She can't accept his words; she has to shake them off, even as their meaning hooks into her. *This is about you.*

CHAPTER FOUR

Sam couldn't read the numbers on the clock, but lunch had to be soon! Quiet Time, when they coloured and drew pictures, had been going on forever. After sliding out of her desk, Sam walked through a row of kids to the window. She peered out but didn't see Chloe tromping across the parking lot. Cars were zipping in, but her sister was nowhere to be seen.

"Sam, you need to get back into your seat right now!" Behind her glasses, Mrs. Jensen was glaring at Sam.

Sam froze. Her teacher reminded her of an owl about to sink its talons into a mouse. If she moved, her teacher might grab her.

"I mean it, Samantha. I'm getting tired of telling you the same thing every morning." As Mrs. Jensen took a step towards Sam, she dashed to the safety of her desk.

When Chloe finally arrived, Mrs. Jensen had a few words to say to her as well. "I realize picking your sister up from senior kindergarten and returning her to school on time is a big responsibility for an eleven-year-old girl, but if you're not a little more prompt, I'm going to have a talk with your father."

"What a bitch," Chloe said, as they were crossing at the lights on their way home. When they were safely across the street, Chloe extracted her hand from Sam's slightly sticky one, which was covered in glue—the invisible glue that looked like Chap Stick and didn't smell as nice as white glue.

Chloe continued, "Mrs. Jensen hates kids with divorced parents. All the teachers do."

Sam didn't care about her teacher. She was with Chloe, and they were going home to play Restaurant. Their father always took them out to eat at restaurants. Mom used to make their food, Chloe explained. But Mom was gone.

In the kitchen Sam prepared their lunch, an easy assembly of cheese and meat slices on brown bread. She wore a white cap and an apron she tied around her waist, just like Dad when he barbecued during the summer. She poured two glasses of pop. Since she was the Chef, she was allowed to "spice up" their drinks. Sometimes she poured sugar into their pop; other times she added Tabasco or Worcester sauce. Today, she just sprinkled pepper and salt. Then Sam set the dining room table and served the food—she was also the Waiter.

Chloe was the Customer. She was wearing a too-large lady's skirt with lipstick and a purse. "Who am I?" she asked.

Sam shook her head.

Chloe picked up the pop, took a drink, and made a sour face. "Disgusting! Bring me something else immediately!" She leaned over to sniff the drink. "It smells awful, too!"

Sam giggled. Chloe was *so* funny.

"Do you know who I am yet?"

Sam shook her head again. She lifted her sister's drink from the table, ran into the kitchen with it, and poured part of it down the sink. Then she brought it back.

"I'm Mrs. Rich Bitch, and nothing satisfies me," Chloe said.

Right, Sam remembered now. Chloe was also Mrs. Sick Bitch, who was elderly and had problems with inflamed joints, and Miss Movie Star, who wore sunglasses so people wouldn't recognize her, and once she was a barking dog who insisted on eating her food off the floor. Chloe could be anyone, but she was always Sam's sister who made Sam laugh.

CHAPTER FIVE

Sam sheds her life in Toronto. Withdraws a small savings bond, gives her notice to both the temp agency and her landlord. She says goodbye, not so much to people, but to the places where she hangs out. The tattoo parlour where she has put a lot of ink on her arms. Church Street, the gay ghetto, where she celebrates Pride and was once queer-bashed. She takes the streetcar west to Kensington Market, which is where she buys fair trade coffee and vintage men's shirts. Strolling down Spadina, she squeezes by the throngs of Asian immigrants to enter the little stores that sell mangoes and coconut milk. Sam loves cooking, especially food she's never tried before. At times she's too adventurous, buys some hairy rambutans, then doesn't know what to do with them. Sort of the same way she picks up girls.

She has a drink at Ciao Edie, her favourite Toronto bar, named with vicious irony after beautiful loser Edie Sedgwick, the socialite fashion model who died at the age of twenty-eight after a lifetime of drug use, depression, anorexia, and electroshock therapy. Sunday night is women's night at Ciao Edie. Deejay Sick plays drum 'n' bass in a place too small to dance but where the women dance anyway. The bar is below street level and decorated in '60s kitsch. Vinyl furniture and shag carpeting are accented by extravagantly tacky lamps with huge ceramic bases and red and green light bulbs. The furnishings notwithstanding, the place attracts the good-looking, the stylish, even though there's no cover charge and no doorman unhooking a heavy rope for particular people.

And despite the cool factor, Ciao Edie isn't unfriendly. All Sam ever has to do to meet a woman is buy her a drink, and before she knows it, the girl is sitting on Sam's lap. Pushing women out of her life is what is difficult. She seems to specialize in fag hags who morph into femmes, women who change their minds about not wanting a relationship.

CHAPTER SIX

Grief was a bad guy. A monster who swallowed Sam's hunger, a pirate who looted her sleep, an extortionist who kept demanding more, more, more. The only break in the grief invasion came in the form of disbelief, in the expectation that her sister would reappear, come back somehow. At the funeral Sam found herself storing anecdotes with the thought of sharing them later with her sister, which made no sense at all. When Chloe's friend Tory arrived with her mother and a cluster of siblings, she fervently embraced Sam, who barely managed to return the gesture. She had never been all that crazy about Tory. During university Chloe and Tory had stopped hanging out, but prior to that they were each other's only female friend. "The Pre-Raphaelite" was Dad's faintly snarky nickname for Tory. When Sam asked him what he meant, he showed her paintings of pale, serious women with masses of curly hair who did, in fact, resemble Tory. Her long, dark skirts worn with a cornucopia of bedraggled scarves added to the impression of old-world-liness. For the funeral, Tory was dressed in a black dirndl skirt accessorized with a solitary black scarf.

Tory said, "I feel so terrible for you and your father."

Sam didn't know how to reply except to nod.

"I brought you this book." Tory thrust a paperback into Sam's hands.

Trying not to look ungrateful, Sam glanced at the back cover. Another grief book. This one was about the power of physical movement to help "move" a person through grief. Uh huh. Everything would be so much better if Sam took a tango class. In high school, Tory signed up for a lot of modern dance classes and was always dropping the name Isadora Duncan. Sam asked Tory if she was still studying dance.

"I'm taking a belly dancing class for fun, but I decided not to finish my dance degree. I'm thinking of doing something more practical." Tory's gaze shifted over Sam's head.

Standing before them was James—Chloe's high-school boyfriend. With an appropriately somber expression, he said, "Hello, Tory, Sam."

Without returning the greeting, Tory gave him a quick, tight look.

Sam hadn't seen James in years. He seemed smaller in stature. He was wearing trendy red glasses instead of contacts, and his hair was a natural dark brown instead of dyed. Except for the black jeans and shirt, he no longer looked like a punk musician. Was he wearing black for the funeral, or did he still wear black to be cool? Sam wore black to be cool but had acquired a new respect for the traditional use of black clothing as a declaration of mourning. It was, after all, the perfect way to let everyone know about a loss. You didn't have to wade your way through awkward conversations, but people knew to leave you alone, to cut you some slack. Why, exactly, had widow's weeds gone out of fashion?

Tory spoke. "I should see how my mother and sisters are doing. Bye, Sam."

She left without a word to James. Sam wondered, had the two of them dated? There was definitely some lingering drama between them. Sam would have to get the whole story from Chloe. Oh right, Sam couldn't. How could she keep forgetting?

Sam felt a pressure against her shoulder. Even though he had never been the type to hug, James had just given her a squeeze.

He said, "Sam, I'm so sorry. It's awful what you must be going through. I, um, brought you some Almond Roca. I remembered you always liked it. I put it over on the table where people are putting food."

Sam stared at him. The old James would have said, "This sucks. I bet you feel like crap." The old James had told her he couldn't understand how she could eat Almond Roca: it looked like rice-covered dog turds. Sam heard herself ask James if he was still in a punk band.

"No. I just do a little composing at home on my computer. I'm at Ryerson, studying graphic design."

Sam had once thought of him as a comet ready to shower the world, but his aura of notoriety seemed to have been extinguished. Perhaps he had never been larger than life. Perhaps Chloe had just convinced Sam that James was the next Sid Vicious.

Although the months after her sister's death seemed excruciatingly slow, Sam kept losing time. Events slipped from her memory like change from a pocket with a hole. She would forget a movie after watching it. The only part of the funeral she remembered was talking to Tory and James. She had listened to the minister speak, saw her father stand up and make a speech, but none of it stuck in her head. Only her conversations with Chloe's friends were sufficiently absorbing for Sam to later notice neither of them had talked about their own grief. Nor did they express surprise over Chloe's drug overdose.

People said stupid things to Sam: "It must be getting easier." "It's terrible when young people get into drugs." She wanted to snarl at them, wanted to snap back equally inappropriate comments: "Yeah, so much worse than seniors on crack." But, of course, she didn't. No excuse for rudeness, stiff upper lip and all that.

People were impatient with grief. Sam understood; grief was boring, immersing yet boring. She read the grief books, which, beneath the sympathy, were just as intolerant and demanding. Grief was a process, badges to be merited, hoops to be jumped through, twelve-steps to be worked, in short— achievements. Not very helpful for her. She'd always been a bit of an underachiever.

The only concession Sam would make was the worst moment was over. Seeing Chloe's body had been the worst moment. Or rather, seeing her head. From the neck down she was covered with a sheet. Her face reminded Sam of a figure in a wax museum. Never before had she worn makeup so tastefully. Sister-doll, Sam kept thinking, sister-doll. She leaned over to kiss her sister's cheek, to regard her sister's face one last time. Sister-doll, your skin is so cold. Dad, you go in the hearse. Dad, you toss sister-doll, what's left of her, into the crematorium. Sam couldn't do it.

CHAPTER SEVEN

Someone will always tell you where an ex-lover can be found, but a dead sister isn't as easy. All Sam has is her sister's old address in Montreal, where she lived with a female room-mate, and the name of the pub where Chloe worked.

Sam moves to Montreal with a suitcase, a sleeping bag, and a knapsack. She leaves her furniture with her father, in-cluding the pieces she inherited from Chloe: an oak lawyer's bookcase with glass doors and a Victorian chaise longue. Chloe, who liked antiques, had purchased them at an auction.

Beside the river, in the Montreal neighbourhood of Ver-dun, Sam rents a tiny apartment on a month-to-month lease. The place is above a store. The hardwood floors are criss-crossed with gouges and tilted enough for a pen to roll, and the paint is peeling from the mouldings and wainscotting. As Dad's boyfriend would say, the place "screams faded charm." But the price is right: two hundred and fifty dollars plus util-ities. What spare money Sam made from various jobs went into inking her arms with tattoos, buying clothes, and going out to Ciao Edie.

She would like to rent on the Plateau, the neighbour-hood on the side of the mountain where her sister had lived, but it is too expensive. According to an article in *The Montreal Mirror*, the free English arts weekly, artists and lower-income people are getting thrown out of their homes on the trendy Plateau because their landlords are selling their buildings to condominium developers.

On her first day in Montreal, Sam goes to the Plateau.

Walks west from St. Denis Street to St. Laurent Boulevard, the dividing line in Montreal between east and west addresses. She then heads north in the direction of her sister's old apartment. Along the way she wanders into a few vintage clothing stores and vinyl record shops. She also stops for a beer at Miami, a bar she recalls Chloe mentioning. It's a punk palace of decay where three people try to sell her drugs. While punks beg on the Plateau, Miami appears to be the only place where they drink. Yuppie colonization is at hand. St. Denis has a Gap and a Starbucks, and St. Laurent has fancy furniture stores and overpriced fusion restaurants serving vertically stacked entrées.

The duplex where Chloe lived is in the north end of the Plateau. Sam rings the bell on the bottom floor. A woman with grey curly hair answers the door. "*Oui?*"

Even though she has taken two French courses at university, in which she received high marks, Sam doesn't know how to answer. The nasal jabber she hears doesn't bear much relationship to the Parisian French she learned at school. In the streets of Montreal people speak the language of *tourtière*, not Molière.

"*Excusez-moi, est-ce que vous parlez anglais?*" Speaking French, Sam feels self-conscious, as if she's wearing a long, dark fur coat, something nineteenth century and Russian. She wants to fling the coat into the gutter but can't move her arms.

"Yes? What is it?"

Sam explains who she's looking for, even though she knows this woman can't be her sister's former roommate—the woman is too old. Chloe hung out with her roommate, whom Sam remembers as being around the same age as her sister. Unfortunately, she can't remember anything else her sister said about her roommate.

"I just bought the building. There's just me and my boyfriend now—we're making it a cottage. I don't know the persons who used to live here," the current occupant tells Sam.

Around the corner from Chloe's old place is a funky café. Peering through the window, Sam sees a purple and yellow room with worn floors the colour of blackened nuts. She can imagine Chloe having coffee here. Sam goes inside. A CD of Hindi hop plays a masala of drum beats and sitar licks. Clove cigarettes perfume the air, and a chalkboard announces various vegetarian specials. This is hippy-dippy land where the citizens tend to be progressive and gentle. Sam sits down in a wooden booth, made more comfortable with the addition of silk-covered pillows. Art lines the walls—multiple portraits of a short-haired, Bambi-eyed girl stitched onto brown velvet.

A waitress hands Sam a menu. The waitress is cute with short hair, tattoos, and low-slung jeans. Her style is boyish, but she isn't. She seems familiar: she is the girl in the pictures on the wall.

"Are you the artist who did the pictures?" Sam gestures around the room.

The waitress uses her tongue to spin her lip piercing around. "Do you like them?"

"They're great," Sam lies.

"They're all for sale." Her eyes flick from Sam's face to her clothes. Sam isn't sure if she's being checked out or, more likely, having the cost of her wardrobe calculated to see if she has potential as a patron of the arts.

Sam hands the menu back. "I'll just have some mint tea."

The waitress tilts her head to the side. "Nothing else?"

"Can you tell me if this place has been around long?"

"A little over a year."

A year. Chloe moved to Montreal from Toronto more than six years ago, lived on the Plateau for almost two years during 1994 and 1995. But there are few traces of Chloe or of the *outré* charm that drew her there in the now-gentrified neighbourhood. Sam sets splayed fingers on the striped brown and orange Latin American blanket being used as a tablecloth. She grinds her hands downwards in frustration, wishing she could leave. Instead she waits for her tea to arrive, drinks a cup, and leaves the waitress a too-generous tip.

CHAPTER EIGHT

During the Christmas of 1994 Chloe came back from Montreal to visit Sam and her father for a week. Chloe had been living in Montreal for nearly a year and looked completely different. Her goth aesthetic had been restyled into grunge, and she gave Sam a copy of Hole's *Live Through This*. Dad told Chloe, "You look like you're going camping." She was wearing a toque indoors, had stopped dyeing her long hair black, and was twisting the ends of it into dreads. She was also wearing bright colours, which Sam hadn't seen her sister do since she was a kid: flared red and purple cords, woven bracelets, and tight white T-shirts layered over long-sleeved shirts. But it wasn't Chloe's new sloppy cool that made her seem so changed. It was something else altogether—Chloe was happy. It was funny because, to Sam, it was the year of the dead: Kurt Cobain killed himself in the spring, and hundreds of thousands of people were murdered in Rwanda over the summer, but Chloe was light of heart. Was it the pot she smoked every afternoon when Sam got back from school? Sam was in grade thirteen, her final year. Grade twelve had been better, or more exciting anyway, but whatever, she would be done soon.

When Sam entered her room, she found Chloe lying on the bed, croaking along to a Cypress Hill CD she later left behind. Looking up at Sam, Chloe said, "Hip hop is so punk rock. I can't believe it was missing from my life."

"Do they play hip hop where you work?" Sam asked, chucking her knapsack onto the floor and joining her sister on the bed.

"Nah," Chloe said. "My boyfriend got me into it."

"Your boyfriend?" Ah ha, the reason Chloe was all smiley-faced. She hadn't had a boyfriend in ages. In fact, Sam wasn't sure Chloe had gone out with anyone since she had broken up with James.

"Yeah, he calls me 'his lady.' He's hilarious."

Sam could imagine him, a long-haired pothead with a bong and a toque matching Chloe's, following her around like a puppy dog. Did Chloe love him? Had they been going out for long? Sam wanted to ask these questions but didn't because Chloe hadn't asked Sam about her love life, not even the obvious question: where's Dyna these days? Since Chloe had moved, she had sent one lame postcard, saying she was living in a cool neighbourhood with a cool roommate. Sam, who was still mad at her sister, hadn't responded. How do you fight with someone you love who lives somewhere else? It was easier to forget their earlier problems, except Sam didn't entirely.

A toke was held out to Sam who sucked the weed into her lungs. The beat of the rap song took over the space in her head. An MC intoned the lyrics in a nasal whine alongside a crush of bass, beats, and guitar licks.

In the evenings, Sam and Chloe played Scrabble in the dining room with their father. Beneath the closed French doors leading to the kitchen, an aroma of fresh herbs wafted. Inspired by their recent trip to Tuscany, Steven was cooking Italian food. He was ten years younger than Dad and had been his student. In the beginning Steven was Dad's pal, a gay guy their father hung out with, but then, after Chloe moved out and Steven moved in, Sam drew the now-obvious conclusion that he was her father's partner. "So Dad's come out," Chloe said. "I guess," Sam said, although he hadn't discussed it with her. She wondered how long it had taken Chloe to work out that their father was gay, but before Sam could ask, Chloe did a swishy imitation of Steven adjusting his cravat. "Who am I?" Chloe asked, giggling. When Sam didn't laugh, didn't answer, didn't do anything besides look at the wall, Chloe stopped.

On Chloe's last night, she proposed a game of poker, something else she had learned from her new boyfriend. Although Sam had never played before, she was a natural. Chloe was a dreadful player—she called too much and didn't raise enough—while Dad was a shark. The three of them played for black olives. After half an hour Dad had a giant storehouse of them, Sam had a modest pile, and Chloe had a lousy three. Dad kept bluffing them on hands that weren't very high. Then he said, "All or nothing for this round."

Sam decided to fold while Chloe matched her father. They turned their hands over: Chloe had three of a kind, Dad had a straight flush. A smug smile hovered on his lips while she handed over her remaining olives.

Steven paraded into the dining room bearing pink glass dishes of tiramisù. Chloe glanced up at him, lifted her hand, and slammed it down on her father's pyramid of olives, which rolled everywhere. One mushed olive flew into Steven's gelled hair. His cheeks went red, but he didn't say anything.

Fuck, Sam thought. Up to now, Chloe's visit had been refreshingly peaceful.

Dad plucked an olive from his lap. "You're being quite the poor loser."

Chloe squished olives into a tight fist, which she raised, and Sam wondered if her sister was going to throw the olives at their father, Steven, or the wall.

The wall.

Chloe amplified the drama. "Do you know why you're so good at poker, Dad? It's because you spent your life faking it, faking Mom was the bad guy, faking you weren't a homo. Now you expect us to act like it's just so cool you've got this... this gay concubine."

Sam's insides became her outsides. Did Chloe dislike Steven because he was a man or because he was their step-whatever? He was scowling at Chloe, which Sam could understand. She, too, felt as if she had just been attacked by Chloe. Sam swung her head in her father's direction, but his expression was hooded. Any anger he felt he muzzled. In a calm tone, he said to Chloe, "I see you still like to toss tables." Then he stood up, took a bowl from the kitchen counter, and began to clean up the olives. As was his way, he declined to play.

Chloe slowly lowered her hand, letting more olives tumble onto the floor. "You're a fucking hypocrite," she said, stalking out of the room.

The hypocrisy of adults had always been Chloe's drum loop, a synthesizer riff she relentlessly played, even though she was now an adult. An adult who couldn't quite hide her glee over the exposure of her father's sins; payback, Sam thought, for all the ways in which her sister failed to measure up in their father's eyes. Sam used to believe everything Chloe said. Now Sam knew better.

CHAPTER NINE

Downtown Montreal is an odd amalgam of the sacred and profane. Strip joints bump up against cathedrals, which are wedged between malls and stores. You can pray, as well as buy brand-name clothing, beer, and lap dances within a one-block radius. The pub where Chloe worked has a sign in the window: "*Plongeur demandé.*" Sam remembers the word "*plongeur*" from reading George Orwell's *Down and Out in Paris and London*; a dishwasher is needed. She enters Le Lapin Blanc and asks the bartender for an application. After she finishes writing down her not terribly relevant work experience, she tells the bartender her sister worked here. This information makes him regard her with more interest. He tells her to wait; he'll get a manager. He presses buttons on a phone, and a thirtysomething guy named Jack comes downstairs and introduces himself to Sam as the general manager. After scanning her resumé, he hires her on the spot, even though he didn't know Chloe. He hasn't been around long, he explains, and there's a lot of turnover. No one seems to make a career out of this place, he adds. Then he frowns as if he is worried his frankness might lead to her refusing the job. Sam feels like telling him not to worry. She has her own agenda, and her limited French makes it impossible for her to work in an office. When he asks her if she can come in later that night, she agrees.

He gives her a little tour. There's a big kitchen; Le Lapin Blanc serves a lot of food. They are half bar, half restaurant, he explains. Enough of a restaurant to be known for their thick steaks and homemade french fries. Upstairs on the second floor people come to play chess. The manager points out the floor, which is tiled in black and white like a chess set. Both the upstairs and downstairs have framed pictures on the walls of the characters from *Alice in Wonderland*: the Walrus, the Cheshire cat, Tweedledee and Tweedledum, the Red Queen, and, of course, the White Rabbit.

Sam barely has time to get back to her apartment, shower, eat, and return. As she steps out of Guy metro, she reads the graffiti written across a boarded-up building: "Montreal Equals Collective Alienation." A little further on, there's a picture of the federal Conservative Party leader with a bubble coming out of his mouth: "We're Going to Party Like It's 1939." Sam grins; she has a feeling she's going to like living in Montreal. But why is the graffiti in English? Is it some sort of Anglo backlash against the language laws dictating signs must be in French? She passes Concordia, an English university, and realizes, no, the graffiti was just written by students.

In the locker room at work, she puts on what the manager calls "kitchen whites": a long-sleeved white shirt and apron, and black and white checkered pants. She has to roll up both the shirt sleeves and pant legs—there aren't any women's sizes. A white cap tamps her crewcut down.

The manager brings her upstairs to the dishpit at the back of the kitchen, where she is introduced to her freakishly tall co-worker, Lemmy. His hair is pulled into a ponytail and dyed shoe-polish black, which has the effect of enhancing the paleness of his skin. He is hunched over, scrubbing a pot with steel wool. His arms are so long that Sam can imagine him boxing with impunity, inflicting damage while remaining out of reach of his opponent.

When he looks up, he tells her, "They've never hired a girl for the pit before." He pauses, then adds, "I hope you're not into Sarah McLachlan because I'm a metal head."

He shows Sam how to wash the dishes and run them through the Hobart machine. It seems straightforward. Then he gives her a tour of the kitchen: here's the line where the food is cooked and you stock plates; here are the silverware bins; here's the supply area where you get more rags and dish-washing soap; and here's the walk-in fridge, but you don't re-ally need to go in there. Back at the dishpit, he puts a Slipknot CD into his boom box. Over the thrash of drums and guitar riffs, Lemmy expounds on his philosophy of metal.

"Headbangers are not devil worshippers," he explains. "What metal is saying is we can conquer Satan with rock and roll."

"I don't believe in Satan," Sam says.

"He wants you to believe he doesn't exist. That way you don't step up and fight evil. You're just a poor fuck it hap-pens to." Lemmy snaps a pair of tongs in the direction of an older Asian man with thick glasses who is cutting vegetables across from them. "Right, Dang?" Dang grunts.

While Lemmy sprays the dishes with water, Sam stacks plates. Lemmy asks her if she's a student.

"No, I just moved to Montreal and don't speak much French."

"I'm what you call a yuffie," he says.

"What's that?"

"A young urban failure. I've worked here longer than any other person except the lady who does the bookkeeping."

Sam feels her heart pound. "My sister used to work here. Did you know Chloe O'Connor?"

"Chloe?" Lemmy stops cleaning the plates. "Yeah, I re-member her. She died, right?" He gnaws on his lower lip, re-vealing teeth that are like bent spokes in a wheel. "Busgirl who liked to smoke up. A couple times, me and her put our money together on payday to get some quality dope. Hey, do you smoke?"

"Once in a while." Because Sam thought Chloe overdosed, Sam made a promise to herself not to take drugs. But last year she broke her vow and tried ecstasy.

"Man, no one will go in with me. Once I asked Dang, and you know what he said?" Lemmy pauses to wave the nozzle in Dang's direction, gushing water onto the tiled walls. "In his country everyone grows pot in their backyard. Powerful shit. Thick like a tree. He bought some here once, and when the guy told him how much it was, Dang thought he was joking. Isn't that right, Dang?"

Dang is slitting lines of fat from a roll of veal and doesn't slow his pace when he answers. "In Cambodia everyone smoke, even my grandmother. In the afternoon, when everyone have their nap, the only people who smoke were old people."

Sam doesn't understand. "Why just old people?"

"Because they been doing it so long they could go to work afterwards. Heh-heh." Dang chuckles like an animated villain.

"Wild, eh? Just talking about it makes me want to go outside and smoke a big doobie," Lemmy says.

A waiter lurches into the dishpit and grabs plates from a pile Sam stacked. He says, "We're down a busboy and we're in the juice. Two of the bus stations are empty. Help me bring out plates."

Sam gathers as many as she can. Staggering under their weight, she follows him into the dining area. He takes off while a busboy rushes over to snatch the plates from her arms. Someone else shows her where the bus station is, and she restocks it with various dishes. When she gets back to the kitchen, everyone is on fast-forward. Lemmy is sorting cutlery for anxious waiters, and he yells at her to run the dishes through. A manager comes in to announce they're slammed, which Sam instantly grasps means busy. The order machine steadily spits out chits. For the next few hours, she works as quickly as she can. Her arms ache, but she doesn't mind. She learns the rhythm of spreading a stack of plates apart like a deck of cards with her left hand while washing them with her right. She likes having her thoughts reduced to a single focus: making dishes sparkle. She's living in the now, *Zen and the Art of the Hobart*. Cleaning up is not as meditative.

Lemmy says, "I'll get the mop and do the floor. You can do the sink and wipe down the machine."

"Sure." Sam bends over water dotted with bits of noodles, which she examines as if she were reading tea leaves. Had Chloe liked working here? The only job Sam remembers her having was a position at the university admissions office, which their father found for her one summer. She was fired for being "brusque." She didn't mind losing the job, but Dad was furious. Dirty water slops onto Sam's sneakers, pushing the memory aside, and she begins to scrub out the inside of the Hobart machine. When she finishes, she notices two small, square metal pans set in an unobtrusive corner. The dishes are encrusted with béchamel sauce.

Sam points the pans out to Lemmy, who has just returned from putting the mop away. "I didn't see those."

Wiping his sweaty cheeks with his apron, Lemmy says, "No problem. Grab them and come with me." He motions towards the exit door, which is propped open with a broken broom handle. Sam follows him down an alley to a blue Dumpster with an attached trash compactor. He reaches his hand out to her and she gives him the metal containers, which he tosses into the compactor. The compactor makes a hideous grinding sound and shakes back and forth but manages to destroy the pans.

"I can't believe you just did that. Are you trying to impress me?"

"No, I do this all the time." Lemmy takes a mashed pack of cigarettes from his front pocket and holds them out. "You want one?"

Sam shakes her head, and Lemmy lights one for himself,

leaning with his back against the Dumpster. His cigarette doesn't quite mask the pungent and competing odours of bleach and rotting garbage. The sky is clouded over and no stars are visible. Goosebumps break out on Sam's arm, and the sweat on her back grows slippery and cool. It is April, but the menace of winter has not yet left.

Sam shoves her hands into her pockets. "Did my sister have any close friends here?"

Lemmy inhales longer than Sam thinks is possible. "She used to go out with Omar."

Omar. The name seems faintly familiar. Was that the name of Chloe's boyfriend, the one who liked hip hop? Sam asks Lemmy if Omar still works at Le Lapin Blanc.

"Nah. He used to be a bouncer here, but now he runs an escort agency. Least that's what he told Joe last time he was in."

"Who's Joe?"

"Bartender who works the day shift." Lemmy suddenly squints at Sam, his focus tightening like a camera lens. Before he can ask her why she's asking him so many questions, she tells him she'll see him inside. She hurries back into the kitchen, then goes to get changed into her street clothes. Omar's name ricochets through her head.

When she emerges from the locker room she finds Lemmy still in his kitchen whites, sitting at the bar with a pint in front of him. He invites her to join him, but she tells him "another time" and hopes he won't ask again. Instead of taking the metro to her apartment, she decides to walk. She wants to be by herself, not packed in beside other people.

An icy wind whizzes through her black bomber jacket. Montreal is colder than Toronto. White teenage punks who have their hair fashioned into tropical cockscombs approach Sam with their hands out, calling *"un peu d'change, un peu d'change."* She gives a girl a dollar and heads south to an industrial area, empty of people, even the homeless. When she turns west on Wellington, she sees the first signs of gentrification: a few refurbished Victorians among low, square brick buildings. The shadowy presence of the middle class is disturbing rather than reassuring—a bottle thrown across the barricades of class warfare. A man with hair the colour of old teeth stands in a doorway drinking a quart bottle of beer. He watches her without moving his head, only his eyes. Because men assume she's a guy, Sam usually doesn't have to feel scared when she walks alone at night, but this man frightens her. His eyes are empty, eerie. Her gender and sexual orientation are less important than the fact that she's smaller than he is. She forces herself not to run, not to show fear. When she reaches Verdun, which is much busier, she realizes she's half-holding her breath. She lets out her breath but still feels edgy. She hurries by dollar stores, pawnshops, and still-open pizza joints. A couple of young thugs walking a pair of bull terriers shuffle by her without a glance. They just roll past. When she gets to her apartment, she runs up the spiral staircase, unlocks her door, then locks it from the inside.

Sam finds out from Joe, the bartender, that Omar runs an escort agency called Arabian Nights. After work she checks the name in the Yellow Pages at a pay phone. Only a phone number is provided, no address. She dials the number. "Hi, can I speak to Omar?"

A female voice replies almost automatically, "He's not here right now. Would you like to leave a message?" Sam leaves her first name and phone number.

He doesn't call. She tries again but he's not there. Apparently he's never there. After her fourth call in four days, the voice on the other end asks Sam what her business is with him. "Uh, personal," Sam says. A frosty pause follows. This time, Sam leaves her first and last name.

Days trickle by. No phone call.

Sam cleans her apartment. Scrubs the kitchen cupboards, the top of the stove, the counters. Mops the floors. She tackled the bathroom when she first moved in but not the bathroom cabinet. As she's wiping down the drawers, she finds an old kaleidoscope. When she was a kid, she had one. Her father gave it to her for her birthday. She remembers lying on her back on the lawn with the kaleidoscope pressed to her eye, bewitched by the medley of colour. But when she peers through the kaleidoscope left behind in her bathroom, the glass inside is greasy, and the colours don't give her the same thrill. Disappointing. During Chloe's last visit, she played with Sam's kaleidoscope. She was stoned and giggled like a kid; perhaps pot brings back the magic. Chloe must have taken the kaleidoscope because Sam hasn't seen it since. If Chloe had asked, Sam would have given it to her.

Sam spins the kaleidoscope-end around. Sees a volcano of blurring colour: a circle becomes a star becomes a pentagram. The light and colour are created by reflection, by a jigsaw of mirrors, which she knows because she did a grade school science project on kaleidoscopes. She continues twisting the end, shifting the perspective.

During a break at work Sam reads a ratty copy of *The Montreal Mirror*. The classified section is full of ads for escort agencies, most of which seem to be hiring, and it gives her an idea. When she gets back to her apartment, she calls Arabian Nights and tells the woman who answers the phone she's looking for a job. A Saturday afternoon interview is offered to her. After she hangs up, she feels her stomach do a free fall she remembers from fair rides: a cocktail of pleasure and fear. If Omar doesn't interview her, she will at least know where he works. But if he does interview her, how will she pretend to be a prostitute? She slept with a woman whom people paid to watch on a webcam, but Sam has never met anyone who fucks for money. What is she going to wear to the interview? She doesn't have anything besides shirts and jeans. She doesn't need to thumb through her closet to check; she just isn't the kind of woman who owns a little black dress.

Arabian Nights is in Chinatown. Sam walks south on St. Laurent through sex trade central, an intersection of streets lined by taverns and peep shows. Pigeons coo, drunks panhandle, and hookers conduct their business in a combination of French and English: "*Pour un* blow job? *Cinquante.*" The smell of fried onions and steamies from *casse-croûtes* competes with the smell of decomposing vegetables. Asian groceries sell shiny eggplants and knobby lychees out of wooden crates. Walking under the imperial-style arches demarcating Chinatown, Sam reaches rue de La Gauchetière, a crooked street paved with bricks where she passes noodle houses and vendors selling sunglasses and baseball caps. She finds the address of Arabian Nights in an industrial building on a side street.

A freight elevator with a barred cage brings her to the third floor. She walks along a wide hall with hardwood floors and a pop machine. Several office suites emit a curious whirring noise. Sam peeks into an open doorway and sees a group of women varied enough to be a United Nations delegation operating industrial sewing machines. First World sweatshops. Is locating an escort agency next to them a recruiting strategy?

The door is locked at the agency suite, so Sam rings the bell. A woman addresses Sam through an intercom, then releases the lock. Sam finds herself in a waiting room, where a trim East Indian woman clad in jeans and a silk tunic sits behind a receptionist's desk. The woman doesn't say anything, just motions Sam to an empty chair. Also seated is a chubby white girl who is wearing a ruffled denim skirt. I should have bought a cheap skirt, Sam thinks. Instead, she's in her usual black jeans with a Bettie Page T-shirt, which seemed like the most sex-workerish item among her clothes. While the girl beside her reads *Elle* magazine, Sam picks up an English newspaper and scans the headlines. She feels as if she's at the dentist's.

"Omar is ready to see whichever one of you has a three o'clock appointment," the receptionist announces. Sam stands up, and the receptionist clangs an iridescence of bracelets in the direction of the hall beyond her desk.

Omar's office is the only room at the end of the hall. He's sitting behind a substantial desk, which appears to be made of solid oak. When Sam enters the room, he stands up. He has dark eyes, dark hair, and skin shaded just deep enough to announce he isn't white. Chloe said her boyfriend was a hip hop fan, yet Sam expected him to be white. She's not sure why. Is it just hard to imagine her punky, petulant sister dating someone so different from herself? Sam continues staring at him. There's a fullness to his face, a pout to his cheeks and lips, a dollop of femininity, which makes him much more attractive than average. He's medium height with shoulders that tell her he has a gym membership and a belly that suggests he skips the cardio machines. While he appears to be in his early thirties, he's dressed in baggy nylon sweats and a Lakers jersey with the sleeves pushed over his elbows. Before sitting back down on his padded black leather chair, he gestures to Sam to park herself in a flimsy wooden chair in front of his desk. Folding his sinewy arms across his chest, he asks, "Have you worked as an escort before?"

"Nope." In fact, she guesses she has less experience than anyone who has walked through this door—she's never had sex with a man. She braids her legs together under the chair.

"Why do you want to work here?" Omar mad-dogs her. He is trying to intimidate her and is succeeding.

"To make money." Sam attempts to sound hard, like

she's been around the block, but she knows she just sounds like a bluffing kid with the wrong answer to a math question.

Omar leans back in his chair, lifts his hands over his head, and clasps them together. "Is there a special reason you need money?"

"Um, no." Sam supposes most women don't like prostituting themselves so Omar wants to know what will keep them at the job. Although she has been hired at places where she didn't want to work, this is tough. She feels as if she's taking an acting class: what's my motivation?

Omar places his forearms back on his desk. "I'll be real. I hire light-skinned black women, Asian girls, and goths."

Sam stares at him. "Goths?"

"You know, white girls who dress like vampires. They're popular with the leather-and-chains crowd. But I don't think I can sell you. From what I can see of it, your body's fine. I have females who would want to get with you, but you aren't their husbands' type. Masculinity in a woman is hard to live up to. Personally, I like the idea of sleeping with a woman who could beat me up, but I'm not most guys."

Sam blushes. No one has ever evaluated her sex appeal before, and she's never known a straight person to do anything besides slide around the fact of her being queer. "I'm not here about a job."

Omar gets up, walks to the door, and closes it before returning to stand over Sam in her chair. A penetrating aftershave surrounds her. Maybe he won't notice she's sweating.

He flashes white teeth in a smile. Claps a hand on her shoulder, hard, and asks her in a perfectly cordial tone: "What the fuck do you want then?"

His tough guy routine is out of a Hollywood movie, but the performance is practised, almost ironic. The intelligence and detachment in his eyes warn her this is just his warm-up act, and that gives her the creeps. She decides not to lie to him. As she looks up at him, her story rushes out. "I already have a job. I wash dishes at Le Lapin Blanc where you used to work with a woman named Chloe. I'm her younger sister, Sam."

Omar's grin evaporates, water turning to steam on a hot grill. "That was a bitch move. Why weren't you truthful?"

She lowers her gaze. "I left you a couple messages, but you didn't call me back."

Omar scowls. "If I want someone to get a hold of me, I give them my cell." He pauses. "I forgot Chloe had a sister named Sam. I didn't put it together."

"If you had, would you have agreed to see me?"

"Maybe, maybe not." Omar strides to the window at the back of his office and gazes out at the market stalls along the streets of Chinatown. He looks as though he'd rather be among the coloured baubles from Hong Kong, the gelatinous buns, and the funk of fish. But then he wheels around and stares at her, his face rigid. "So why're you here? Tell me. Now."

Either he's a volatile guy or talking about Chloe gets to him, Sam thinks. In a gentle voice she says, "I just want to know what Chloe's life was like in Montreal."

The tension seems to drain from him. His expression doesn't exactly soften, but he no longer looks angry. She said the right thing or, rather, didn't say the wrong thing. Intuitively she understands there is something he doesn't want to tell her, something she is not supposed to ask. If she asked him the wrong question, he would have thrown her out.

He says, "Your sister wasn't the type of girl I ever thought I'd be with. She was so serious. At work, I was always bugging her, asking her, 'What're you thinking about? How come you don't talk to no one?' After a while, we talked. And it was like she could really feel my shit. It was special with her. She wasn't like other girls, even smelled different. Didn't wear Chanel or Obsession but some kind of oil."

"Patchouli." Sam can almost smell it. Can see the little jar of glistening, dark liquid sitting on the bathroom shelf.

"Yeah, that's it." A hesitant smile plays across his lips. He leans over his desk, traces a whorl in the wood with his fingers. To Sam, it seems as if he's caressing a memory of his own of Chloe. Then he glances at the flashing light on his phone and straightens his posture. Picking up the phone, he cups it with one hand. "Listen, I've got more girls to interview. Why don't you come with me to a party tonight? There's someone I want you to meet. She used to live with your sister."

The roommate. Sam was on a roll. "Where's the party?"

"Give me your address. I'll pick you up around midnight." Omar pushes a pen across the desk, then taps his finger on top of a pile of business cards held in an antique brass holder.

Stalling for time, Sam examines the business card. Below a logo of a cocktail glass are the words "exotic, elegant, multilingual escorts." How did he go from working in a bar to running an escort agency? What would Chloe think if she were alive? Sam wants to ask Omar about his relationship with her sister, but instead she flips the card over, writes her phone number and address on the back, and gives it to him.

He slides the card into a drawer. "You know, I can tell in five minutes whether a woman can do this job or not. What did you think of the woman sitting next to you?"

Sam shrugs. What she can remember is the woman seemed neither exotic nor elegant, but then most businesses engage in misleading advertising. Is his question a test of her intelligence or is he bonding with her about girls, which some straight men like to do with dykes? He seems to want her to like him, which isn't the same as him liking her. While she's curious about him, she can't say she likes him. He's nothing like her sister's high-school boyfriend. He's not like anyone she's ever met.

Sam asks, "Do you ever hire someone, even if you don't think they're going to work out?"

"Yeah, but it never pays." Omar walks her to the door. He pauses before extending his hand to her. His handshake is a bit too firm. The next potential recruit totters in on a pair of platform sneakers.

CHAPTER TEN

When Sam was twelve, she couldn't wait to be a teenager.
Teenagers were cool. Sam had an instinct for cool, for knowing the right clothes to wear at school in order to be accepted, but she was also drawn, like Chloe, to rebellion and
nonconformity. Sam understood that her sister was kind of
cool, kind of a loser. While Chloe played Sex Pistols and
Nick Cave records and was interested in Sid and Nancy, she
didn't have a subculture look: she didn't dye her hair or wear
white makeup. Her only friend was Tory, who lived on their
street. Chloe and Tory were always talking about how much
they hated the preppies, the in-crowd kids, but they didn't
know how to make friends with the cute boys wearing eye-
liner at showings of *The Rocky Horror Picture Show* at the Roxy.
Mostly Chloe stayed at home and fought with Dad. When
she was out, the house felt empty to Sam. Her sister was this
large, buzzing presence whose emotions Sam felt acutely.
Chloe's frustration and desire enveloped Sam like the
patchouli oil her sister drenched herself in. Patchouli oil
bought at a Yonge Street head shop. One time Chloe took
Sam there. The place gave her a little charge. While Chloe
thumbed through a rack of posters, looking for a picture of
Sid and Nancy to add to her collection, Sam examined the
black T-shirts pinned to the walls. A large glass case running
the length of the store displayed drug paraphernalia and
patches stitched with the names of bands and pictures of
pot plants. The patches could be sewn onto jackets, pants,
and knapsacks. After buying a jar of patchouli oil from the

display case, Chloe pointed out the hash pipes and rolling papers to Sam. Out on the street, Chloe unsealed the stopper on the patchouli, turned the bottle upside down on her finger, and smeared a spot of the dark oil on the collar of her black sweater. "Perfume lasts longer if you put it on your clothes," she told Sam.

A dab of feminine wisdom lost on Sam, who wasn't interested in wearing perfume.

Chloe added, "It doesn't last forever, but nothing ever does."

In the fall, Sam would begin junior high. On notepads she wrote: "What Is Going to Happen to Me?" She wanted to be ready. She wanted to reach past her childhood to the risk and shimmer of the city and adventure. A poster on the street advertised an all-ages show, which was being held at a nearby church. She asked her father if she could go.

"Only if your sister takes you," he said.

Chloe gave a world-weary sigh. She was eighteen; she was over the whole all-ages show thing. Sam couldn't remember Chloe ever going to one, but she claimed she had. Nonetheless, she agreed to accompany Sam.

Sam's first gig. Church basement, low ceilings, lots of rooms, stream of kids, and the indescribable thrill of being around teenagers when you weren't quite one. On stage the band was setting up. They were called the Vegetarians. "We're part of a youth direct-action group who do benefits for different animal rights organizations," the lead singer announced over a microphone. While his fellow band members tuned their instruments, the singer jumped off the stage to hand out pamphlets about factory farming. Sam stuffed one into her pocket.

The singer got back onto the stage and sang-screamed, "Fuck fast food, fuck fast food, fuck fast food." Three words plus three chords. Sam leaped into the mosh pit, got bumped around from boy to boy like a pinball. It was fun. She ran to get her sister.

"C'mon, let's dance."

Chloe shook her head. "Maybe later." But Chloe didn't join her; she stayed on the sidelines watching the band. When they finished their first set and left the stage to take their break, Sam saw Chloe scamper after the singer, a tall, skinny boy with blue hair who looked her age. Sam crept over to them because she wanted to tell him she liked his band. As he leaned over a drinking fountain noisily slurping water, Chloe tapped his shoulder, her fingers resting for a moment on his sweaty bare skin, accessible through a hole in his tattered T-shirt. He jerked his body up, regarding Chloe with such raw curiosity that Sam found herself staring at her sister as if she had never seen her: a lanky girl in jeans and a black sweater, messy red hair reaching below her shoulders, silver studs caulked along the edge of her right ear.

"Great songs. Too bad about the name of your band, " Chloe said.

Sam was shocked. Why was her sister being mean to him?

"What's wrong with our name?" His voice was tinged with a familiar huffiness. He sounded, well, like Chloe.

"Too obvious."

"Have you got a better one?"

"The Battery Hens." Even though Sam figured it had probably taken Chloe his whole set to come up with the name, she looked terribly smug.

He didn't tell her then how much he liked the suggestion, but his interest in her swelled across his face. He didn't crack a smile, but he couldn't take his eyes off her.

Sam spent the rest of that summer watching James's shows, helping her sister sell Battery Hens T-shirts, and handing out pamphlets on animal liberation. Mostly people threw them on the floor, but Sam read them and became a vegetarian. She and Chloe went to a demonstration where attractive, young women who had little need of makeup carried signs that said, "Beauty Without Cruelty." They were part of the Compassion Campaign launched to protest cosmetic companies testing on animals. When Sam and Chloe's father left town for a conference, the band came over for several days. The boys had crests of brittle dyed hair, which they let Sam touch. They wore ripped T-shirts and black vinyl shoes. They were all radical vegans who were obsessed with food. Every one was thin, and they talked about the joys of soy, the horrors of milk, which produced mucus in your nose, and their sugar highs from the chocolate bar they shouldn't have eaten. The first night Chloe dyed her hair black. Within a week, she bought herself some vintage clothing from Kensington Market, took out some vegetarian cookbooks from the library, and became vegan. Her indiscriminate indignation became focused as a gob of spit. When Chloe saw a beagle on the street, she would rant about how their obedience made them a favourite of researchers who would take them from animal shelters and cut out portions of their brain in labs. Sam cried the first time she heard this. She wanted to become vegan, but Dad wouldn't let her. He wouldn't let her dye her hair either, but she did get permission to buy her own clothes, to go thrifting with Chloe. Sam worshipped her sister more than she had when she had been a little kid. Chloe's new life was so cool, so right on. Sam believed in it and in her without realizing there was a difference between the two.

PART TWO
RISKS

CHAPTER ELEVEN

It is just after midnight when Omar calls Sam from his cell-phone. While they talk, she watches him from her balcony as he paces back and forth on the sidewalk in front of her building. Above her, the night sky is rippled with clouds, grey finger curls. Sam leaves her apartment, meets him on the street. His illegally parked car is chrome-coloured with a sleek body. She has no idea what kind of car it is, but the last time she saw something similar was in a James Bond movie.

She climbs into the front seat. "Nice ride."

"Thanks." Omar presses a button and her window slides down. The air is mild and the wind feels soft against her face, portents of summer.

"Who's having this party we're going to?"

"Hells Angels."

Her mouth sags open. "You're kidding me."

"I'm a member of the Hells Angels."

"Were you when you knew my sister?"

"Yeah, I've always been a hood. When I was younger, I stole cars, ran dope, collected."

"Collected what?"

"You know, money."

Sam gets it. Loansharking, extortion. Wow. She feels as if she's slipped into a different life, been enchanted.

Omar shifts gears, speeds up unnecessarily—a boy showing her what he can do with his toy. "I could smear any banger in the city back in the day. Now I just run a business."

The car careers along a southern boulevard beside the

river. The street is quiet, with only pizza delivery cars and the occasional cab passing them. Sam stares out her window at the river illuminated by street lights surrounded by fluttering moths. The river is a dusky colour barely distinguishable from the sky. She hears a rushing sound and realizes they are driving by the rapids. Earlier in the week, she hiked here through tall, shaggy wild grasses. The river surface is serene; the real pull of the current would not be felt until you were in the middle of it. Omar has the same smoothness coupled with an undertow. He's a pimp and a gangster. Is he really taking her to a party? Did he kill her sister and is he now getting rid of her? Sam considers opening the door and hurling her body out of the car, tumbling until she lies in a heap, bruised, bloodied, and with limbs studded with gravel. Or is she overreacting? Maybe his life isn't like a Hollywood movie. Maybe he has downtime in which he celebrates birthdays and Christmas like everyone who stays on the right side of the law. Glancing at Omar, Sam tries to imagine him eating turkey and opening a box of socks sent by a great aunt living in a nursing home, but, unbidden, another image forms— Omar strangling a crumpled elderly figure.

He gets off the highway and winds the car through a nest of suburban streets, stopping when they reach a circular driveway lined with expensive vehicles: Ferraris, Jaguars, Porsches, and Harleys. The house is a Mediterranean villa whose entrance is flanked by gigantic Ionic columns made of peach stucco—a mansion contrasting starkly with the neighbouring ranch-style homes and fir-tree-lined suburban lawns. The building is pure ego, owned by someone who doesn't care about blending in with his surroundings. A Café del Mar CD drones from an open window.

Sam and Omar climb a trio of wide stone steps, and he opens the unlocked front door. They enter the villa without bothering to remove their shoes, stepping into a spacious interior that looks as if it were purchased in one ginormous shopping spree. Everything is very modern, a magazine showcase. All the rooms are painted a crisp white. The chairs in the living room are in crazy shapes while still maintaining an ergonomic yin-yang. Two couches are covered in white fur, and the cabinets and shelves are made of glass and steel. Hors d'oeuvres and wine are being served by young waiters in typical hotel attire, complete with cummerbunds. Most of the male guests are well-dressed and in their thirties, forties, and fifties with much younger girlfriends. The girlfriends have the look of professional anorexics and are clad in couture garments: a pair of pants made out of silver buckles, a blue vinyl and chiffon dress. Omar, wearing black leather pants and a neon green mesh shirt, has the appropriate rakish élan while Sam feels like riff-raff in the same black jeans and Bettie Page T-shirt she wore to the interview.

Sam nudges Omar with her elbow and murmurs, "I thought Hells Angels were a bunch of white trash bikers, not guys in Versace suits."

"That's just at the lower ranks. You'll see some bikers. But you'll find doctors here, along with lawyers, accountants, and businessmen. Lots of businessmen." Omar places his hand on the arm of a waiter and asks him in English to bring over a Scotch and soda. The waiter swivels his head expectantly at Sam, who tells him she's happy with any kind of imported beer. After the waiter leaves, Omar lightly punches her shoulder. "Cool tats."

"Thank you." Sam has everything on her arm from Bettie Page to the Amazon rainforest to Inuit symbols. She loves getting tattoos. According to some book she read, endangered tribes tattoo themselves. With the disappearance of both a mother and sister, Sam feels a little endangered.

"I have a tattoo." Omar shifts his shoulder towards her. Beneath the netting of his shirt, she can make out graffiti-style words inked in black on his bicep: "Only God Can Judge Me."

"Guess you're not Muslim."

The waiter returns, presenting Sam with a tray holding a bottle of beer and a glass. She picks up the bottle, leaves the glass.

Omar raises his drink in the air. "Damn straight. My mom left Egypt to get away from all that. After my father was killed in the Six Day War, my mom quit believing in God or Allah. Anyways, my tattoo is props to my man Tupac Shakur, rest in peace."

Sam stares at him. "What do you mean?"

" 'Only God Can Judge Me' is a Tupac cut."

Sam sucks down some of her beer. Did he send her the postcard with the image of Tupac? At his office, he seemed genuinely shocked to meet her. Did someone who knows him send her the postcard as a clue to lead her to him? If she asks him any of these questions, she's going to sound like a cop or a weirdo. Perhaps she should start by asking him whether he shared Chloe's interest in conspiracy theories? As Sam tries to think of a casual way to steer their conversation towards presidential assassinations, a man wearing a leather jacket and leather chaps over jeans comes over. He and Omar exchange a handshake in which they bang their knuckles, then rub their thumbs together in a circle. Accompanying the man is a blonde S/M Barbie wearing a latex cat-suit unzipped far enough to reveal a silver ring threaded through her navel. In the highest spike heels Sam has ever seen, the woman towers over her companion.

"How's business?" the man in leather asks.

Omar sighs. "I've got clients like no tomorrow, but the Serbian girls who were working for me all took off for Miami."

The man in leather tsks. "It's always a cycle—you got too many clients, not enough girls, then you get the reverse. And the fads, that's what gets me going. I put all this money into setting up a dungeon a few years ago, and you know what my clients want now?"

Omar shakes his head.

"Fur. I've had to order custom-made fur bodysuits. Beaver, lynx, rabbit, I got it all. I tell you, you just never know what's going to happen in this business."

Sam thinks she should have such problems. The leather man's girlfriend sits on an ottoman and roots through her purse for a package of cigarettes. Her long legs are pressed together in a perfect L-shape, like a pantyhose commercial. When she brings out a cigarette, Omar takes a Zippo lighter from his pocket and flicks it on. He leans forward, cupping the flame for her. She thanks him with a saucy smile before wandering away with the man in leather.

Omar whispers, "She's fine."

"Her shoes look like they could be used to slaughter rats. Besides, isn't she with the guy you were talking to?" Sam has a sudden vision of walking into a bedroom and finding Omar naked with a knife wound, his blood soaking into a white carpet.

Omar's eyebrows shoot up. "Are you kidding me? He's a fag."

Sam takes a gulp of her beer only to discover the bottle is empty. The man in leather is a Leather Daddy? "There are gay men in Hells Angels?"

"Sure. They're discreet; they bring female escorts."

Sam remembers Omar said he would introduce her to Chloe's roommate. "Where's the woman I'm supposed to meet?"

"I haven't seen her. She's coming from work." Omar takes his cell from his pocket, a flat silver bar. He opens it with one hand and punches a button. After a moment, he asks, "Where you at?" Snapping the phone shut, he glances at Sam. "She's here already, upstairs. Just wait." He vanishes into the crowd.

Sam sets her empty bottle on the floor and sits down on the ottoman. In front of her, a widescreen TV is showing porn. Two trailer trash girls pretend to be college cheerleaders who pretend to passionately fuck each other. When one of them inserts pink talons into the other, Sam flinches and looks away from the screen. There's plenty of action around her. A middle-aged man in brown leather is cruising a young woman in red leather. Behind Sam, a group of men are speaking in French about the rising condo market, or so she gathers since some of the words are the same in English. Meanwhile, Fetish Barbie complains in English to anyone who will listen that the ecstasy she took is making her grind her jaw.

Omar returns with a woman who doesn't walk into the room so much as make an entrance. Eyes dart like fireflies in her direction. The woman is striking, tall and slim with breasts barely encased in a tight orange dress with a keyhole neck. A swirl of blue-black hair, dark velvet eyes, and cheekbones like cut glass also help to draw people's attention to her. The only feature disturbing the pretty symmetry of the woman's face is her bumpy, elongated nose. Yet she's no haughty model. There's a wry twist to her mouth, which both acknowledges the effect of her looks and invites people not to take her too seriously.

While Sam feels herself respond to the woman, she is careful to keep her expression blank. The best way to get a beautiful woman to pay attention to you is to pretend not to notice how beautiful she is.

The woman says, "I'm Romey."

"I'm Sam." She sticks out her hand. Her fingers are given a languid squeeze by a long-fingered hand whose nails are surprisingly short and free of polish.

"So, what do you think of the party?"

Sam gazes around at all the leather clothing. "This wouldn't be the place for a membership drive for People for the Ethical Treatment of Animals."

Romey rewards her with the requisite dry smile. Then she joins Sam on the ottoman and begins to unhook the laces on both of her long black boots. Sam watches the deft movement of Romey's hands and notes the oddly masculine heaviness of her many silver rings. When she has unlaced her boots, she pivots around and places her feet before Sam. "Can you get them the rest of the way off?"

Sam quickly and efficiently tugs the left boot, then the right one, free. Although she's never been so in thrall, she's careful not to seem supplicating. Romey is stunning, but Sam's desire for her is more basic, a smell she wants to put her face in. Romey wiggles her bare toes. She has perfect feet and toenails; she must see a pedicurist on a regular basis.

Romey says, "That's better. Those boots are a bit tight."

Omar sits down on the floor in front of them. Waves a sealed plastic bag containing white powder in front of Romey's face. "Want a bump?"

"I really shouldn't." Which, Sam knows, means yes.

Omar looks around. After standing up, he grabs an empty jewel case, shakes a line of powder onto it, and cuts the dope with a newly minted fifty. He rolls the bill into a tight tube, then holds it out to Sam, who has never done coke before. She and her friends take ecstasy while the fucked-up kids at the clubs do crystal meth. Coke is an '80s drug, a drug that goes from your nose to your brain, which she finds creepy. She feels a hand on her shoulder.

"Want to share a line?" Romey asks.

Sam nods. They bend their heads together, sniff, and let the drug race into their bodies. Romey's long hair tickles Sam's cheek, and their thighs are pressed together. Sam has never met a woman who both turns her on and intimidates her. She's not just nervous or self-conscious but anxious, like it's *all too much*. She's got this pang, a sort of panicky feeling in her chest. When she's heard people talk about love at first sight, she thought they were idiots. How can you love someone you don't even know? But looking at Romey, Sam thinks, you could be big. The coke kicks in. Even though she's wide awake with her eyes flying everywhere, she feels as if she's wrapped in cotton batten. She and Romey are sitting together on the floor with their heads on the ottoman while Omar sits across from them with his legs sprawled apart. Omar and Romey smoke du Maurier cigarettes and discuss the movies they've watched. Both of them rent a lot more movies than Sam would have expected. Time breathes, contracts, and expands. An hour or so goes by. Buzz of a pager.

Romey says, "Your married lady, beeper boy?"

Omar takes a pager out of his pocket, clicks a button, and reads the number on the display. "Nope, it's my mom. She was visiting her cousin in Ottawa, and I asked her to call me as soon as she got in. I should go see how she's doing."

"It's like two in the morning!"

Omar puts his pager back into his pocket. "I haven't seen her all week."

"You're high."

"I've just had one line. I'm fine."

"You're such a mama's boy." Romey flips onto her side so she faces Sam. "Can you believe he only moved out of his mother's place two years ago? And then he bought a condo in the suburbs because it's four blocks from her house."

Omar holds both of his hands up. "It takes me ten minutes to drive downtown and my building has a gym and a pool."

"Gee, a pool," Romey replies sarcastically. Her breasts kiss Sam's elbow, shooting twinges of sensation between Sam's legs.

Omar reaches over to give Romey's knee a pat. "Do you want a ride home?"

She does a hair-flip thing—the mark of a true girly-girl. "Of course."

Omar turns to Sam. "Are you coming?"

Sam wonders what he imagines the alternative is. She's out of it, she doesn't know where she is in the city, and she hasn't learned anything about the relationships these two had with her sister, let alone whether what the postcard alleged is true. Sam forces herself to sit up. "I didn't even get to talk to you guys about Chloe."

Omar and Romey exchange a parental glance, a let's-talk-later-not-in-front-of-the-kid look. Seems as if they're hiding something. Sam has always prided herself on holding the better hand in any interaction, on holding back, but these two are out of her league. Romey reaches for her boots and starts to put them on, this time without Sam's help. Romey didn't seem to need assistance the first time either. From a little pocket on the side of her left boot, which Sam didn't notice earlier, Romey takes out a business card and hands it to Sam.

Romey says, "That's the address of the bar where I work. If you want to get in touch, I'm there Thursdays and Fridays until late. Sometimes Saturdays."

"Okay." Romey works at Le Triangle d'Or, located downtown on St. Catherine Street. As Sam puts the card in her back pocket, the edge scores her finger, pricking her. She touches her tongue to the glistening bead of blood—claret laced with salt.

Omar drives back as though they were in the Indy 500. Sam is quiet, trying to take in the events of the evening like a too-rich meal. Omar puts music on, some R&B diva whose name Sam can't remember but whose hit song she recognizes. She has so many questions she wants to ask she doesn't know where to begin. Like, what happened between her sister and Omar? Were they together when Chloe died? What's Romey's story? She seems like a woman who has one. Could she have sent the postcard? Sam can't decide what to ask, how to ask it.

Before Sam knows it, Omar parks the car in front of her apartment. She's run out of time, but then something occurs to her. A question flies from her mouth. "How come you two weren't at my sister's funeral?"

Romey glances at Omar, but he looks away, checks the rear-view mirror as if someone is following him. His eyes in the mirror are a burnished brown. They remind Sam of her father's eyes, except Omar's are more intense—fire, not ice.

Omar says, "We didn't find out in time to go."

Although she can't say why, Sam is sure he's lying. She leans forward to scrutinize Romey, who is sitting in the front seat. "Didn't my father call you?"

"Chloe wasn't living with me anymore. She moved out July 1st, quit her job," Romey explains.

"We didn't know where she was," Omar says. "We thought she'd moved back to Toronto. She took her stuff back to your father's house."

"She did?" Everything Sam knows about her sister's death rips open, stitches pulled from a wound. Sam inherited Chloe's furniture, so the scenario Omar is describing could be right. Chloe could have brought her belongings back to Toronto, but, if so, she didn't stick around. Didn't say "hi" or "bye" to Sam. Where was Chloe between the beginning of July and the middle of August when she was found dead in a New York hotel room? Sam always assumed her sister went to New York for the weekend and bought some bad drugs. She thought Dad was the one who retrieved Chloe's stuff. Guess not. The only thing Sam is sure of is that Omar and Romey know more than they're saying.

Romey looks as if she feels sorry for Sam. "It was nice to meet you," she says, a signal to Sam that it is time for her to get out of the car.

During work on the following Thursday, Sam moves like a mean machine because she can't wait to see Romey. All week it is as if she has been carrying Romey in a tiny, unopened box, saving her up. As Sam slicks gel into her hair after her shift, she thinks of Romey lying beside her in that clingy dress. Romey's probably not a lesbian, but that hasn't stopped lots of women from having sex with Sam.

Shortly after midnight, Sam makes her way through downtown. The streets are filled with drunken university students who have just finished their classes—gaggles of shrieking girls wearing flared jeans and tube tops in too-cool weather, and packs of frat boys who leap on one another's backs and break into exaggerated fisticuffs. Older tourists with Boston accents shuffle out of restaurants with Surf and Turf specials.

The bar where Romey works is below street level, and Sam halts at the bottom of the stairs when she sees the red neon outline of a naked woman in the window. Only now does the double meaning of the name of the club—The Golden Triangle—sink in. Three guys with moustaches and workboots torpedo past her into the club; one of them turns to grin at her reluctance to enter. She takes a deep breath and marches in after him. She keeps her eyes on the ground and doesn't realize she has to pay a cover until a jock on steroids grabs her arm and demands five dollars.

Le Triangle d'Or is a '70s throwback. Strings of beads sway against one wall, while another wall is covered with hand-painted murals of swingers playing guitar, smoking dope, and locking their limbs into tantric sex positions. There is a platform at the back with a metallic gold bar from which an attractive, well-muscled Latina hangs sideways, posing like a kid on a jungle gym. As she does nearly naked aerobics to a pop song, Sam stares at the woman's triceps, not her breasts.

Sam glances at the bartender, but the woman is busy making a batch of cocktails at the other end of the bar. The customers are mostly here alone, chain-smoking. The mirror behind the bar is hazy; Sam can't remember when she was last in a bar with this much smoke. There is an advantage to the lack of visibility. She doubts any of the men in the room will look at her closely enough to realize she isn't a guy. She turns away from the bartender in order to check out the chicks. She has never been in a strip club before, and the girls are more varied than she would have thought. While a few women are biker babes with bleached blonde hair and bad silicone jobs, most are not. Sam is surprised by the spectrum of skin colour, age, and body type. There's a duo of pierced and tattooed girls with shaved heads who are young and junkie-thin in ratty teddies they probably bought at Value Village. When Sam was twenty and between jobs, she shaved her head. Removing her hair made her into someone whom adults were afraid of. Whenever they looked or stepped away from her on the street, she felt two things: safe, and a cool rush of power. Freaking out everyone you know must be part of the reason some girls take their clothes off for money. One of the punkettes cruises Sam whose attention is diverted by the sight of a woman in her forties with short hair dancing on a cube for a rapt man, her wide hips spiralling in his face. While the phrase "soccer mom" comes to Sam's mind, the older woman is hot. She's unselfconscious as she rubs her hands over her breasts, as if she is dancing for a lover. She may not love her job, but Sam gets the feeling she doesn't mind it.

Sam scans the room for Romey but doesn't see her. Sam doesn't see any obvious dykes either, so maybe Omar knew what he was talking about when he didn't even consider hiring her as an escort. Men might rape a woman who competes with them, but they won't pay for the privilege of watching her remove her clothes.

Sam has to go to the washroom. She tries to tell herself she doesn't have to pee, that she's just nervous about seeing Romey. Fuck. Sam *does* have to go. At the back of the bar, she finds men's and women's washrooms. Going into the men's means less potential hassle, but men's bathrooms are so skanky. On the other hand, the women's washroom isn't likely to be used by many people. The strippers probably have their own bathroom in some other part of the building.

But when Sam opens the door, a cocktail waitress immediately snaps at her in French. Sam can translate: wrong bathroom, buddy. She's too flustered to remember how to say in French, "I'm in the right place," so she thrusts her breasts forward as much as she can in her loose T-shirt. When the waitress shoots Sam a dirty look, she knows the woman has figured it out—she's just making it clear she doesn't think Sam deserves to be there. Ignoring her, Sam goes into the stall. This bullshit happens to her all the time; once she got tackled by a male security guard. She's used to it, but it's still annoying. Back in Toronto, she knew where all the public, single-stall washrooms were.

When she gets out of the bathroom, Sam sees Romey— she's onstage. The music has changed to raunchy post-punk, and she is wearing a black bra, panties, and red platform sneakers. A black cat mask covers her eyes. She weaves her hands in front of her face as she lip-synchs a song Sam knows only too well: "She Walks on Me" by Hole. After Chloe died, Sam played Hole a lot and not just because the CD was a gift from her sister. The perpetual outrage of both the songs and Courtney Love reminded Sam of Chloe.

Romey struts across the stage, flinging her bra off. Soon she's not wearing much more than the pout on her lips. Sam can't take her eyes off the stage. Romey is like certain actresses: watching them brush their hair is interesting. Yet the striptease isn't sexy. When Romey spanks her ass with a slow-motion slap, a phony smile plastered across her face, it's as if she's telling these guys "fuck you" and "pay attention to me." She's parodying porno, not being it. Because she's so good-looking and charismatic, she can get away with the attitude. For her finale, she slithers around on the floor with the same derisive wink and a nod to a song by Tori Amos, who is famous for protesting violence against women.

Romey's performance is a rebuke, but Sam isn't sure to whom.

After she leaves the stage, the punkettes come on for a Sapphic duo in which they snake their hands over each other. As Sam tries to decide whether they are authentic, she feels a hand on her back. She looks up. Romey is standing beside her with her mask removed, and her eyes are like melting tar.

Romey asks, "Did you enjoy my show?"

"Absolutely." Sam sounds like a pompous idiot. How can she be appreciative without being a pig? While nervously stretching her fingers, she struggles to think of something to say.

The bartender, a woman who was born male, impatiently drums spangled nails on the counter in front of Sam. "*Quelque chose à boire*? Can I get you something, honey?"

Sam orders a beer and asks Romey what she wants. She tells the bartender to bring her a chocolate martini.

The bartender's eyebrows are already arched. "Not your usual ginger ale?"

Romey doesn't answer, just twitches her nose at the bartender, who moves towards a creased twenty dollar bill, which is thrust out, demanding a drink and promising a tip.

"Your last song was a strange choice," Sam says.

"I enjoy pushing the envelope. One time I showed up in a nun's habit and the manager sent me home. I told him he was making a big mistake, I would have made him a lot of money, but he wouldn't listen. If he was French, he would have been like 'Yeah, right on, fuck the church,' but, no, he's Italian, like me."

Romey is talking very quickly. Is it the adrenaline of getting off stage, or is she, like Sam, feeling nervous? Romey was cool as anything at the party, but then they were both high, so who knows? Sam still can't think of anything to say. Romey is so close Sam can distinguish the separate fragrances of Romey's lemony perfume, almond-scented shampoo, and peppery deodorant. Her skin is damp, and Sam wants to lick the sweat from her neck. Romey adjusts her cleavage, exposing the pale moons of her breasts. She tucks a few bills further down her bra, and Sam's eyes follow the flush of her nipple peeking out of shiny fluffs of material. Sam is aware of two distinct sensations in two different parts of her body: the clunk of her heart in her chest and an ache between her legs. Relax, Sam tells herself, chill. After a moment she asks Romey if she likes stripping.

Romey shrugs. "We call it dancing. Taking your clothes off is only demeaning if you hate doing it but do it anyway— just like any other kind of job." While the frustration in her voice is real, her words seem rehearsed.

Sam says, "I understand—you're renting your body, not giving it away."

The corner of Romey's mouth dips up. "I see you've read the theory." She continues in a softer tone. "I'm not crazy about lap dancing, but I love being onstage. Used to be you could just table dance, but not these days. Fortunately, I've got regular clients that are different from most, young freaks wanting something out of the ordinary and grateful older men who like my jazz numbers and spend a lot of money on me without trying to grab me. The men I stay away from are the good-looking ones. Some girls actually date them."

"But not you?"

"God no. I'm a lesbian."

"You are?" Sam's voice cracks.

"Can't you tell?" Romey reaches over and strokes the top of Sam's crewcut as if she were an expensive pet.

The bartender reappears with their drinks. Sam pays for them, but neither she nor Romey lift their glasses from the counter. Romey's hand is still entangled in Sam's hair. Sam puts an arm around Romey's waist, pulls her close. "You're so fucking hot." Sam has never talked to a girl in such a tacky, obvious way before, or at least not until they were in bed together.

Using her knee to nudge Sam's legs apart, Romey fits her thigh between Sam's. Cupping Sam's ear, Romey whispers, "If you stay in this bar, you're going to have to give me some cash."

Sam steps back from her, thinking, you minx. But she reaches for her wallet and pulls out her last twenty, resentful at having to pay for something she always gets for free. Was Romey flirting with her or working her? Sam rolls the bill tight as a joint and plunges it into Romey's bra with trembling hands. She's a dyke, and Sam realizes turning straight girls isn't the hardest game. Doing what they expect is easy, but watching Romey as she grips the bar with her arms and rocks back on her heels, Sam knows nothing about her will be. Romey's smile fades, and her eyes grow thoughtful, her coquette routine fizzing. She says, "I've got to make some money now. Why don't we see each other on Sunday? Saturday night, I've got plans with Omar."

Sam broods over those plans, even though Romey said she was gay. How often does she see Omar? "I'm working Sunday. How about Wednesday?"

"Okay."

Romey leans over the bar, providing a great view of her ass, and fishes a pen from somewhere. She scribbles her address and a time on a cocktail napkin, presses it into Sam's hand.

"I live in St. Henri, not far from you."

Sam places a hand on Romey's arm, unwilling to let their conversation end just yet. Sam wants to find out a little bit about Chloe. This time, Romey isn't going to *completely* distract her. "I want to ask you something. Do you know if my sister was investigating anything before she died?"

"I don't understand what you mean."

Should she tell Romey about the postcard? Sam's instinct is to be a bit coy. "Like a conspiracy theory, whether it was true or a hoax."

"That's kind of out of left field."

Sam shrugs.

"Well, she talked a lot about how fucked up governments are. Maybe you should talk to this guy at the anarchist bookstore. Chloe used to volunteer there, and she had this friend, a black guy, who was a conspiracy freak. I saw him there about a year ago so he's probably still around. I can't remember his name, although I was the one who went by the store to break the news to him about Chloe."

"How did you find out my sister died?"

"From Omar. Your father called her work, told them."

Sam gives Romey's arm a little squeeze. "Thank you."

"For what?" Romey tosses her hands in the air, then leans forward to kiss Sam goodnight. Sam backs away, giving a sideways salute with two fingers. Romey turns Sam on way too much. If Romey kisses her, Sam is going to throw her onto the floor.

A middle-aged yuppie approaches Romey to ask for a private dance. With a glance at Sam, Romey nods her assent, then marches off, bills flapping like streamers from her thong. Sam wants to punch the guy's soft gut. After leaving her beer at the bar, Sam swaggers out of the club. It isn't Romey's fault Sam feels so insecure; it's the homophobic shrapnel lodged in her skin.

Business is slow on Sunday afternoon, so Sam helps Dang prep the vegetables. To peel the garlic, she uses Dang's technique of banging the cloves against the counter, then rolling the skin between her fingers. She can't stop thinking about Romey. Sam has never felt this captivated. She always resists getting in too deep, doling out her affection in incremental lumps, stingy cubes of sugar. When she tells the women she sleeps with she doesn't want a girlfriend, doesn't want to get close, she isn't lying. They lie to her when they say that's fine. She is Player and they are Drama. Sam has always thought being the dumper makes her superior, but now she wonders. Like the dumpees, she winds up with nothing. Sam hopes it will be different with Romey.

A waiter scuds into the kitchen and lowers a tray of dishes onto the counter where Sam is working. The double doors to the kitchen swing open again, and one of the Somali busboys rushes in and storms up to the waiter, giving his shoulders a shove. Everyone working in the kitchen looks up. Sam doesn't know the name of the waiter but has noticed the busboy, Hassan, who has the cheekbones of a model, an aristocratic attractiveness he enhances by ensuring his uniforms of white shirts and black pants are Hugo Boss. While getting a refill of pop one day, Sam caught him peering at himself in the mirror behind the bar.

"*Tapette*!" Hassan tosses the word at the waiter like a hand grenade. "In my country we put people like you in jail."

The waiter puts a hand on his hip. "Well, buddy, you're in Canada now, and we've got different laws here."

"He's a *tapette*." Hassan looks at Sam and Dang for support. "You know what I'm saying?"

"Yeah, he's gay. Why do you care?" Sam asks. Unspoken sentences swim through her mind: I never knew *tapette* meant faggot; so am I; fuck you.

The waiter butts in, "If you're so crazy about pussy why does it bother you that I suck cock?"

Dang waves his chef's knife in the air. "What's the problem here?"

Hassan folds his arms across his chest. "He tried to offer me to a customer."

Sam's curiosity gets the better of her. "What do you mean?"

The waiter smirks. "A customer asked if we had some Black Label beer, and I said, 'No, but we have black busboys.'"

Sam rolls her eyes at the waiter. He knows better but doesn't care. Now he's pretending to massage his crotch while looking at the busboy lasciviously. Hassan gives him the finger before dashing back into the dining area. Returning to her task, Sam sniffs her hands. Dang's method of peeling garlic leaves a residue; her hands reek of garlic. To take away the smell, she goes to the bar and asks the bartender for some lemon slices to squeeze onto her skin.

Joe hands her a couple of lemon wedges in a square glass, then flicks his head towards the other end of the bar. "Someone here to see you."

Sam looks over and sees Omar at a table in the back. He's smoking a cigarette and watching sports on the television screen. Why didn't he call first? He has her phone number. It's as if he wants to surprise her, the same way she surprised him, what he called a bitch move. She walks over to him, holding her lemons. "You're looking for me?"

Omar taps a pillar of ash into an ashtray. "I thought we could have a drink when you finish your shift."

"I'll be another twenty minutes," Sam warns.

As she cleans the Hobart, she wonders why he's here. Is he going to confess he sent the postcard? Or maybe he'll tell her what exactly Chloe was up to before she died? Sam knows Omar's hiding *something*. She planned to see him again but first wanted to hear what Romey had to say about his relationship with Chloe. It's like poker—what isn't chance hinges upon the order in which you make your moves.

When Sam joins Omar, he is talking on his cell. He covers the mouthpiece with his hand and asks her what she wants to drink. Holding up her full glass of Coke, she tells him she's good for now.

"Nothing else," Omar barks into his cell. Sam glances over at Joe, sees him hanging up the phone behind the bar. Even though the place is dead, Omar ordered drinks using his cell. How pretentious.

Pale gold afternoon sunlight filters through the leaded glass windows at the front. To keep from being blinded by the light, Sam slightly shifts her chair. When Omar finishes tucking his cell into his pocket, he asks her how she likes her job.

"More than I thought I would," Sam says. Working at a place where looking and acting feminine is both impossible and unnecessary is an incredible relief. She didn't realize how much pressure she felt at her office jobs.

Omar seems completely uninterested in her answer. He lights up a cigarette, blows smoke in her direction. "I had dinner with Romey last night."

Sam wafts the smoke away with her hand. "She mentioned she was doing something with you."

"Yeah, I see her regularly because she's my best friend. And she tells me everything. Like she told me you wanted to know if Chloe was investigating a conspiracy."

Sam examines Omar's face. "Was she?"

"No." Omar's eyes tighten into dark pins. "She just had kooky ideas about things. *I* might be able to tell you about some serious shit, but Chloe? Nah." He slowly shakes his head back and forth, then stops. "Someone's just told you a crazy story. And you don't want to check up on a crazy story because that means dealing with crazy people." His knuckles rap the table in front of Sam. "Bad idea."

She can't believe it. He came to see her to give her a warning. She didn't know whether to take the postcard seriously, whether to even believe the political conspiracy exists—now she thinks it's a possibility.

Omar continues in a more casual tone: "Your sister was a nice girl trying not to be, that's all."

Sam sighs. If he's not going to tell her anything about what Chloe was looking into, maybe he'll talk about the real issue. "Why would a nice girl kill herself?"

Omar's cellphone rings. Setting his barely smoked cigarette in the ashtray, he digs his cell out of his pocket and starts speaking in Arabic. From living in multi-culti Toronto, Sam can identify the most common foreign languages, even though she doesn't understand them. When Joe brings over a beer, Omar doesn't raise his head. Whoever he's talking to rates his full attention. Finally, in English, he says, "Okay, Mom, we'll go to Home Depot. I'll talk to you later." He closes the phone, leaves it on the table.

Sam smirks at him.

Omar frowns, and she realizes he hates being laughed at. He puts his elbows on the table and leans forward so he's looking down at Sam. "You want the four-one-one on Chloe, this is it. We broke up. I bailed on her. I was cold. But I had to be. You see, the truth is—I wasn't good enough for her."

Sam almost laughs but stops herself; he's one part charm, two parts threat. But his line? That's a joke. She's told girls, "I'm not good enough for you." She said it regularly until a woman called her on it, told her, "You mean you can't or don't want to live up to my expectations." The woman was right, which Sam demonstrated by never again speaking to her or feeding a woman that line. Now she repeats Omar's words with a measure of incredulity. "You broke up with my sister because you didn't think you were good enough for her?"

Omar continues to look intently at Sam. "When I was with Chloe, I didn't think about anyone else. But we lived in different worlds. Sooner or later, she was going to get over her drama with her daddy, go back to school, and forget about me."

"But she didn't." Sam sets her glass on the table, making a wet ring, lifts it, and makes another ring, overlapping the first one. What he is saying makes sense, but she doesn't buy it. There is more here than his excuses. But how can she get him to tell her what he's hiding?

Sam says, "Chloe never played by the rules. She might have gone into the escort business with you."

Omar yells, "What? Chloe, a whore! That's a nice way

to talk."

Sam concentrates on making another wet interlocking ring. She's made him deviate from his script in which he intimidates her, then makes her feel sorry for him. When she speaks next, her tone is dry and mocking, a weapon from her father's arsenal. "I was thinking more along the lines of running the business. She'd investigate niche marketing and order the fur suits while you handled security."

Omar's hands square into fists. "Go to hell."

Sam shrugs. "If you won't talk to me, I'll talk to Romey." She's not afraid of him right now. It's when he's calm that he's scary.

Omar doesn't answer immediately. Instead, he shakes out his fists, as if he's trying to toss away his anger. When he finally speaks, his voice is smooth and cold. "I'll hurt anyone who gets Romey into trouble."

Sam knows better than to ask her next question but can't help herself. "You two are just friends?"

Now it's Omar's turn to look amused. "You need to check yourself. Romey's not into guys." The smugness leaves his eyes. "For real, Chloe would have dumped me if I hadn't dumped her."

Sam's voice wobbles, "Who are you trying to convince?"

"This conversation is over." Omar chucks a ten dollar bill on the table, grabs his cellphone, and fades out the door, not even bothering to talk to Joe.

Sam notices her fingers still stink of garlic. The lemons don't mask the odour; they add to it. Omar is guilty. She just doesn't know of what.

Even though Sam feels as if she's coming down with the flu, she heads over to the anarchist bookstore. Before she sees Romey, Sam wants to find the conspiracy freak who was Chloe's friend and talk to him. If anyone would know if her sister was investigating a political conspiracy, he would. Maybe the conspiracy freak even sent her the anonymous note. He's black so maybe he's a Tupac Shakur fan. Omar's tattoo is probably just a coincidence.

Sam gets out of the metro station and trudges north on St. Laurent. She feels exhausted and is glad Librairie Alternative turns out to be close to the metro. There is no sign, only a sheet spray-painted with a black anarchy symbol, which hangs in a second-floor window. An industrial-looking glass door opens at street level onto a flight of stairs. At the top of the stairs is another door leading to the bookshop, which Sam enters. A square room lined with shelves holds a meagre selection of books. Sections are labelled "Feminism," "First Nations," and "Antiglobalization." Most of the books are in English, but there are also materials in French and Spanish.

A woman sits behind a desk, reading a magazine. Beside her, an electric kettle begins to produce steam, which she either ignores or doesn't notice. While the woman appears to be in her mid-twenties, she is wearing her dark blonde hair in slightly preposterous twin braids. Her pierced eyebrow only partly subverts her dairymaid look. Sam clears her throat to get the woman's attention. She flips her magazine shut, and Sam sees she's reading *Bust*, a feminist publication that is more trendy than political. In English, the woman asks Sam if she needs help.

"I'm looking for someone who works here or used to work here. All I know is he's a conspiracy freak and he's black."

"You mean Francis? Yeah, he works here," she replies. Her hand darts to her eyebrow piercing. The skin surrounding her eyebrow is puffy and pink like an insect bite.

She probably just got the piercing, Sam thinks. "Can you tell me what days he comes in?"

"We're a volunteer collective, and we don't give information out to people who haven't been vetted. I mean, I have no idea who you are." Her voice soars uncertainly at the end of her sentences, transforming them into questions, which Sam finds annoying.

Water from the kettle slops onto the woman's desk, leading the Swiss Miss to at last unplug the cord and pour the boiling water into a nearby mug. She adds, "We have a bulletin board at the back where you could leave a message for him."

Sam sighs. Who knows when this guy will read the message. And what should she say? "Do you have a pen and some paper?"

While the woman rummages through the desk drawers, the floor abruptly shifts beneath Sam's feet. If she doesn't sit down, she is going to pass out. She surveys the room for a chair but sees only the one behind the desk.

The woman places a pencil in front of Sam but no paper. "I'll check the printer tray at the back." She gets up.

Sam hauls herself onto a corner of the desk, taking care not to knock over the steaming cup of tea. She hunches forward, pressing her elbows into her thighs and the heels of her palms against her eyeballs. Vapour scented with cardamom whorls upwards from the tea, moistening Sam's face and hands. The room and its contents flow away from her as she reels backwards. She feels as if she's being pulled out of her body. She sees herself lying on an autopsy table, skin white, wrinkled, and powdery, as if it has been sprinkled with flour. Her hand is stained with ink: the officials are trying to identify her. Can't they tell who she is from her tattoos? But the body on the table has no tattoos; Sam is wearing a different skin, an unmarked one. No, not exactly unmarked—she's cut open in places. Blood and tissue trickle out of holes in her body. She tries to tell herself, it isn't me. But the real her has escaped. Where has she gone?

"Are you okay?" The Swiss Miss is patting Sam's shoulder. "Would you like a cup of chai?"

Sam shakes her head. When the woman touched her, Sam's fatigue and her dream, which felt more like a trance, disappeared like a palmed coin. Sam has the strange impression the woman made the hallucination happen, brewed it with her tea.

"I've got to talk to Francis. He was friends with my sister, who died. He may have information about her death," Sam says. She wants to take charge of the situation, but instead she's acting crazy and desperate.

The woman pins Sam's face with cool, light-coloured eyes. Are they blue or grey?—they are no closer to one than the other. There is a skein of lines at the edges of her eyes suggesting the woman is older than she looks, is in her thirties.

The woman says, "What's your name?"

It isn't a question so much as an order. Her tone has lost all of its previous perkiness. The woman has shifted, traded one persona for another.

"Sam O'Connor."

"I'm Amanda Tupper." Her step, as she walks off, is light and on the balls of her feet like a ballet dancer. She returns with a piece of paper, which she gives to Sam, who writes down her name and phone number. Amanda folds the paper into an origami crane, perches it on the desk. She says, "I'll call Francis tonight." After a pause, she adds, "You're not from here, are you?"

"No," Sam admits. She's not going to tell the woman she's from Toronto. From a few conversations at work, Sam has learned that trashing Canada's largest city is a defensive sport with Montrealers.

Amanda sweeps her gaze over Sam. "Black clothing without artful rips. I'm guessing Toronto."

Sam's eyes drop to her black jeans and black Puma T-shirt and she immediately regrets doing so. Then she just doesn't care; she wants to go home and sleep.

As Sam opens the door on her way out, Amanda calls,

"If you want to talk, I'm here every week." Then she picks up her magazine and pretends to read it. Sam wonders why this strange person would offer to see her again. People are friendlier in Montreal than in Toronto, but still. Sam's boots slap down the stairs.

The next day, Sam calls in sick to work and sleeps until four o'clock in the afternoon. When she wakes up, she feels fine. Whatever strange bug she picked up is gone. There is a message on her voice mail: "The hawk is in flight. Tell the mice to take cover. I repeat, tell the mice to take cover. I can be reached at the following number...." The words are spoken by a man with an elegant baritone—a classical music radio announcer. Sam presses the number nine on her cordless phone to listen to the message again. What the hell does it mean? Who or what is the hawk? Who are the mice?

Sam dials the number left on the message. When a man answers, she informs him, without bothering to contain her annoyance, that he left a stupid message for her.

The man replies with a question. "Would it be safe for me to draw the conclusion that you are Sam O'Connor?"

He probably has call display. "It wouldn't be dangerous. Who are you?"

The man clears his throat. "I'm Francis. I was a friend of your sister's. I got a message *you* wanted to get in touch with *me*."

Sam sighs. The conspiracy freak who works at Librairie Alternative. She guesses she owes Amanda a thank-you. "Yes, I'd like to talk to you about Chloe, preferably in person."

"I can understand. You never know when the government's listening in. The problem is I'm kind of occupied this week."

"Are you busy right this second?"

Francis pauses and admits he is free.

Although Francis agrees to see Sam, he doesn't make it easy. He wants to meet her at a place called The Orange Julep, but he isn't sure of the address. He says, "You can't miss it. You'll see it as soon as you get out of the metro."

"I really don't know Montreal very well," Sam says.

Finally, reluctantly, he provides her with another address, which includes an apartment number, so she assumes it's his home.

She grabs a map, runs out the door, and takes the metro to the northwest part of the city. When she gets out at a stop near the end of the orange line, she sees she's next to a highway in one of those non-neighbourhoods that responded to urban sprawl by burping up car dealerships, fast-food chains, and big-box stores. As she walks along the highway, she is blitzed by the noise of wind and traffic. Commuters are heading home. The grey light of an overcast afternoon is slinking into darkness. Just before reaching an industrial sector, Sam turns right onto a tiny street. The address, written down on a piece of paper in her coat pocket, leads her to a cement high-rise, generica built by greedy developers in the '70s. She walks across the parking lot to the lobby, stopping just before the entrance at the sight of an old-timer sitting on a stool operating a ventriloquist's dummy. The old guy is bald with fat orange sun freckles covering his head. He has a basset hound's jowls, low-slung and wobbly, and he's wearing a blue polyester suit that has been around since disco. Beside his white-shoed feet is a cardboard sign: "Presenting the Amazing Mister Horn and Jimmy." The dummy is about three feet tall with red hair parted on one side and thick-lashed, brown glass eyes with thin, curved eyebrows. He is dressed in a plaid flannel shirt and tan trousers. In a strange way, the dummy reminds Sam of her father.

"*Bonjour*," the man calls to Sam.

"Hello," Sam responds.

"Eh, you speak English. *C'est pas grave.* Jimmy and me,

we're English. Right, Jimmy?"

Sam watches the dummy's head bob up and down. Then the dummy's mouth flaps open, and, in a high, squeaky voice, he announces he's hungry.

"A dummy eating food? Don't be funny!" Mister Horn replies.

The dummy bangs its arm up and down. "I want my dinner. Give it to me. I do so eat!"

"You're pulling my leg." Mister Horn stretches his right foot.

The dummy slaps Mister Horn's leg. "You liar! We went to McDonald's on the weekend. Liar, liar, pants on fire!"

Mister Horn stares up at Sam. "What do you say? You got some change for Jimmy and me to get a burger?"

Sam is unprepared for the sleight of hand changing a performance into a panhandling routine. When she reaches into her jeans pocket to get a coin, a rumpled five dollar bill falls from her pocket to the ground. She picks it up and hands it to the man. It is the most money she has ever given a panhandler.

She rushes into the lobby of the apartment building. When she gives beggars money, she can't stand to look at them. She's embarrassed but can't tell if her embarrassment is for them or for her. Checking the piece of paper again, she punches the code of the apartment building into the intercom. An older woman answers. When Sam explains she's meeting Francis, there is silence, then the buzzer goes off.

When she reaches his apartment on the fifth floor, the door is barely nudged open. Francis speaks to her through a thin strip. "Who is it?"

Sam grits her teeth. "Sam O'Connor. We spoke on the phone."

Francis undoes a chain lock but doesn't move the door open any further. He peers at her over the rim of his glasses. "Can I please see some identification?"

Sam takes out her wallet and gives him her driver's licence. She feels as if she's crossing a border. Perhaps in his mind she is. At the same time, his behaviour seems affected.

Francis examines the licence for several minutes before giving it back to her. "I guess you must be who you say you are." He speaks with reluctant generosity as if he is giving her the last piece of his favourite cake. In the background, Sam hears the older woman calling to him, asking him whom he's talking to. Francis holds up a finger, then shuts the door in Sam's face. A few minutes later, he joins her in the hall, having put on a coat and boots.

"This way." He opens a nearby door for her with a flourish of his arm. Sam enters a stairwell, and they jog down several flights of whitewashed concrete stairs to reach the ground floor. He brushes past her, through a door that looks like a fire exit but doesn't set off an alarm. Outside is a fenced-in area of grass where people are playing with their dogs. Francis strides by the grass and continues on away from the road, cutting through the backlanes. His legs are long so Sam has to run every few steps to keep up with him. When they get to the highway, they walk single file.

"What's with the cloak and dagger?" Sam yells into the wind. "Why didn't we go out the front door?"

Francis shivers, his torso twisting in a shimmy. "I never use the front door. I can't bear the ventriloquist and his dummy." His eyes flick skywards. "What, dear Lord, did I do to deserve them?"

Sam found them quaint yet understands his repulsion.

"Where are we going?"

"The Orange Julep for steamies." Just ahead of them, an enormous orange fibreglass ball is perched on top of a hot dog stand. Sam and Francis make their way across an expansive parking lot to the ordering counter. Around them, people are sitting in their parked cars, and girls in stretch pants and roller skates whiz along the pavement carrying bags of food. When a man rolls down the window of his car, a skater girl hands him a hot dog and a cardboard carton holding soft drink containers.

Even though the wind is raw and blustery, teenagers swarm the ordering counter. The air smells of potatoes and fried onions, and static-filled classic rock filters through poor-quality speakers. Francis orders the trademark orange drink and a hot dog from a teenager whose face is exploding with acne. Sam asks the kid for a large fries with mayonnaise. Out of a combination of new-found preference and a desire to seem native, she now orders her fries with mayonnaise. While she waits for their orders, Francis goes and sits down at a nearby picnic table. When the food arrives, Sam pays for it since he hasn't given her any money.

Sam joins Francis. The wood of the picnic table soaks the back of her jeans, but she decides to just deal with it because he doesn't seem to be the easygoing type. In his long parka, he won't notice the dampness of their seats.

"This place is weird." Sam says. "Don't get me wrong—the food's fine." As if to prove it, she gobbles up a french fry.

Francis folds his arms together. "I love The Orange Julep. I know it's kind of shoddy, but it was built in the Forties. Generations of teenagers have hung out here. We're all addicted to a kind of post-war, Archie-comics nostalgia, I guess, because how can we be nostalgic about our own youth: the Vietnam War, the FLQ crisis, and Watergate?"

Although Sam has eaten in cafés that brand their mismatched dinnerware as ironic, and she remembers Chloe and James going to seedy taverns, in which he championed the working-class patrons, Francis's take on eating at a cheap hot dog stand is unique. But he *sounds* reasonable. His voice is so dignified, so confident, so white. Meanwhile, Omar, who is Egyptian, talks like an urban African-American.

Sam studies Francis as he eats his hot dog in judicious bites, managing not to spill any chopped onions onto the table. From his reference points, she guesses he's around forty. He's average height and weight. With his wire-rimmed glasses and short, unfashionable afro, he isn't a nerd so much as out of date. He is wearing plain black slacks, and Sam notices the corner of a pressed white handkerchief poking out of the right pocket of his grey button-down shirt. He does, however, have one strange feature, which Sam identifies only after several minutes—his earlobes are missing, and he appears to have been born that way.

When he finishes his hot dog, Sam offers him some of her fries. He shakes his head. He is waiting for her to talk to him, a time-honoured modus operandi, which she knows because she has watched the same television cop shows as he has. Understanding what he's doing doesn't alter the effectiveness of his method. She pushes away her half-eaten yellow carton of fries and asks him if he sent her a letter.

He raises an eyebrow. "I don't know you. How could I have sent you a letter?"

She says, "I know this is going to sound crazy, but I moved to Montreal because someone sent me a typed, anonymous postcard, which said my sister was investigating a political conspiracy when she died. The postcard suggested my sister was murdered."

Francis slips his hand into his breast pocket, removes his handkerchief, and begins to wipe his fingers one at a time. When he finishes cleaning his hands, he folds his handkerchief into a precise square and tucks it back into his pocket. Only then does he respond; he asks her if she brought the postcard with her.

Sam bites her lip. "No, but it's at my place. If you want, we can go get it."

Francis nods. "It's okay, I believe you. I'm sorry to disappoint you, but I never sent you anything like that."

Sam turns away to watch the cars race along the highway. The noise of the wheels has a repetition that can be mistaken for rhythm. The difference is rhythm has purpose, rhythm ends up somewhere.

Francis clears his throat. "Chloe and I shared a world view. Detractors would call us paranoid, but I prefer 'justified suspicion.' She believed, and I still believe, that all the facts of any event are never known, that some information is always being withheld, that what we see isn't all there is. What we see is only a reminder of what we don't know."

Sam tries to laugh but makes more of a choking sound. "I don't know anything, that's for sure. Until I got the postcard, I thought my sister died of a drug overdose. My father lied to me for years about how exactly my sister died. If I can't trust him, how can I believe anyone?"

Francis offers her a sympathetic grimace. "If I had my mother's Bible here, I would place my hand upon it and swear to you I didn't send you that postcard."

Sam wants to believe him. After all, he believes her. And he doesn't seem to care whether or not she likes him. When she first met Omar and Romey, they wanted her to like them. Their friendliness felt a little like flattery, was too shiny somehow. Sam asks Francis if he thinks her sister killed herself or was murdered.

He rubs his chin. "I don't know. The last time I saw Chloe, she told me, 'If anything happens to me, don't believe it's an accident.' When I heard she overdosed, I assumed she'd been telling me she intended to kill herself. But murder is within the realm of possibility."

"Why do you say that? Do you know if she was investigating something?"

"She was, but she wouldn't tell me much about it. Just that it was off the radar screen of the usual political conspiracy theories, and she needed to find another source. I guess she wanted corroboration."

Once again, it seems as if the author of the postcard is right. Is opening a secret like opening a wound? Because Sam feels a new pain wrap around the old. Omar claims not to know anything. Fine, he's lying. But Romey? How could she live with Chloe and be her friend and not know what was going on in her life? Is Romey lying as well?

Francis says, "Was your sister murdered? You have an anonymous letter and her statement that if anything happened to her, it wouldn't be an accident. What are the chances that both the letter and her statement are a joke? How likely is coincidence as an explanation?" His question is rhetorical, but he pauses to hold his hands together as if in prayer. Sam catches a glimpse of his palm, pink as a cat's tongue. He continues, "To claim that events occur by chance or by error rather than design is an ideological position, one of denial. In conspiracy theory, a coincidence is usually meaningful, a link, a revelation."

Sam wonders how such an obviously educated man came to be living in a dumpy apartment with his mother. Then again, believing the universe to be at the mercy of inscrutable, corrupt, and all-powerful forces means you are a victim with all the hopelessness that implies. Taking action for social change requires an optimism absent from the ramblings she has found on the conspiracy theory websites she recently trolled at work—a computer station with Internet access has just been installed on the second floor. The websites have the same strident tone as the left-wing ones, but there are no calls for mobilization, no petitions being signed, no anti-authoritarian protests being held against the puppet masters, no marches with people yelling, "One-two-three, smash the Illuminati!" In the conspiracy theory mentality, there is a disengagement with the world, a nihilism. Was nihilism at the core of her sister's outrage? Sam wants to believe her sister investigated a cover-up to expose injustice, but Chloe was, as their father said, a girl who liked to toss tables.

Sam realizes Francis is asking her a question.

"Do you believe your sister was investigating a political

conspiracy?"

Sam shrugs. "I think she was sticking her nose into something."

"Ah." Francis shakes his finger at her. "You're not a believer. But you see, for a hoax to exist it has to imitate something genuine. Take psychics for example. For most of them, it's a sham act, a scam, but a few are the real article. If there weren't any that were real, how would the fakes know what to fake?"

Sam doesn't follow his argument, but she thinks she sees where he is going. "You think something happened to my sister?"

Francis nods. "Six weeks before Chloe died, we went to Paranoid—that's a conference for conspiracy theorists. She met this fellow there, and they started seeing each other. I thought he was a racist, but Chloe said the fact that he fought in the Gulf War and developed Gulf War syndrome justified some of his attitudes. We had an argument about it, and Chloe stayed with him. If I recall correctly, what she was looking into had something to do with the Gulf War. Perhaps *he* sent you the postcard."

Sam reaches over the picnic table as if she is going to grab Francis by his lapels. "What's this Gulf War vet's name? How can I find him?"

"His first name's Bernie, but I couldn't tell you what his family name is. He's a big guy, handsome, although who knows what he looks like now—as I mentioned, he claimed to be suffering from Gulf War syndrome. He lived in Detroit, which is where the conference was held. I have a good friend who runs an alternative bookstore down there; he might be able to help you."

Sam's brain begins to churn out, collate, and staple various considerations. She has a credit card; she can rent a car. She might not be able to get time off work, but on the other hand, what was the worst thing they could do? Fire her? She could always find another job as a dishwasher. "Would you come with me to Detroit?"

"I wouldn't mind visiting my friend," Francis says. "But I don't think I can help you with Bernie. He was part of some kind of militia organization, and they aren't too fond of blacks."

"A militia organization?" Her sister's politics were messy and punk rock, not skinhead. "Was she serious about this Bernie guy?"

"He was pretty taken with her, but, frankly, she seemed as if she was trying to convince herself she liked him." Francis lifts the lid on his drink, puts his napkin and hot dog carton inside, and then reseals it. "I wouldn't be able to go for another month or two. I've got a lot going on in my life right now."

Sam wonders why he always has to sound so mysterious. "What did you mean on my voice mail about the hawk and the mice?"

"Oh, I was just kidding around." His head is ducked down and his tiny ears are tucked so close to his skin that he reminds Sam of a mouse. He doesn't seem to have any problem hearing, but she suspects he hears differently from, well, everyone else. A gust of wind buffets their table and his empty cup rolls onto the grass. Sam gets up and retrieves the container for him. They dispose of their garbage and walk back to the metro in a not-uncomfortable silence.

As Sam is pushing against the swinging doors at the metro station, trying to open them against the hard suck of the wind, she hears Francis yell her name. He jogs over to her and she steps back from the door.

He's panting a little as he speaks. "The person who sent you that postcard obviously knows something. He or she could even have killed your sister. That card is evidence, and, if I were you, I wouldn't show it to anyone. I would put it in a safe place."

Sam nods. If Chloe was murdered, the postcard probably was sent by her killer. A killer who wants someone to know what he or she got away with. What other motivation could exist for sending the letter? Francis's warning is sensible. When he wants to, he can summon gravitas. Meanwhile, she's been running around questioning a member of the Montreal underworld. She's being reckless, but how else can she find out what she needs to know? She isn't used to being Mission Girl. She's a slacker, a—what did Lemmy say? A young urban failure.

Before striding away, Francis gives her shoulder an avuncular pat—her fear and confusion must be showing. She hopes he will be in touch. More importantly, she hopes Romey hasn't lied to her.

Sam is so busy thinking about her meeting with Francis she accidentally gets out of the metro one stop too soon. She walks home along Wellington Street. The street lamps are covered in plastic orange sunflowers that appear to be singing. Speakers hidden behind the flowers are tuned to a pop radio station, a sound that is momentarily dowsed by church bells. Montreal, with a history of French Catholicism, has many churches, and her neighbourhood seems to have more than its fair share. Her neighbourhood also seems to have a million pizza joints and *casse-croûtes*, all of which have crane games. Looking in a window, she watches a three-pronged claw dig through stuffed toys held in a glass box lit by a streaking fluorescent tube. Surprise—the chubby boy standing in front of the game wins a panda. What were the chances? Unlikely. Unlikely as the idea Sam's sister was murdered because she was investigating a conspiracy related to the Gulf War? Improbable isn't the same as impossible.

In front of Sam's apartment, a group of teenagers are shooting dice. They are white but wear bandanas over their scalps. Hip hop is now so huge that what Sam thinks of as "black" is stretching like a piece of gum. She slows her pace to watch the outcome of the craps game, to see one kid collect wadded-up five dollar bills from two of the others. The parked cars on her street are rusted, and someone has fixed a smashed rear-view mirror with duct tape. These kids have more of a claim to hip hop than the sprinkling of middle-class black kids she grew up with. On the other hand, it isn't too hard for Sam to imagine the white teenagers who live in Verdun winding up in jail, abandoning their passion for hip hop, and joining white supremacist biker gangs. Some people have the power to recreate themselves; other people do not.

Chloe's boyfriends—James, Omar, Bernie—are so different from one another, or, at any rate, it sounds to Sam as if they are. Maybe, for Chloe, that was the point. At the end of her first year of university, Chloe broke up with James. After she left him, she ordered a cheeseburger at a mall, thus ending two years of not eating meat and dairy. Within a week, she ate another cheeseburger and emptied the fridge of soy milk. Sam was furious at the time. How could Chloe just change her politics? How could her beliefs be so yoked to a relationship? Sam asked her, "If James was a cute guy in a Christian youth group, would you have become a Baptist? Would we have handed out religious tracts?" Her sister didn't have an answer, except to yell at Sam to leave her alone.

CHAPTER TWELVE

Some kids in her grade nine class talked about getting drunk, and Sam asked her friend Paul what it felt like. "Fucking great," he said, which didn't really answer the question, so Sam decided to get drunk on her own. When she got home from school, she went to her father's liquor cabinet and took out a bottle of rum. That's what Paul drank: rum and Coke. It tasted sweet, he said. Sam poured herself a large glass of rum and took a sip. Gross. How could adults like this? It was like drinking chemicals. Sam added some Coke, which made it a little better. She gulped the glass down and poured another one. At first she didn't feel anything, then—whoosh!—the thoughts in her head tumbled, like a barrel over Niagara Falls. Paul was right—getting drunk was fucking great. She felt as if she could do anything, talk to anyone…. After putting on her sister's Violent Femmes record, she screamed the lyrics to "Add It Up." She called Paul, and they took turns playing different songs for each other, holding up their respective phone receivers so the other person could hear. Battle of the bands. Punk and goth versus classic rock. The music was so loud Sam didn't hear Chloe come in.

"Are you out of your mind?" Chloe stamped over to the record player, lowered the volume, then turned back to Sam. "Oh my God. You're drunk!"

Sam told Paul she had to go.

"Do you know what time it is? Any minute now Dad's going to come home to this little after-school special." Chloe put the Coke back in the fridge, stuck Sam's glass in the dishwasher. "I can still smell the booze." Chloe ran upstairs. When she returned, she was waving around a burning stick of incense that dripped grey ash onto the floor.

The thick herbal smell made Sam's stomach lurch. She charged in the direction of the bathroom, but the contents of her stomach flew from her mouth onto the bathroom floor.

Chloe came in. "I can't believe you." She picked up the fuzzy blue bathmat, which was now speckled with vomit, and tossed it into the tub. As Chloe ran cold water over the mat, Sam remained hunched over the toilet, throwing up again and again. Chloe sat on the edge of the bathtub, waiting for Sam to finish.

When the spasms ended, Sam stood up and studied herself in the mirror: her face was grey, and there was a dribble of vomit on her chin. Chloe wet a washcloth and handed it to Sam.

Voices drifted in from the kitchen. Chloe said, "Go to your room, okay?" Before dashing down the hall, she winked at Sam. Ignoring Chloe's instructions, Sam followed her sister to the kitchen where Dad had arrived. Standing beside him was a stranger, a man who held up the bottle of Captain Morgan's rum. Shit. Sam had left the rum on the counter.

Chloe strode over to the man and stuck her face up to his, exhaling on him as if he had demanded a Breathalyzer test. "I drank it," she announced.

The man stepped back, his face puckered with distaste.

Dad said, "This is my friend Steven, and I think you need to apologize to him." Their father's tone had never been icier, and Sam crept into her room. Later that evening she went to see her sister. Chloe lay in bed, reading. She seemed to be engrossed in a biography of Marilyn Monroe.

"So what happened?" Sam asked.

Chloe looked up. "I got grounded for two weeks."

Her sister did that for her? Wow. Sam's heart suddenly

felt too big for her chest, as if she's happy and she might die. "Thanks."

Chloe waved the book she was reading. "The Kennedy brothers probably had her killed, but we'll never know. They were saints, good guys, while she was a screwed-up Hollywood slut. People don't want the truth—they reach for the explanation that fits their world view."

Sam didn't respond, but she understood Chloe was also referring to their father, who tended to cast the two of them into separate roles: the fair daughter and the wicked one. Even though Sam had messed up for a change, Chloe allowed her sister to keep her privileged status.

CHAPTER THIRTEEN

St. Henri, where Romey lives, is a schizophrenic neighbour-hood. An upscale market and expensive condominiums are blocks away from public housing and abandoned factories. On her way to Romey's place, Sam passes a funky second-hand store, a massage parlour, a French bistro, and a Caribbean restaurant. Yet, the area seems somehow appropriate for a woman who, Sam senses, is complicated.

Romey's place is on the third floor of a triplex. After Romey opens the door on the second floor landing, Sam follows her up another flight of stairs into a spacious apartment festooned with clutter. Without apologizing for the disarray, Romey goes into the kitchen to make coffee while Sam looks around the living room. A posse of dying plants is stashed in one corner of the room while opposite them on a small table is a shrine dedicated to the Virgin Mary, a statue surrounded by votive candles in coloured glass cups. The shrine doesn't seem to be camp. Newspapers, magazines, and CDs are strewn across the hardwood floor, plastic trolls stand in a row along a windowsill, and dozens of tasteful black and white postcards of nude women are tacked onto the walls. There are also a few photographs, which Sam examines, noting the absence of women who look as if they are or were a girlfriend. Instead there are pictures of people who appear to be elderly relatives and photographs of Omar. In one picture Omar is cooking hamburgers on a gas barbeque in a backyard. Behind him, Romey sits in a hammock with her arm draped around a small, plump older woman who has the same rounded cheeks as Omar. A strip of pictures from a photo booth reveals Omar crossing his eyes while Romey sticks out her tongue and pulls her lips apart with her fingers. Sam studies it for a moment. Who knew the two of them were capable of silliness? A second strip from the photo booth dangles upside down; a tack holding the top has fallen off. She flips the photos back up and sees her sister, which gives Sam a buzz. It's as if she found something she thought she had lost. In each image Chloe and Omar are together, touching; his hands protectively clasp her waist, her fingers smoosh his hair. The expression on Omar's face is serious, almost wounded, while Chloe smiles dreamily. They were, Sam realizes, smitten with each other.

"Here's your coffee."

Sam spins around and Romey hands her a demitasse of espresso. How cool and European, Sam thinks, taking a sip. She nearly chokes. The coffee is strong and quite bitter.

Romey laughs. "Cream, sugar?"

Sam shakes her head, then takes a seat on a couch with a red velvet throw. Romey joins her, sitting closer than Sam would have expected. Are they on a date? Sam can't tell. Romey isn't wearing makeup and is dressed quite casually in black jeans and a hoodie covered with black and white, Japanese-style comics of teenage girls with swords. But on the other hand, her hair is slightly damp as if she has just taken a bath. Of course, it's probably safer not to think of this as a date since Sam isn't even sure she trusts Romey. Her best friend is a thug who practically threatened Sam.

Romey says, "You can have those pictures of your sister if you want."

Sam gulps her coffee as if it is a shot of tequila. "No, you keep them. I have other pictures of her. But I was wondering, how did you guys meet?"

Romey sets her own espresso down on the floor—there's no coffee table. "She answered an ad I put in the paper. I wanted a female roommate who smoked and was messy. Turned out she smoked pot, not cigarettes, but that didn't bother me. She was the only girl who answered. Everyone else who replied was a guy. I remember one of them told me he had feminine qualities."

Sam has to smile at that. "So what did he think were his feminine qualities?"

"I don't know because I hung up on him. I was so fed up with men. I kept sleeping with them, thinking it would be different if the guy was an artist, older. Once I even slept with this blind guy who said he was great in bed because he was so tactile."

Sam can't keep herself from asking, "Was he?"

Romey wrinkles her nose. "No, he was nothing special. Anyway, I wanted to live with a woman, but not another dancer. There's too much competitiveness, has she got nicer boobs than me, that sort of thing. Along came Chloe, and we got close, like that." Romey snaps her fingers, and Sam glimpses a tattoo on her wrist, a black triangle.

"So you met Omar through Chloe?"

"Yeah. Omar's never gotten over her. Those two were madly in love. But, you know, it would never have worked."

"Why not?"

Her frown is dainty. "Omar's mom came here from Egypt with, like, five hundred dollars. She could barely speak English, didn't speak any French. He grew up in a shitty apartment, and they were always scrambling for money. He wound up running with a gang of West Indian guys. One's dead now, another one's in jail, and the other two got jobs in the straight world and married their girlfriends. Omar loved Chloe, but I'm not sure he would have given up the thrills and chills for her."

"Maybe she wouldn't have wanted him to."

Romey looks at Sam with disbelief. "Your sister was a proper girl from a proper home. No offence, but she was slumming. There was just a lot of chemistry between them." Rolling her eyes, Romey adds, "God, they used to be freaking loud."

Sam says, "They had stuff in common. They both lost a parent." When Romey doesn't respond, except to draw her body back, Sam realizes her tone was too snappy. Listening to someone talk about her sister having sex makes her feel perverted, as if she is having sex with her sister. Maybe she's too uptight, but she suspects Chloe would feel the same way. Sam remembers her sister once saying she was glad Sam was six years younger because it meant they would probably never fuck the same guy. Turns out Chloe need not have worried.

Romey fumbles with a pack of cigarettes she takes out of the front pocket of her sweatshirt but seems to change her mind—instead of lighting up, she sets the pack on the floor beside her coffee. Now she's not even looking at Sam, who tries to think of something to say to her. Is the awkwardness because they don't know each other very well, or is it about attraction, or something else altogether, something relating to Chloe? Sam doesn't know. But another question occurs to her. Asking it, she feels her heart thump, lay down a bass line. "Were you out to my sister?"

Romey leans back against the arm of the couch. "I told Chloe I was bi, which was what I called myself at the time. She didn't take it seriously at first. She didn't believe me. People don't. My mom doesn't." She bats her lashes, but the set of her mouth is flinty, hard.

This doesn't tell Sam what she wants to know, which is how homophobic was Chloe? But Romey's manner is a diversion. She has an essential insolence that Sam finds terribly appealing. She remembers the sarcastic way Romey took her clothes off. No. Don't think about that. Don't think about Romey naked. Don't think about doing things to her.

Sam asks, "Did Chloe ever talk to you about me?"

Romey gives her a sardonic smile. "The only time I remember Chloe talking about you was when I was admiring a dress in her closet. I went, 'Hey, you have a real vintage Diane Von Furstenberg,' and she just stared at me. She had no idea what I was talking about. She said you gave her the dress, you found it second-hand. From that, I figured you for this fashion plate girly-girl."

Now it's Sam's turn to grin. "If I was a girly-girl, I would have kept that dress!"

Romey's eyes lock on Sam's. "Don't take this the wrong way, but Chloe was kind of heavy. At first I thought maybe she also liked girls, but she didn't. She *really* didn't. She was bitchy about women, always putting down the waitresses at work. I don't know why she liked me. And there was something about her, I don't know what, but something about your sister I couldn't tear myself away from." Romey stands up from the couch in a fast awkward movement, as if to prove she can, however, tear herself away from Sam. Walking over to a CD player Sam hasn't noticed—a pile of laundry lies on top of it—Romey presses a button, and loopy ambience streams from an invisible set of speakers. The band is Air, their first CD from when they were just popular in France. A great CD to have sex to, Sam thinks, as she watches Romey shift the Virgin Mary statue slightly, centring it. Sam asks Romey why she has a shrine.

Romey flops back onto the couch. "I pray to her sometimes."

"You're Catholic?"

"Of course." Romey flings her hands around. "I'm Italian." Her hands fall back onto the couch, her baby finger resting against Sam's thigh.

Sam feels a flurry of breakneck beats in her chest and shifts away in case Romey didn't mean to touch her. "You're a Catholic lesbian who takes her clothes off for money. No contradictions there!"

Romey launches an arm outwards. "I know, I know. According to my family, I'm going to hell. But I can't *not* be

Catholic anymore than I can't *not* have a family even though, yeah, they're both fucked up. It's who I am. I can't break it down better than that." Her explanation, or lack of one, is interrupted by the ringing of a phone. Romey doesn't pick it up—just stares at it without speaking. A disembodied voice emerges from the wreckage on the floor. Then a click and a whir followed by Omar's voice. "Rome, pick up, it's your homeboy. Guess you're still out on your date…"

Sam thinks, a date. Oh my God. They *are* on a date.

Romey scrambles across the floor, tossing items of clothing out of the way to reveal an answering machine whose buttons she begins to stab. Omar's voice is abruptly cut off. When Romey sits back on the couch, her cheeks are flushed. Omar tipped Romey's hand.

Sam doesn't want to embarrass Romey, so she continues the conversation. "So, um, do you go to church?"

"Huh?" Romey is still flustered. "No, but I go to confession sometimes. And I tell the priest the truth, which I never used to do." She thrusts her chest forward, observing Sam from under half-lowered eyelids to see if she is having an effect. She is, but what turns Sam on are not Romey's breasts so much as the effort she is making to get Sam's attention. They are tapping into sex, sugaring a maple. Sam has this sudden insight—at work, Romey has to be in control of sexual situations, but that isn't how she likes it in her personal life.

Sam says, "When you were a kid, what did you lie about to the priest?"

Romey says, "I liked girls, but I never told anyone. I was the slut, you know, the girl at parties who was always drunk and making out with some guy on the staircase. I told the priest about kissing boys to get penances for what I felt about girls. Being a slut was camouflage, you know?"

"No, I don't. I never bothered with boys." Sam pounces then. Moves over, bringing her face close to Romey whose lips, even without lipstick, are so full. And she smells lovely, of something light and fresh and herbal. She closes her eyes and Sam kisses her. After a moment, Romey wriggles onto her back while Sam gets on top and pins Romey's arms above her head. Romey makes little noises, then lifts her pelvis and slides it against Sam's thigh.

Opening her eyes, Romey stares at Sam. "I wanted you the first time I saw you."

Sam doesn't tell her she felt the exact same way. She always holds back to have the edge and to make sure the words aren't going to be stolen later on. She runs her finger over Romey's lips, then darts a tongue in and out of Romey's mouth in a rhythm suggestive of the one she will feel when Sam works her way down. Under Romey's sweatshirt she's not wearing a bra. Her breasts swell in Sam's palms, her nipples temper against Sam's fingers. Instinctively, Sam knows Romey wants her nipples to be pinched; no gentle caresses here.

Romey isn't content just to be touched. She slips her hands under Sam's shirt, then beneath an unwieldy bra. The delicate rub of her fingers soon kindles flames in Sam's nipples. When it comes to making love to women, Romey's no amateur. To avoid surrender, Sam fishes Romey's hands out and tamps them to the couch. Lifts Romey's shirt, exposing her breasts. Stops touching her in order to observe those burgundy-brown nipples, those very round breasts, which Sam can tell are natural because they fall ever so slightly.

Romey giggles. "Do you like what you see?"

Sam stares at her. Tries not to think about the fact that Romey probably says this to men all the time. "Not bad."

Romey opens her mouth in mock outrage. "Fine!" She pulls her shirt down but Sam pushes it back up. Romey reaches for Sam, who grasps Romey's wrists with one hand while raising the other hand as if to say *you're going to get it*. The threat is empty, but when Romey's wrists are released, she flips over on her stomach and tilts her ass up. Sam spanks her. Slapping Romey's ass, Sam feels heat shoot through her like a sparkler.

"You're a top. Lucky me." Romey jiggles her butt in Sam's hand.

Sam has never been called a top before, but the word feels right, as if she's being given something she already owns. In high school, she imagined having a cock and using it to fuck the mean, pretty girls. At the same time, the word "top" makes Sam anxious. She isn't sure what she's supposed to do, what's expected of her, but she takes a stab by telling Romey she has to undress.

"Okay," she whispers. "Let's go into my bedroom."

Her room is dark, but she opens the black, gauzy curtains to let in a thin stream of light. Romey removes her clothes without fanfare and lies before Sam on her futon. Sam gathers her up, runs rough hands over the silk of her. Sam's lips kiss a path from Romey's collarbone to her cunt. Sam scores the trail with her tongue, a line of fire tracing gasoline.

Afterward, Romey lights a few candles and Sam strips down to her boxers and a T-shirt. Romey had offered to make love to Sam who said, no, she was satisfied. "I hope it isn't always going to be like that," Romey said. Sam felt her chest catch; Romey used the word *always*—there was going to be a next time. "It won't be," Sam promised. "I like to come too."

Sam strokes Romey in a contented haze. The slate of her skin is almost blank. Her only piercing is a wedge of gold embedded in her navel, and she has just the one tattoo on her wrist. Women always finger Sam's tattoos, ask her the names of the shops where she got them done, occasionally ask about the meaning of a particular symbol, and then flash Sam their own, inevitably smaller, markings. The inquiry is routine, boring, yet Sam feels oddly annoyed Romey isn't following the protocol. Catching Romey's wrist, Sam runs her thumb over the black triangle, feels thick tracks of skin. The tattoo isn't decorative; its purpose is cover-up. The ends of the scars, where the tattoo doesn't reach, are a gleaming silver. Sam edges her thumb along each line of scar, feeling Romey's muscles tense. She doesn't stop Sam, but Romey's permission is reluctant. There is usually only one reason a person has these kinds of scars on their wrists; Sam is overwhelmed with a feeling of tenderness.

After a moment, Romey withdraws her hand, sits up and winds her legs—flexible from dancing and working the pole, Sam thinks—into a yogic position. "I haven't been with anyone in awhile. I've had affairs with some of the other dancers, but they're never butch enough. The last couple years, I've just picked women up at Pride, girls who are too young for me."

"How young?"

Romey begins to laugh. "How old are you?"

"Eighteen," Sam lies. She watches Romey's jaw slump, but when her eyes narrow with suspicion, Sam tells her the truth. "I'm twenty-four."

"That's cool. I'm twenty-eight." She reaches over, grasps tufts of Sam's crewcut and holds the sections into pigtails. While Sam squirms, Romey leans her head back to observe. Then she stands up and puts her sweatshirt and jeans on without bothering with a bra or underwear. Sam lies on top of the sheet, her hands folded behind her head, watching Romey.

Romey pats her stomach. "*Ho fame*, I'm hungry. C'mon, I'm going to treat you to dinner with my filthy lucre." When Sam doesn't immediately get up, Romey leans over and licks her chin. "I can taste me on you!"

She is affectionate while Sam is less demonstrative. Sam tells herself Romey's screwed up, she's tried to kill herself, and she's friends with Omar who did God knows what to

Chloe. But Sam's admonitions to herself fail to close the muscle of her heart. From the beginning, Romey sews herself into Sam's skin, sinking barbs she can't feel at first. When Sam does feel their sting, she makes no effort to pull them out.

Sam and Romey spend every day together. They have more sex than Sam thought was possible, bouts that leave them ravenous with a more prosaic hunger. Romey introduces Sam to Italian food, takes her to the Jean-Talon market where they buy organic tomatoes, braids of garlic, fresh basil, pungent cheeses Sam has never heard of, and red peppers they broil until their blackened skins can be slipped off under cold running water. Between prepping meals at work and being around Romey, Sam learns a lot more about cooking great Italian food. She learns to curl her fingers when using a chef's knife so she doesn't slice her hand. She learns to begin with oil, herbs, and heat, to wait for their perfume before adding more ingredients. She learns about the importance of the right ingredients: blocks of parmesan so rich they leave a greasy smear on her fingers, fresh pasta dusted with flour, and organic cream.

At work, Lemmy asks Sam if she's met a guy. She guesses she's acting way too cheerful. Can't he tell she's a lesbian? She regards him as if he has three heads. "No. I met a woman."

Word gets around. Now they know she's out, the gay male waiters are chummier with Sam. The older woman who does the bookkeeping and writes the paycheques is noticeably cooler. Not unpredictable. A "Jesus Saves" button is often pinned to the woman's lapel.

Two days a week of work at Le Triangle d'Or pay Romey's bills. If she has to go to the dentist, she picks up extra shifts. Sam doesn't have full-time hours at the restaurant so she, too, has time. And Montreal is full of cheap thrills. Romey unfurls the city beneath the glamorous image, cracks open the dark, brittle places. Thrift stores along Monk in Ville-Émard where Canadian hockey legends Mario Lemieux and Gilles Meloche grew up, and people drink beer on their balconies long before the sun sets. The Italian district of St. Leonard where Romey makes a monthly trek for what she considers to be superior coffee. In St. Leonard, they go into a place Romey calls a "sports bar," which isn't really a bar at all. You can't buy alcohol, just coffee and juice. In the "sports bar" they play foosball and drink espressos and pear juice at a counter with old Italian men.

In the southwest where Sam and Romey both live, they bike along the canal and the river, stopping to shoot pool in a dive called The Dew Drop Inn, where everyone speaks English, and the television is tuned to a hockey game in which the sportscaster announces the plays in English. The neighbourhood is Point St. Charles, an Anglo-Irish ghetto, where about a third of the population is on social assistance. The reason they are on welfare, according to Romey, is because they're unilingual. Romey is fluent in English, French, and Italian. When Sam's plumbing backs up, she asks Romey to call the landlord, even though it isn't too hard to say "*Il y a un problème avec la toilette.*" If she stays in Montreal, Sam will have to learn some French.

Romey and Sam take a trip east of downtown, have a late afternoon beer at Foufounes Electriques ("Electric bum cheeks," Romey translates), a punk bar with a half-pipe in the interior for skateboarding. From Foufounes, they go into a sex shop. Inside an emporium of sleaze, they examine a smudged glass case of plastic dicks. They reject a pink rubber obelisk with ersatz veins in favour of a black and white striped silicone candy cane designed to press upon the G-spot, a dildo more like a sex accessory than a cock. When they get home, Sam cuts Romey's thong off with a Swiss Army knife, and they christen their dick. The next morning,

Romey hides Sam's boxers and makes her go commando when they go to get croissants at the market. Sam isn't always the top, and the hunger with which Romey takes Sam's nipple into her mouth demonstrates, as words cannot, that Sam is a desirable woman, not a freak.

One night they don't have sex because Romey has cramps. As Sam rushes to the pharmacy to get pain medication, fills up a hot water bottle for her, and makes herb tea, she doesn't feel disappointed. Looking after Romey is just as important as having sex with her. Sam thinks, I'm in love. Except maybe with Dyna in high school, Sam has never been in love. Her lust always crumbled into guilt and fear when the women she slept with began to glow with soft feelings for her. But her response to Romey's affection, to the hearts and arrows Romey may as well have inked all over both their skins, is to stay still, to breathe love in.

Romey doesn't discuss her feelings. She's quieter than every other woman Sam has dated. Femmes aren't supposed to be strong, silent types, but Romey is. Sometimes she talks a lot, but she is capable of sitting on her balcony and smoking her du Mauriers for hours without saying much of anything. Sam can riff about her day or not—Romey is as comfortable with Sam's silence as she is with her own. Women usually present Sam with full narratives of their lives, their traumas, their dawning awareness of their sexual attraction to other women. But Romey offers her history as though she were a croupier dealing cards. When they run into people Romey knows, she introduces them to Sam but that's all. There's the guy at the Atwater market who sells flowers. Even though Romey never buys flowers, she always greets him. Sam finally asks, "How do you know him?"

Romey says, "We went to CEGEP together." CEGEP is Quebec's system of junior colleges.

"What did you study?"

"I took a bunch of different courses."

"Do you ever think about going to university?" As she says it, Sam feels like an asshole, is reminded of her father. *What's your plan? You know you can't be a dancer forever.*

"A university won't take my application. I never got my diploma from CEGEP. I quit." Words spat on the ground, shower of dark hair tossed with a sharp movement of her head.

Sam drops it—the same way she dropped trying to find out what happened to her sister. After their first date, Romey and Sam don't talk about Chloe. All of Sam's efforts to find out who sent her the postcard, what exactly Chloe was investigating before she died, what Omar is hiding, are abandoned. Sam tries to set aside her memories of her sister, to tuck them into bed like a tired and cranky toddler you hope will sleep for awhile. When Sam is away from Romey, however, thoughts of Chloe intrude. While washing racks of dishes at the restaurant where Chloe used to work, it is hard not to think about her. The problem is, Sam doesn't want to. She remembers her father telling her she was going to Montreal for her own reasons. Maybe he's right—maybe she moved here to get over Chloe. Or maybe Sam's just afraid to try to find out more about Chloe's death in case it screws up things with Romey. Even though she isn't hanging out with Omar these days, she talks about him fondly. Whenever he has some kind of Egyptian community event to go to, he takes her. "I'm his beard," Romey laughs. He's not gay, of course, but his girlfriends have a tendency to be heroin-using drama queens. His current girlfriend is married to someone else. Meanwhile, Omar's mom really likes Romey. "You should marry her," his mom says, stabbing her finger at Romey. And the truth is, Romey acknowledges, their friendship has outlasted all of their lovers.

As Sam is leaving work one afternoon, she runs into Francis, whom she last saw more than two months ago. He's standing in front of Le Lapin Blanc talking to one of the Somali busboys whose name it takes Sam a minute to remember: Hassan. The busboy who informed her they put fags in jail in his country.

Sam trips down the steps of the pub to join them. They are pointing out marks on the ground where some drunken kids chalked a hopscotch game on the pavement and filled it in with signifying numbers—"13," "69," and "666."

"Hey, Francis, Hassan. You guys know each other?"

Francis looks up at her. "That would be a correct assumption."

Hassan interrupts: "*À bientôt.*" Without waiting for Francis to reply, he flounces off. There's an effeminacy in his manner of departure that makes Sam wonder for the first time if he's gay. A curtain opens on the argument she witnessed between him and the waiter, revealing both the staged drama of what she saw and another hidden dialogue. Had Hassan rejected the waiter's advances, only to have the waiter take revenge by reaching for racism, a reliable weapon, never far from one's side? And fearing being outed, had Hassan responded with homophobic overkill?

Sam asks, "Is Hassan your boyfriend?"

Francis laughs, displaying his teeth and a flash of tongue. "That would be an incorrect assumption. Hassan and I play chess together. He's one of the few people who can beat me."

"You knowing someone I work with is quite a coincidence. Oh wait, you don't believe in coincidences."

Francis kicks a stone from the hopscotch game into the street. "Now that's not an accurate paraphrasing of my theories. Besides, in this case, there's a simple explanation. I've played chess here for years. It's how I met your sister. And you got a job here to gather information about her. Speaking of Chloe, I'm sorry I didn't get back to you. I kept meaning to, but I've been busy doing all these interviews with a journalist."

"How come?"

"He's writing a book."

"About you?"

"About my father." He gives her a small frown, a warning not to pursue the topic, then continues. "Anyway, I've been chatting with my friend Ray in Detroit. He told me there's this fellow who runs a group for men with Gulf War syndrome. Ray thinks it might be a good place to try and find the guy that Chloe dated. Do you still want to go?"

"Of course," Sam lies. The truth is she almost forgot about their conversation, their plans to go to Detroit. As she and Francis discuss dates, times, and car rental arrangements, Sam's thoughts shift to her sister and the Gulf War conspiracy she was allegedly investigating. Except Sam feels as though she were taking out an old toy that no longer conjures a secret world. A toy like the kaleidoscope she found in her apartment, which she gave to Romey last night. As they sat drinking beer on Romey's balcony, Sam goofed around, aimed the kaleidoscope in the direction of the sky as if it were a telescope. She shifted the tube at the tangle of stars as if she were able to zero in on distant planets, as if she were discovering a big new faraway world, instead of watching a tiny canvas of subtly moving colour. A canvas she ignored, even though it was directly in front of her.

After Sam sees Francis, she goes to Meow Mix with Romey. Meow Mix is Montreal's dyke night, held irregularly at an old-style cabaret club with chandeliers hanging from the ceiling and a stage with red velvet curtains. Preening dyke hipsters come to watch a short stage show followed by their own show—their personal romantic dramas.

Just inside the door a curvy woman with long black hair and short bangs takes their money and stamps their hands.

As she inks Romey's knuckles, she glances up. "Where's your bad boy pal tonight?"

For some reason Romey colours slightly. "I haven't seen him lately."

"Too bad." Wet cranberry lips arch into a smile.

The club is almost full and buzzes with energy. Most of the clientele are women in their twenties and thirties but there are also a few men, both gay and straight. Sam asks Romey if the woman at the door was referring to Omar.

"Yeah, he tags along with me sometimes. It's so pathetic—he's gotten lucky twice, which is one more time than me."

Sam is surprised to hear this. Women must be intimidated by Romey. Either that, or she's more of a Catholic girl than she seems. "Did Omar sleep with the door girl?"

"Uh huh. She's bi."

The show begins with a burlesque dancer who has a pretty body but a not very interesting peek-a-boo routine. Sam asks Romey if she has ever thought about dancing at Meow Mix.

She rolls her eyes. "Every now and then some artist chick gets a job at The Triangle. They quit within six months, then wind up doing performance art about it for the next three years."

"So?"

"So, I'm not one of those girls. I'm not a dancer who is 'really an artist.' I'm just a girl who takes her clothes off for money. Don't try and upgrade me."

"I don't think I was," Sam says while wondering if Romey's right. Sam does think Romey underestimates how funny and smart her dancing is. She is way better than the woman they just saw.

Next up are drag kings performing Devo. "Are we not men," they sing and pantomime with flower pots on their heads. The vixens and studs in the audience smirk—the crowd is too cool to laugh. Devo is followed by a performance artist who, the MC informs everyone, has come all the way from Berlin.

When the artist walks onto the stage, she is naked. A stage light pinpoints an object in her hand: a bundle of black suture thread with a curved needle stuck into it. She begins pulling frantically at the thread, letting it web across her body. A joker in the audience yells *"plotte,"* which Romey explains to Sam is French for both vagina and a ball of yarn. After the artist has partially unwound the suture thread, a stage hand approaches her to give her a bucket, which she tilts, allowing the audience to see it is filled with ice. The stage hand gets on her knees, takes an ice cube from the bucket, and rubs it over the belly of the naked artist. When the ice cube melts into transparency, the stage hand picks up another ice cube and repeats the procedure. Just as Sam is beginning to be bored, the stage hand ducks back behind the curtain. The artist then threads the needle and reaches down to pierce her stomach. She pulls the needle through her skin a second time, making a stitch while the audience collectively grimaces. The light beamed onto her pale, concave belly reveals dots of blood. The artist gives the audience a merry smile, but as she continues to sew her skin, her expression and posture become more taut and fearful. She's leaking but cannot contain what is inside of her. She is trying to mend herself, except she is the source of her pain.

When she exits, she receives a smattering of applause. Sam can't decide if she liked the performance or not.

The show is over. Women who know the routine begin stacking tables and chairs along the sides of the venue, and a queue forms for the bar. Sam offers to get drinks. As she is waiting in line, a hand waves across her eyes. It's Deejay Sick, house deejay for Ciao Edie. Of all the women Sam could run into from her hometown, she's relieved to see Deejay Sick because there is no drama between them. Born in Japan, Deejay Sick is too thin and androgynous to sexually attract Sam. Always joking, dancing, or working the turntable, Deejay Sick is an agitated hummingbird. With a tip of the brim of her black cowboy hat, Sam greets her friend. Tonight, Sam's a sweet transwestite in jeans and a black gabardine shirt with front patch pockets and pearl white snaps. The only problem with the ensemble is it covers up her tattoos.

Leering at the wall of women, Deejay Sick asks, "Someone caught your eye?"

"No! I have a girlfriend these days." Sam cranes her neck around, looking for her lover amidst the art dykes with low-slung pants revealing curved tummies. She finally spots Romey standing in a corner talking to a short, chubby man with a goatee. What is Romey doing talking to a guy? Does she know him from somewhere? Hopefully not work! Sam points out her lover to Deejay Sick with a certain pride. Even in just a shirt and jeans, Romey is so gorgeous! She catches them staring at her and wanders over. When Sam makes introductions, she gives Romey's butt a slightly territorial squeeze. Romey shakes Deejay Sick's hand but otherwise doesn't contribute to the conversation about the relative merits of Montreal vs. Toronto. As soon as Deejay Sick leaves, Romey clutches Sam's arm. "I just ran into this woman I slept with, and she's taking T. I didn't even think of her, I mean him, as all that butch. You're more butch."

"What do you mean by butch?" Sam asks. Calling herself queer is easy because it embraces so much. It is like saying she's a rebel; how can she not want to be a rebel? But Deejay Sick says she's a "boi" as do a few other women Sam knows. Some of them bind their breasts, but Sam doesn't care to. If she did fall further along the masculinity continuum, she doesn't think she would call herself a "boi." Boys don't grow up; Sam isn't sure she's grown-up, but she wants to be.

Romey jacks her lip up. "Are you ashamed of being butch?"

Since they have just reached the head of the line, Sam raises her palm to tell Romey to hold onto her scorn for a minute. Then Sam orders their drinks: a beer for herself, a Cosmopolitan for Romey. While Sam likes the way Cosmopolitans taste, she isn't going to be seen in public drinking a cocktail. She doesn't like the word, but, yeah, she's butch.

"Are you ashamed?" Romey persists.

Sam shakes her head. "It just sounds so old school."

"*Plus ça change, plus c'est la même chose.*" Romey pauses to pick up her drink from the counter. "Taking hormones though, that's another story. But I'm not surprised. When we slept together he didn't take off any of his clothes, not even his baseball cap."

Sam crosses her arms. Romey is so close-mouthed, except when it comes to sex, where she overshares—like the time she told Sam she got wet at work dancing for an attractive straight couple. "I don't want to hear what it was like to fuck a tranny boy, okay?"

"What's the big deal? It was casual, just a hot fling."

An image swims into Sam's head—the transman licking Romey, the bill of his baseball cap turned around to facilitate it. What the Berlin artist did to her skin couldn't be worse than the way Romey is ripping Sam open. She hates herself for feeling so jealous—it isn't like her. Or maybe it is—she's never gotten close enough to another woman to find out. Why did Romey suggest going to Meow Mix anyway? In Sam's life, going to a dyke bar with a woman she is sleeping with signifies the end of the initial frenzy of lust, which is also when Sam looks for a new partner.

After tipping the bartender, Sam leaves the lineup. Romey follows her, asks, "What's the matter with you tonight?"

Sam stops, takes a swig of her beer. Her breasts are

swollen, but admitting her crummy mood is related to PMS is almost as embarrassing as discussing her insecurities. Instead she tells Romey about running into Francis, and her decision to visit Detroit with him.

"I wish you didn't have to go." Romey moves in front of Sam to straighten the collar of her shirt, then pats her lapels. Her hands linger on Sam's breasts. Romey's touch is casual, but Sam's body responds with desperate speeding desire, a vial of crack shuffled from seller to buyer. But fucking Romey isn't going to satisfy Sam. She wants to wring more out of Romey, out of them, than an orgasm.

Sam says, "If you told me a bit more, I wouldn't have to go anywhere."

Romey drops her hands. A wariness creeps into her eyes. "What do you mean?"

"I feel like I don't know you," Sam bellows. "You and Omar, you guys have never given me the whole story." What she is saying is, she suspects, half on-target and half ludicrous.

Penitent fingers snag Sam's belt loop, but she withdraws from Romey's reach. Offering equal parts apology and need, Romey trails after Sam, who is almost disgusted. Her lover is responding to Sam's nastiness with a weird submissiveness. Romey is tough, and Sam wanted to break her but didn't expect it to be so easy.

When Romey stops to bum a cigarette from one of the drag kings, Sam ducks back to the bar. There isn't much of a lineup anymore. She orders a pair of shooters and offers one to an older woman standing beside her. They cross arms and sling their drinks down. Then Sam feels a light knock-knock on the back of her head. Her cowboy hat pitches forward, covering her eyes. She grabs at it, but it falls to the floor. When she settles her hat back on her head, she glances up to see Romey sucking on her bottom lip. Sam's drinking partner melts away—she knows drama when she sees it.

Romey says, "Can you take me home?"

Sam nods.

They walk over to Parc Avenue to get a cab. When Sam turns her head to the right, she can see the giant cross on Mount Royal. During the day, the cross is a tangle of metal and wire, but at night it becomes a majestic totem. The beacon reminds her of the international fireworks competition that began this week; she and Romey sat on the flat tar roof of her building and watched the comets of colour on Île Ste-Hélène, cracking pearls glowing in a whoosh from green to red, thunder enmeshed in light. The desire to create a storm is universal; the ability to contain fire separates the winners from the losers.

They take a cab to Romey's place. She asks Sam if she's coming in.

"Of course. I much prefer to fight in person," Sam replies.

Romey offers Sam a tiny fragile smile. Inside her apartment, Romey makes them fresh drinks and brings one to Sam, who is sitting on the couch. Romey sits on the opposite end. She sets her drink on the floor and doesn't touch it. Instead she lights a cigarette. Blinking as if to barricade tears, she asks, "Do you think I'm a bad person?"

Sam shakes her head. Watches the tip of her lover's cigarette glow orange as she inhales.

Romey places her cigarette in the ashtray. She slides her hands into her dark, shiny hair as if she is nervous. "When I was growing up, I never got along with my brother. He was always calling me names, hitting me. He got picked on because he was fat and he took it out on me. When I was twelve, thirteen, I remember getting up super-early in the morning so we wouldn't have to take the bus to school together. But in high school my brother grew six inches, filled out, got friends, and was easier to get along with. We would play the same Led Zeppelin records, bitch about our parents. Then in my first year of CEGEP my brother took me to a party where his friend Paulo got me drunk and raped me." Her speech reels crazily like a spool of film unwinding. "My brother was in the next room and he didn't do anything. Afterwards he said I made a big deal out of nothing. And my parents didn't want me to go to the police—they told me to just try and forget about it, to stay out of Paulo's way. It was crazy. So I, um, tried to kill myself." Romey pauses for a moment. "It's a selfish thing to do. Not that you mean to be. There's a curtain between you and the rest of the world. The world looks normal, but you're on the other side. In the hospital I realized what I did was wrong. My parents were terrified. They showed up with this old Italian lady, a witch doctor who was supposed to get rid of the *mala*, the evil eye someone must have put on me. They don't have much education, my parents. Grade school, that's it. My brother even visited me, almost as scared, but he wouldn't apologize. He just sat there smoking, and I bummed one from him. That's when I first started smoking." Picking up her cigarette, Romey takes a long drag.

Sam would like to tell her how sorry she is, but the words seem inadequate. She wants to hold Romey but waits for her to finish her story.

When Romey continues, her eyes are lashed with tears. "I knew I could never do something like that again, so I left home. My parents begged me not to—Italian girls don't leave home. But I just couldn't live in the same house as my brother. He still had Paulo over. Anyways, I told Chloe about what I did, took her with me when I got this tattoo." Romey lifts her wrist up. "I tried everything to get rid of the scar, aloe vera, vitamin E, you name it. And I guess that's why I didn't go to Chloe's funeral. One part of me felt too guilty. I hadn't been a good enough friend to her, I didn't deserve to go. But another part of me was pissed off at her. I told her how fucked up it is to kill yourself, and she went ahead and did it anyway. Like it was a personal 'fuck you' to me."

Sam can understand this. Taking a deep breath, she says, "You know, Romey, I'm in love with you."

Romey crushes out her cigarette. Moving to the other end of the couch, she rests her chin on Sam's shoulder. Sam can feel Romey's chest lift, can feel the heat of her breath, can smell the smoke of her cigarettes. Why isn't she saying anything? Doesn't she love Sam? Sam wants to take her words back but realizes there is no point; she told Romey the truth. And Sam loves Romey so much she doesn't care whether or not Romey loves her back, as long as Romey lets Sam be with her.

"I wish you didn't have to go to Detroit," Romey murmurs.

Sam disentangles herself. Turns so she's facing Romey. "I have to tell you something. I came to Montreal because I got an anonymous letter claiming Chloe was killed while investigating a political conspiracy. According to Francis, Chloe was looking into something to do with the Gulf War. Are you sure you don't know anything about this?"

Romey jerks back. "No! Are you sure the letter isn't someone's idea of a weird joke?"

Sam doubts that. "I don't think so. And I know my sister—she was a hothead. If she stumbled onto some kind of political cover-up, she would have tried to find out more. And someone could have hurt her." At home, Chloe had acted as if youth and attitude could protect her—that other people, like her father, would respond with maturity and refuse to engage. But when Chloe left Toronto, she slipped into the lives of people far removed from her middle-class family. "Just before Chloe died, she dated this guy in Detroit. If I can find him, he might be able to tell me more."

"I hope he can." Romey reaches over to seal Sam's hands

in her own. "I love you, too, Sam."

Relief courses through Sam. Love—this is what counts. Love is more important than the stories she and Romey have to tell each other.

When Sam's boss refuses to give her time off to go to Detroit, she gives him her notice. No one seems surprised, especially not the manager. A few days before Sam is supposed to leave, she and Romey go to the Tam Tams, the weekly drumming and toking festival at the foot of Mount Royal. Summer has arrived in a hurry with blasts of dry heat. Throngs of people gather in the park to enjoy the weather, to enjoy themselves. On the steps of a monument with a marble statue of one of the so-called founding fathers of confederation, white men with beards and Guatemalan vests pound on drums in frenetic unison. Below them, a gang of student-age dykes with identical short haircuts dance with varying degrees of self-consciousness beside a group of teenage boys, who are playing Hacky Sack. Two women in vintage cotton sundresses give bowls of water to their big bruisers of dogs, which look like they were rescued from the pound. In another example of familial love, a bald white man and a black woman with a foot-high nimbus of hair grasp the right and left paw of their confident, ambulatory toddler. A few other people are selling stickers and jewellery in a laid-back way, not bothering with stalls. Such an absence of capitalist zeal would never happen in Toronto, Sam thinks. The whole event has the sweetness of homemade cake.

Romey spreads out a blanket for them. Sam sprawls on her back, hands stretched out and touching vibrant green grass not yet bleached of colour by the sun. The air is redolent with dope. A woman in orange pantaloons comes over to them to ask if they would like to buy organic menstrual cups. Romey replies that she works in a G-string and anything besides tampons doesn't cut it.

The woman smiles at Sam. "How about you?" she asks with gooey earnestness.

"No thanks," Sam says. The woman bows her head as if in prayer and meanders on. Sam wonders aloud how many more politically correct products people are going to try to sell to them.

Romey bursts out laughing. When Sam asks her what is so funny, she just pounds her hands against the blankets. Finally she gasps, "You know those President's Choice salad dressings, 'Memories of Thailand' and so on? I just thought, 'President's Choice Menstrual Cups, Memories of Feminism.'"

Sam grins. "You're bad."

When Romey takes some suntan lotion out of her purse, Sam offers to put it on her. Sitting up, Sam draws down the straps of Romey's little blue sundress and smears the cream onto her skin. It has only been hot for a week, but her neck and shoulders are the colour of toasted coconut. All of her is, except her tattoo and the scar, which shines like porcelain. Sam dabs extra lotion on the area, as she knows it is more vulnerable to ultraviolet rays. Then she puts lotion on her own pale, freckled, tattooed, cancer-soliciting arms and shoulders. Because she is wearing black jeans, she doesn't need any lotion for her legs. Finding non-dorky shorts was impossible (the camp-counsellor style was big this year), and summer makes her feel defenceless enough. Now that she's not wearing a jacket, and her breasts are visible in her T-shirt, people have stopped calling her "*monsieur*" and "buddy." Metro ticket collectors and grocery clerks pause for a moment, then ask for her bank card or give her change without using any pronouns.

A shadow slices the grass in front of Sam. Using her hand to shield her eyes, she makes out Omar standing over them. He's wearing a pair of black wraparound shades, which remind Sam of 3-D glasses. Romey springs up to kiss him on both cheeks, but he doesn't kiss her back, just stiffly holds his cheeks to her. When she finishes greeting him, he crouches on the grass beside them. Looking sideways at Romey, he says, "Thought I might find you here."

Romey flicks her eyes in his direction but only for a few seconds. "I've been meaning to call you."

Omar doesn't answer. He removes papers, a pack of cigarettes, and a baggie of pot from the pocket of his vest and begins to make a joint, rolling it on his knee with casual expertise. He licks the end closed, lights it up, and begins to smoke. He doesn't offer any to them. After a few tokes, he begins to lecture Romey. "We're supposed to be best friends, but I haven't heard from you in over two months. I bang chicks, but I still call you. You bang chicks, and you still call me. I even get involved, and you still hear from me. But you? You never get serious about your, what do you call them, Romey? Your fuck buddies." He pauses to look meaningfully at Sam.

"I'm sorry." Romey's eyes widen. "I really am."

Omar raises his joint to his lips again and puffs his cheeks in and out like a giant toad. "I thought, 'why's she bugging?' We haven't had a fight, nope, no unkind words. Then it hits me." He leans over and snaps his fingers in Romey's face. She flinches but doesn't move away from him. "She doesn't want me to tell her new girlfriend the whole down-low on why Chloe and I stopped seeing each other."

Sam props herself up on her elbows.

Omar pinches out the joint, then turns to Sam. "You see, the reason Chloe shot herself was because she walked in on me and Romey banging."

"How could you," Romey rasps.

"Did you really sleep with him?" Sam cries.

Romey nods her head, and Sam's heart feels as if it is clamped with steel pins. The three of them sit in the hot grass, not speaking. Omar canvasses the crowd with his eyes, but his body remains still, listening, waiting. A stranger breaks the peculiar tension—a shaggy-haired boy sitting beside them asks Omar to leave. He says, "You're creating a bad vibe, man."

Omar snaps, "Why don't you bounce out of here, cave boy?"

Sam says, "I'll leave." She stumbles down the hill, knocking into groups of people and muttering apologies. She's hurt and pissed off. How could Romey do that to Chloe? Romey's explanation of why she didn't go to Chloe's funeral omitted some important details, reminds Sam of the way Romey confessed to the priest about boys in order to receive penance for her real sin: wanting to kiss girls. How many layers does Sam have to peel away to get the truth from her lover? How far would Romey go to protect the best friend she used to fuck? Would she lie about a political conspiracy? Would she cover up a murder? Or did she just turn away from certain facts? She's good at that.

When Sam reaches the street, she hears footsteps behind her and spins around.

It's Romey. She puts her hand out as if to touch Sam, then seems to think better of it. "I'm so sorry."

Sam longs for the comfort of Romey's touch while knowing it is impossible since she is the cause of the pain. Turning from Romey, Sam begins to walk down the street.

Romey dashes after her. "Don't you want to know what happened? Don't you want to know why?"

Sam stops so suddenly Romey bumps into her. Sam moves to the side of the curb and sits down on the grass. She plucks a strand of timothy-grass and begins to chew the end. "Okay."

Romey drops to the ground beside Sam. Words race from her mouth. "I was in love with Chloe. She wasn't my type sexually, but I didn't have enough experience with girls to know that yet. I knew Omar found me attractive, and I thought, maybe all three of us could get together, take care of each other's needs. What can I say? I was young. One night we were smoking up, listening to music, and feeling the peace, and Omar kept talking about how he thought women together were hot, so I, um, leaned over and kissed Chloe." Romey pauses, her face flushing. "And do you know what she did? She wiped her mouth and said, 'Don't be a pig.' I felt so ashamed, you see, because I wasn't very comfortable about liking girls. And I felt humiliated. She was my best friend, and she had just reduced me to the level of the guys I take my clothes off for. She refused to talk to me about it, to talk to me at all, so I fucked Omar three days later. I wanted to hurt her, and I figured I couldn't get any lower in her eyes. And I guess I was also trying to prove to myself that I was bi, that I wasn't a dyke." As she tells her story, her hands pat her body looking for a pocket containing her cigarettes. The gesture begins absently but intensifies until she glances down and realizes her dress has no pockets. Her cigarettes are in her purse, which is back on the blanket where they were sitting. Romey's head swivels towards Omar. Seeing he hasn't left yet, she turns back to Sam to gauge her reaction.

When Sam is sure she has Romey's full attention, she spits out the piece of grass she was chewing. How can Romey imagine her explanation offers Sam anything? Omar cast an emotional grenade, but the professional arsonist is Romey, who stuck around to watch the fire. Romey fucked Omar and fucked over Chloe. Words bang in Sam's head like the tam-tams. Fuck. Bang. Gang Bang. The gang's all here. When Chloe refused to have sex with Omar and Romey, they punished her by letting her know they went ahead and did it anyway. But Omar and Romey didn't hive off because all three were connected in the same cat's cradle, no move possible to set these friends and lovers free.

Romey wipes her eyes with her arm. "I'm sorry I didn't tell you. I was afraid of how you would react."

"Don't." Sam thrusts her hands out—she doesn't want to hear any more. She walks away from Romey. Keeps going all the way down Parc Avenue to the subway.

That night at work she cleans cutlery in a daze of misery, not speaking. She feels like bad poetry, a soppy country and western song—nothing anyone wants to hear. She puts the same rack of plates through the machine three times. During break, as she shakes fries in a bowl with a pinch of salt, she wonders why she's making herself dinner since she's not hungry. Beside her, Dang is using a paintbrush to spread bar-beque sauce over a giant rack of ribs, cooking them part way so the cooks can make the orders more quickly. He indicates the ribs with a swish of the paintbrush. "That's my country when I left. Everyone dead." Before the Khmer Rouge came to power and murdered his parents and seven of his eight brothers and sisters, Dang was rich. His family owned a restaurant, he was attending university, and he spent his days driving around on a moped. He says, "When bad things happen, you never forget." This is the first time Dang has talked to Sam about his life, and she's touched by his subtle commiseration with her.

After work, Sam sits down at the bar and drinks one beer after another. Maybe Chloe forgot about her promise never to leave Sam. Maybe her sister killed herself because her best friends hurt her. It isn't hard for Sam to imagine Chloe blundering into death with the same graceless outrage with which she lived her life. If it weren't for the postcard, Sam could believe it. But whoever sent the postcard was right about the gun, was right about Chloe investigating something. That's two out of three. Good odds for the author of the letter being right about murder. Much better odds than Romey or Omar telling the whole truth to Sam.

She orders shots, splashes them into her mouth. The tequila scorches a hole in her throat, melts her brain. The bartender is arguing with a waitress, but Sam can't make out what they are saying, even though they are speaking in English. Words don't make sense anymore because, as her father's boyfriend likes to say when he drinks, she's all liquored up. When Steven drinks, his Cape Breton accent emerges. After last call, Sam leaves the bar, teetering down the steps to the curb. One of the waitresses skitters after her. "Are you okay?" she asks. Her fingers smooth Sam's gelled hair.

No, I'm not, she thinks as she pitches forward and pukes. She can't seem to stop puking. Some cops walk by, their gait constrained by the weight of the gear riding on their hips. Their batons look particularly lethal; more so than their guns.

"*C'est quoi le problème?*"

"*Elle est soûle.*"

The cops leave Sam's line of vision. She sits up and wipes her mouth with her shirt. The waitress lends Sam money, then convinces a cab driver to take her home. Sam has to pay the waitress back tomorrow—she has kids to look after. Did Sam know that? Sam didn't but doesn't care. She doesn't care about anyone or anything. At least that's what she tells herself.

It takes twenty-four hours for Sam to recover from her hangover. It's the worst she has ever had. She leaves the house to pay back the waitress, then returns home to bed.

Over the next few days, Romey doesn't call Sam, and Sam doesn't call her. Sam keeps waking up at dawn, unable to go back to sleep, her brain kneading information like dough. The last time, the only other time she had insomnia, was in the months following Chloe's death.

Sam's doorbell rings a few hours before she has to get up to drive to Detroit. Even though it is well after midnight, Sam opens her door. She is half asleep but wakes up as soon as she sees Romey standing outside. Without a greeting, Sam lets Romey in. When they get upstairs, Sam stares at Romey, who is wearing a tiny silver dress with black platform shoes: she has come straight from work. They gaze into each other's eyes, sex and anger jangling, competing for priority.

Sam seizes Romey's shoulders. "I could kill you."

"Really." Romey pauses. "How would you do that?"

Sam places her right hand on the stem of Romey's neck. "I'd strangle you."

Romey produces a slight smile. "I'm stronger than you so I don't think you can." It is true—when they wrestle, Romey usually wins. She's a little bigger than Sam.

Sam kisses Romey. Except it is less of a kiss and more of a plunder. Nonetheless, Romey immediately moans. When Sam grasps Romey's nipples, they are pointy. After a moment, Romey wriggles away. She says, "Let me take a shower."

Sam shakes her head. "You're not allowed."

When Romey opens her mouth to protest, Sam puts a finger against her lips. "Don't talk. Just use your mouth to make me come," Sam says, shoving her boxers down to her ankles and kicking them off. Romey kneels down, leans forward, and gutters her tongue along the seam of Sam's cunt, straying on her clit. As Sam's hands rest on the sides of her lover's head, clamping her in place, Romey lifts her tongue ever so slightly. She slides it down, then up, so each lick overlaps half of the previous lick, a backstitch sewing Sam's desire tight. With a fist wrapped around Romey's hair, Sam's commands soon veer towards pleas. When her pleasure twists free, she loosens her grip on Romey.

Romey lies on her back on the floor, pulling her dress up and panties down but keeping her high heels on. She plays with herself, something Sam always does for her. Sam stares at Romey, aches to touch her, to feel her, to see her bouncing on *their* dick, but instead watches her like a creepy voyeur. Romey's finger jiggles and her belly lifts in orgasm while Sam feels both turned on and distant. When Romey finishes, Sam puts her boxers back on and sits on her futon mattress. Romey observes Sam as if she understands something Sam does not.

"I can't do this," Romey says. "We should break up."

"What?" All of Sam's anger smudges away. She has been ignoring Romey to punish her, not to end the relationship. Fear trickles along Sam's skin. "Romey, no."

"I need some space." Romey hauls her underwear up, yanks her dress down. Then in an almost calm tone, she adds, "I hope you find what you're looking for in Detroit."

Sam stands up. She can't accept Romey walking away. Their passion isn't waning—they just proved it. "Why are you doing this?"

Romey's face crumples. "Sam, you don't love me."

Sam reaches over and clasps Romey's shoulders. "You're wrong. You're the only woman I've ever loved." This sounds over-the-top but happens to be the truth.

Romey tucks her elbows up over her ears. Monkey no hear. She starts to cry softly. "Sometimes I've wondered if you are with me as a way to feel close to your sister. Maybe I'm just part of some weird grief process."

"That's not true." Her protest is automatic but, as she thinks about it, Sam realizes Romey is wrong. Looking into Chloe's death is what has made it possible for them to get this far. Chloe's death produced voluptuous possibilities: she might have married Omar or adopted Labrador puppies; she could have been a professor, a businesswoman, a spy. The contemplation of her futures makes her more than she might have been and makes Sam less. When Chloe's death cancelled her opportunities, Sam stopped allowing herself to take any. If someone got close to her, if it was possible for her to take a lover she might care about, she sabotaged the relationship. But here, in Montreal, understanding this for the first time, everything is different. A tsunami of hope washes over her. "Romey, I do want to be with you. I want to stay in Montreal. We can get married. We can have kids if you want."

"Does this mean you've forgiven me?"

Sam wavers before saying, "Yes." While she's no longer mad about how Romey treated Chloe, Sam hesitated because there are other considerations. What if Omar is hiding something even worse? Romey may have to choose between her lover and her best friend.

Romey sighs. "I don't know about you and me."

Then again, maybe there won't be a choice.

"Don't do this to me, to us. Is Omar the only meaningful relationship you're going to have?" Even though she knows she is making a mistake, Sam can't seem to shave the frustration from her voice.

Romey swings her elbows down and shoves Sam's chest, pushing her away.

"I'm going now," Romey says. Her eyes are darkened windows locked down.

"Don't wait too long to come back. I have a use-by date." Sam is full of shit, testosteronic. But Romey strides out of Sam's apartment without a second glance. Sam wants to follow but grief holds her fast.

PART THREE
WARNINGS

CHAPTER FOURTEEN

During her third and fourth years of university, Chloe could not stop talking about the Kennedy assassination. As far as she was concerned, the lone gunman theory was crap. Certain facts, she argued, were indisputable: a president was killed, and the Warren Commission established to investigate the assassination operated in secrecy; minutes of its meetings were classified top secret, and much of the evidence was sealed for seventy-five years; witnesses who heard and saw people shoot from behind the fence on the grassy knoll weren't called. His own government killed him; it was as simple as that.

Chloe's obsession with the Kennedy assassination was not an isolated incident. Gradually, her interest expanded to other conspiracies, which she addressed, wherever possible, in her papers for her political science classes. Mind, she didn't believe all conspiracy theories—she was a skeptic when it came to alien abductions and the alleged dangers of fluoride, agnostic with regard to the idea the Apollo moon landings were faked—but she was unwavering when it came to political assassinations.

Sam was baffled by Chloe's new-found passion for conspiracy. It was as if she had wandered into a revival tent filled with snake handlers and been converted. But, as far as Sam could tell, no like-minded individuals had brought Chloe into the fold—her worship was solitary. In fact, in terms of a social life, she needed to get one. She had made no new friends since her breakup with James and the cooling off of her relationship with Tory. Except to go to class, Chloe didn't leave the house. And, as long as she kept her grades up, Dad didn't force her to get a job.

The only things Sam could identify as having been responsible for her sister's conversion were books. Her scriptures were: Noam Chomsky's *Manufacturing Consent* and Michel Foucault's *Discipline and Punish: The Birth of the Prison*. When Chloe began to refer to herself as a Foucauldian, Sam decided to read *Discipline and Punish*. She tried for months to read the book but couldn't get through it. It was dull. It was an historical account of the development of the panopticon, an architectural model of a prison building that allowed an observer to watch all of the prisoners without the prisoners being aware of whether or not they were being observed. Who cared?

While her sister's influence led Sam to become a vegetarian, the path of conspiracy buff was not for her. But perhaps she was just bitter over the way Chloe had abandoned vegetarianism. It was an issue that caused their relationship to pulse with friction when, for example, Sam left the following note in the fridge: "Dear Number One Sister: In future, please don't let your bloody hamburger meat touch my tofu. Sincerely, Number Two Sister." The irony of the greeting and sign-off was not lost on Chloe, who retaliated by tantrum.

When Sam returned the Foucault book, she found her sister lying in the dark in the basement den watching the *X-Files*. She was supposed to be reworking the outline for a research paper, an historical survey of éminences grises. She had recently had a crushing meeting with her supervisor, who had characterized the outline as sloppy and unfocused. Chloe should be examining no more than three examples of decision-making by unofficial advisors and provide detailed background, covering the socio-economic, historical, and cultural context of each situation.

"Here's your book back." Sam dropped Foucault onto

the portion of the Ikea couch Chloe wasn't lying on.

"Did you like it?"

Sam shrugged. "I don't think I got it."

An advertisement came on. Chloe swung her legs onto the floor and sat up. "Sam, listen to me. The people we need to be afraid of are multinational corporations and state governments who only let us see what they want us to see. What Foucault adds to this is the idea that we need to examine the way in which the government has made surveillance normative."

Sam nodded. Was normative a fancy way of saying normal? She didn't ask because she didn't want to sound stupid, plus she wasn't sure she really cared.

Chloe wasn't daunted by Sam's silence. "For example, take bank machines. We don't even think about the cameras that watch us withdraw money. We don't even consider that those cameras can match faces with identities and economic transactions. Basically, the government can find out everything about everyone."

"I guess," Sam said. "I'm going out. Catch you later."

Chloe held a pillow to her chest. "Where are you going?"

"Don't know yet." A lie: Sam was going to a gay bar, something she had never done before. She wasn't sure why she didn't tell Chloe, but Sam thought maybe it was because she wanted to have an experience that was hers alone, something to which Chloe wouldn't be able to say, "When I was your age, I did that."

"Are you going with Dyna?" Chloe singsonged Dyna's name.

"Yeah. What do you have against her, anyway?"

Now it was Chloe's turn to shrug. "She seems trashy." The *X-Files* were back on, and her attention was once again burrowed into the screen.

Dyna Kouropoulos was Sam's new friend. Dyna was a year ahead of Sam, so they didn't have any classes together. They had met outside the side doors where everyone smoked. Even though she didn't smoke, Sam liked the smokers—they were the bad-ass kids. Dyna was an incest survivor, a fact she tossed like a Molotov cocktail into unrelated conversations. She wasn't beautiful—she had a big nose and a spritz of acne running across her square-jawed face—but guys paid a lot of attention to her. She had long brown hair and a pretty body, but so did lots of girls, so why, Sam wondered, were the boys always sniffing at Dyna? Why couldn't Sam stop staring at Dyna? Why did she ooze sex, as if being molested when she was a kid had sprayed her skin with pheromones? The other girls hated her, called her a slut and worse. All the girls, except Sam who knew Dyna wasn't really a slut. If you didn't like having sex with boys, it didn't count. To Sam, Dyna described getting up in the middle of a blow job in order to make a sandwich and fantasizing about chopping off the penis she had been sucking. Although she couldn't remember the first time she had sex, she knew she had lost her virginity to her father. What she did remember was going horseback riding and thinking to herself, if a boy ever asked, she would tell him she broke her hymen from riding a horse. But no boy ever got that story. After guys fucked Dyna, she told them her father had raped her. Their reactions? Shock, horror, embarrassment, and occasionally contempt. But none of it seemed to make a difference to her. "I've never been in love," she told Sam. "I can't decide whether I hate men or feel sorry for them."

No one at school talked like Dyna. As casually as she would lend a pen, she handed over her most squirmy secrets and feelings, something which Sam admired but which also made her feel afraid for Dyna, protective. Sam couldn't stop thinking about her. The two of them spent every day together. They ate lunch, spent their free periods together, had coffee after school. On weekends, Dyna liked to go to punk clubs, even though she didn't like the music and didn't look like a punk. She wore white Lacoste shirts with super-tight jeans; Chloe dubbed Dyna's style "preppy gone bad," which Sam found annoyingly apt. What Dyna said she liked about punk was the anger, but Sam also noticed the looks Dyna showered on the skinhead boys. Personally, Sam was over punk. One day Dyna suggested they go to a gay bar.

Walking into the gay bar, Sam felt nervous, exposed. She thought, everyone will know I'm gay. If she ran into a neighbour, that person would know the truth about her, and she wouldn't be able to retract it. But once she was in the bar, Sam realized she was being silly, paranoid—no one here cared about her. She was disappointed to see she and Dyna were the only women in the bar. The reason Sam agreed to go to a gay bar was to see lesbians. But the place they were in throbbed with men: alert hunters studying a dance floor of gyrating quarry displaying naked muscular chests.

The few seats in the bar were taken, so Sam and Dyna leaned on a square pillar, which was covered in mirrors.

"Check it out—these guys are all hunks!" Dyna said.

What struck Sam about the men was their pleasant scent. The place was packed, but all Sam could smell was aftershave and gel, as if the men had just taken a shower and put on antiperspirant. Punk bars were as full of guys, but they stunk of beer, smoke, sweat, and, not too infrequently, vomit. Two men with moustaches necked beside Sam. The sight was both slightly shocking and a relief. She and Dyna were in a bubble, away from incursions, or so Sam thought, until an older man came over to them and put a beer in her hand.

"Thanks," Sam said. Without thinking about why he might have brought her a beer, she proceeded to drink it.

Dyna glared at the man. "We're lesbians."

The man stared at Sam for a moment, then left.

Dyna explained, "He thought you were chicken."

"What?"

"A young boy. He bought you a drink because he thought you were a fag."

"Oh." Sam felt stupid. She drank the rest of the beer as fast as she could. She wanted to get drunk but was afraid to order another beer in case the bartender asked for ID and threw them out. Dyna was bolder; she went to the bar and returned with two more beers. When they finished their drinks, Sam cupped Dyna's ear, ostensibly so Dyna could hear Sam above the music, but in fact Sam just wanted to touch her. "Are we lesbians?"

"Do you want to be?" Dyna yelled.

Sam nodded and Dyna kissed her. Sam had only ever kissed a boy or two at a dance, but this was different because she was kissing someone she wanted to kiss. She was kissing Dyna, whose lips were fuller, whose mouth opened just enough to hold Sam's tongue. There was a feeling like the blooming of flowers in Sam's chest, and she pressed herself closer to Dyna. Running a tongue along Dyna's slightly crooked front teeth, Sam felt their hard edges, an imprint she wanted to keep forever. She opened her eyes and saw their reflection in the mirror: a gawky boy-girl with freckles and pale lashes kissing a taller girl-woman, who was wearing enough mascara for both of them. Sam closed her eyes; she wasn't sure what they were doing could survive scrutiny, could survive—high school. But when Sam opened her eyes again, she saw Dyna's eyes were also open, were, in fact, peering around.

When they walked out of the bar, Sam was plastered. She had spent all of her money on beer and needed to take a cab home, so they stopped at a bank machine, where they had to wait for two teenage boys to finish getting their money. Sam felt so loose, so loud, as if she couldn't be contained, as if the best parts of her, the love and affection she carried deep within her, were flowing like lava from a volcano. She stumbled against Dyna, then put an arm around her, reaching up to kiss her.

"Lesbians." The teenagers stood with legs apart, scowling at Sam and Dyna. Even though it was December, the boys weren't wearing coats. Their hair was unwashed, their jeans dirty.

Sam thought, lesbians? How pathetic! The boys hadn't even called them dykes, let alone carpet munchers. Did they think Sam was going to cower and be ashamed? Well, she wasn't. Not after tonight. She said, "Nothing gets past you guys!"

One of the boys looked uncertain while the other one glanced at the ceiling, then flicked his eyes meaningfully at the other boy. Without a word, they trudged out the door.

Dyna said, "I'm not really a lesbian. I just thought it would be easier with you."

In an instant, Sam's cockiness vanished. She got it: Dyna thought Sam would be easier to keep at bay than a boy. Everything Sam felt, everything she wanted to feel, was not possible. Dyna had wound a tight thread around Sam, intending to weave the two of them together, but instead Dyna had cut off Sam's circulation.

Sam looked at the ground. When they got out of the bank machine, she was too stunned by Dyna's comment to notice the boys waiting for them. The first punch to Sam's stomach seemed eerily normal, an appropriate accompaniment to Dyna's rejection. As Sam's palms smacked the cold, raw ground, she realized the security cameras in the bank machines had temporarily provided them with protection.

Chloe looked up from her morning coffee. "What the hell happened to you?"

"Is it that bad?" Sam ran from the kitchen to the down-stairs bathroom to examine herself in the mirror. While Dyna had screamed, the boys kicked Sam's legs and ass. Then one of the boys stopped what he was doing to Sam to seize the hood of Dyna's coat and pull her to him. Sam scrambled up from the ground to lunge at the boy holding Dyna. What Sam had got for her efforts was an elbow in the eye. An eye that was now puffy and bruised the colour of an eggplant.

Chloe stormed into the bathroom without bothering to knock. "Did Dyna do this to you? Are you guys having some kind of twisted dyke relationship?"

Twisted dyke relationship? With shaking hands Sam ran a washcloth under cold water. Was her sister no better than the idiots who had done this to her, who would have done worse if two big men wearing chaps and leather jackets hadn't chased the boys away? In the mirror Sam glared at her sister's reflection. "Get. Out."

"She did do this to you, didn't she?"

Sam pressed the cloth to her swollen eye. "No, she did-n't. But I'd like some privacy. Don't say anything to Dad, okay?"

"Like I ever have." Chloe flounced off.

By some strange instinct, Chloe's assessment was par-tially true: Dyna was the one who had really hurt Sam.

Sam told her father she got drunk and fell on some stairs, and he grounded her, but Sam's misdeeds were trumped within days by Chloe, who dropped out of school. Her su-pervisor deemed a second thesis outline unacceptable: Chloe had failed to deconstruct the concept of conspiracy theory and éminence grise.

"We live in a culture of secrecy—that's what I'm deconstructing. But I'm not going to deconstruct my deconstructions. That's insane!" Chloe railed to Sam, who didn't have much to say to her sister or to anyone because she couldn't stop thinking about the night she was attacked. After their rescue, Dyna had hailed a cab. The two of them had got into the back seat, and Dyna had held Sam's hand. Speaking in a low, fierce voice, Dyna had said, "I can't believe this shit still goes on, but I guess I shouldn't be surprised. Even though we've got feminism, men keep raping women. Men are such fuckheads." When the cab had stopped in front of Sam's house, she had invited Dyna to sleep over, but she had shaken her head. "I don't think that's a good idea." Sam had croaked, "I just want you to hold me." She had been telling the truth, but Dyna hadn't been able to meet Sam's eyes, had stayed in the cab. Now Dyna was dating a guy. So much for men being "fuckheads."

When Chloe announced she was visiting Montreal for a weekend, Sam barely paid attention. But when Chloe called on Sunday night to say she had decided to stay there, Sam was furious. How could some people just take off? How could some people dump the people they loved? When their father drove Chloe's stuff up to Montreal two months later, Sam remained at home, pouting. She missed her sister, but Chloe's absence felt like an echo of the other aches in Sam's life.

CHAPTER FIFTEEN

Sam parks the rental car in front of Francis's building and waits for him. He asked her not to ring the buzzer because the noise will disturb his mother, a nurse who works shifts. The discount car rental place gave Sam a Pontiac Sunfire, a low-end sports car, which she rented for four days, from Friday morning to Monday evening. A phone call and her credit card will allow her to add days if she needs to. She flips the radio station dial, searching for a sound to incinerate her thoughts of Romey. But all Sam sees are a slow succession of images from the night before: Romey's face scrunched with pleasure as she came; her cheeks streaked with tears and mascara while she cried; the brisk movement of her long legs as she stalked out of Sam's apartment. The radio doesn't help. Romey keeps trespassing through Sam's mind.

When Sam left her apartment to get the rental car, she noticed a package in her mailbox, a plastic bag containing a book and a kaleidoscope, which Sam took out. Her fingers tightened around the tube and she felt herself flush. How dare Romey return Sam's gift? Except—it wasn't Sam's gift. The tube was a different colour, a two-tone swirl of mulberry and lime. She held the kaleidoscope to her eye, twisting the end to make the corners of the five-pointed star collapse into itself. The psychedelic colours were familiar; Sam flipped the kaleidoscope upside down and found her name written in blue marker in her own childish handwriting. Chloe had stolen, then abandoned, the toy their father had purchased for Sam, and now Romey was giving it back. Sam dug the second item out of the bag—a thick, greasy paperback biography of Sid Vicious and Nancy Spungen. A Post-it was stuck to the top of the book: "Chloe left these behind. I found them the other day. Romey." The note wasn't even signed *love*. Sam turned the Post-it over with foolish hope, but there was just a ridge of tacky paper lined with lint and fuzz, no further message, no indication Romey was feeling as miserable as Sam. She chucked the bag and its contents into her knapsack.

Sam had locked away her capacity to love until Romey, the safe-cracker, jacked Sam open. Now Romey is trying to leave Sam. "I want space" generally means "I don't have the inner resources to dump you, but give me time to line up a distraction, and I'll do it." Sam hopes Romey will be less predictable but doubts it. Thank God, Sam is going away; if she stayed in Montreal, she wouldn't be able to keep herself from showing up at Romey's door. The trip to Detroit has become a diversion from the present rather than a visit to Chloe's past. Searching for a beat to pump through her head, Sam twists the radio dial around and around. She can't find any music. Instead the news comes on. Where the hell is Francis? Sam is about to get out of the car and bang on his door when she spots him scurrying towards her, holding the ventriloquist's dummy upside down, the feet grasped between his thumb and forefinger and held away from his body as if the dummy stinks. In his other hand, Francis is carrying a hard plastic beige suitcase. Sam rolls down her window and pokes her head out.

"Open the trunk." Francis is panting so hard it takes Sam a few seconds to understand him. Sweat gleams on his forehead.

Sam checks the area around the steering wheel to see if there's an automatic button to pop the trunk.

"There's isn't time for that," Francis says.

Sam boosts an eyebrow but does as he asks—gets out of

the car and opens the trunk using her keys. He sets his suitcase on the ground and tosses the dummy into the trunk,
shutting it with a thud. When he steps aside, Sam re-opens
the trunk and examines the doll Francis flung so ruthlessly
one knee is bent backwards. Sam straightens out the
dummy's leg and notices the name "Jimmy" sewn onto the
front pocket of his checkered shirt. Sam swivels around to
face Francis. "What are you planning to do to Jimmy?"

Putting his arms akimbo, Francis gives Sam a fierce look.
"I'll have you know this is the first time in my life I've ever
stolen someone else's property. I know it's a sin, but that man
just doesn't know the effect his doll has had on me for the
six years he's eked out his living in front of my apartment."

Sam scowls. "You can't snatch Jimmy." She scoops
Jimmy out of the trunk and into her arms.

Francis returns the frown. "The Disney generation, you
can anthropomorphize anything. It wasn't a kidnapping I had
in mind but, rather, murder. Now if you'll just hop into the
car, turn right at the next light, we'll reach one of the city
dumps. There's a small fee for dumping your trash into a
giant pit, but I'll be happy to pay it."

"There's no fucking way." Sam clutches Jimmy to her
chest. "Besides, I'm not letting you destroy that poor homeless man's livelihood."

Francis rolls his eyes. "Bleeding-heart liberal. Well, kidnapping is another option. I could leave a ransom note offering Mr. Horn the safe return of Jimmy if he promises to
live in front of another apartment building."

"Forget it." Sam stomps back to the front of the building and sets Jimmy on the pavement, folding his plastic arms
into his lap. There is a histrionic element to the drama with
Francis, as if they are playing roles, and he knows Sam won't
let him carry out his threats.

When Sam gets back to the car, the trunk is shut, and
Francis is sitting in the front with his eyes closed and his head

sloped onto the headrest. He has changed the radio station, and classical music soars forth. Without opening his eyes, he informs Sam they will be meeting Amanda in fifteen minutes.

Sam lowers the volume on the music. "Who's Amanda and why are we meeting her?"

"You know Amanda, you met her at the anarchist bookstore. She put us in touch. She's coming with us. I tried calling you, but you're never home. If you're not home much, you know you should really invest in a cellphone. Anyway, Amanda can share the driving with you and give you some money towards gas. And she might be able to help you find this Bernie fellow. She's Librairie Alternative's resident expert on right-wing groups."

Amanda was a weirdo Sam never thought she would see again. "Why can't you help me?"

"Because I don't feel like tagging along with you to meet libertarian wackos who view the development of Federal Reserve banks by President Roosevelt and the revocation of the gold standard as disasters that have led to America's subjugation to the Illuminati."

"Who exactly are the Illuminati?" Sam knows they are part of the conspiracy theory lore, but no one ever seems to produce any names.

"They're an alleged cabal of conniving Rhodes scholars and international bankers who are often described as being Jewish, which is not a fact but rather anti-Semitic fantasy. Supposedly, the Illuminati are responsible for multiple, nefarious plots—everything from killing Princess Di to starting the Gulf War. If you want to know more, you can ask Amanda."

Sam turns onto the highway, which is now glutted with solo commuters jockeying for position. A driver of a Mercedes does a U-turn and nearly takes out a bag lady and her shopping cart. Driving in Montreal is a race of fear Sam takes as a personal challenge. She sighs. "Where are we picking up your friend?"

As Sam drives by Toronto she feels nostalgic, even though she is with strangers: Amanda, who sits beside Sam drinking a thermos of organic, fair trade coffee, and Francis, who is napping in the back, his breath a steady yo-yo. The white noise of highway traffic puts him to sleep.

Just after Chloe got her driver's licence, she took Sam west on this highway. They went on a little road trip to the Western Fair, where they ate fresh-made donuts, rings of batter bobbing and browning in oil, then flipped into a tray of sugar. They dared each other to go on the Zipper, where they tumbled and flopped like laundry in a dryer. But, for Sam, the biggest thrill was watching men and women toss rings and darts, and boys woo girls with fluorescent-coloured toy animals. Sam sensed and envied the players' desire rippling beneath the games. Then she won at Whac-a-Mole. Being a winner felt terrific, much better than the prize itself of a giant koala bear, which she immediately handed to Chloe with the same nonchalant shrug as the teenage boys streaming by.

"Are we going to have a proper meal soon?" Amanda stashes a map above the glove compartment, blocking a corner of the windshield. She has been munching on apples and granola bars, which evidently aren't sufficient. Since they are still an hour from the border, Sam suggests pulling into a McDonald's.

"I'm a vegetarian." Amanda replies petulantly.

Soon she will be asking Sam how many more miles it will be before they get to Detroit. "Me too. McDonald's has veggie burgers now."

Amanda sniffs. "So what? They put food additives and sugar in everything. Plus I'm sure the soybeans they use are genetically modified." Even though the air conditioner is on, she opens the window. A gust of wind sweeps in, bearing the rank smell of manure. They are surrounded by farms on their second or third crop rotation. Sam wrinkles her nose, and Amanda rolls the window back up with a sigh. She has already informed Sam the hydrofluorocarbon gas in air conditioners contributes to global warming.

"If the food is mass-produced and isn't *au naturel*, Amanda thinks it's suspect. And she calls me paranoid," Francis speaks for the first time in hours.

"Everyone's paranoid. Our fears just find different hosts," Amanda says.

Francis pokes his head between the front seats. "Speaking of paranoid, do you think you two could fix yourselves up when we cross the border? Sam, you need to put on a shirt that hides your tattoos, and Amanda, your facial piercing has to go. I'm afraid, however, that I can't do much about my skin." In the rear-view mirror Sam sees an expression of mischief in his eyes.

"How come you have so many tattoos?" Amanda asks, dragging the tip of a finger along Sam's forearm, mapping out a black and white tattoo of a chick with a fauxhawk riding a skateboard. It must be the air conditioning that makes Sam shiver, makes goosebumps pop up on her skin.

"I like them," Sam replies, keeping her eyes on the road. Like Romey's dancing, Sam's tattoos are a way of saying "fuck you" and "pay attention to me." Except this explanation leaves her lust out of the equation. Once she got a tattoo, she wanted another, the same way a crack addict wants another hit of the pipe. Before she moved to Montreal, she was getting a sleeve.

They reach the border at the end of the afternoon. In a gas station bathroom just outside of Windsor Sam puts on a white shirt that belongs to Francis, while Amanda removes her eyebrow piercing with the aid of the mirror on the visor. A black star tattoo bursts from Sam's knee, but she doesn't think the border guards will check her lower body.

At the American border a black woman growls at them from a protective glass shield: "Citizenship?" The woman is wearing a green and brown uniform, a duet of the military and fast food franchises.

Before either Francis or Sam has a chance to speak, Amanda says, "I'm American." A slender arm slides past Sam's chest, thrusting a passport into the outstretched hand of the woman in the booth. Francis and Sam hand over their Canadian passports, but the woman barely gives them a glance. Instead, she thumbs through Amanda's document, then gives all of their documents back to Sam, who notices Amanda's passport is stamped with one country after another: Belize, Mexico, Colombia, Hungary, and the United Kingdom. After the border guard asks a few more questions about where they are going and how long they are staying, they are whisked through. Given how often Amanda travels, Sam is surprised they have no problems. The word "American" must be her secret password, her Masonic handshake. Being white, blonde, and pretty probably also helps propel her through the world. But Francis has another theory.

"Did you see the way Amanda got us across the border? She's a spy working for the American government. It's encoded on her passport."

"Ha, ha," Amanda says.

"Her parents are Americans who moved to Ottawa. Who would move to boring old Ottawa after living in Boston? Her father attended an American Ivy League university but went to work for the Canadian government." In the rear-view mirror Sam sees Francis emphasize the word "government" by lifting his fingers and making quotation marks in the air. He continues, "They were supposedly hippies but they never did drugs. They got involved in the peace movement. In other words, they infiltrated the peace movement. Amanda's followed in their shadow so to speak. Is it really credible that a multilingual graduate in psychology from McGill University would choose to work part-time for a non-profit organization? Then there are her jaunts to foreign lands. Clearly, she's on assignment."

Amanda looks up from the map. "Sam, take the next exit." She doesn't offer an explanation for her travels, but Sam fills in the blank: trust-fund baby. Amanda has the self-assurance verging on arrogance that comes from wealthy parents and a good education.

As Buffalo is quite close to Toronto, Sam has visited that city a few times, but this is her first time in Detroit, home of techno, Motown, and the automobile. She has heard the city never recovered from the race riots of the '60s, but the balkanization of Detroit still shocks her as she makes her way through rush-hour traffic. The corporate culture is close to the border, beside the river. Steel skyscrapers rise over streets where men in three-piece suits power-walk with their earpieces extended, a secret service legion in better clothes. A few blocks further on, prosperity ends. Sam drives by dark, empty factories and storefronts boarded up with plywood. Victorian mansions with cornices and turrets are missing their doors and windows. They have been stripped the way hubcaps are taken from an old car, except here the valuables are being purloined by delinquent yuppy renovators. Every street has a vacant lot: a ravel of weeds and smashed-up concrete. Billboards advertise condominiums and the second coming of Christ. Sam wonders if the religious messages are intended to reassure the few pedestrians, who are mostly black and down-and-out. You can't afford a condominium, but that's okay because eventually you'll inherit the earth. She coasts along one street after another, keeping an eye out for a bank machine to get money in American dollars, but there are only cheque-cashing businesses. When an automatic teller is finally spotted, they all get out only to discover the machine is busted.

The quest for American currency is abandoned, and Sam drives to the home of Francis's friends, Ray, who runs a small left-wing bookstore similar to the anarchist bookstore in Montreal, and his wife, Elena, who is an administrative assistant at Wayne State University. They live in a two-storey wooden house not far from downtown. Ray is sitting on the steps outside his house. He is white but wears his hair in long grey dreadlocks, which give him the appearance of a small, thick-branched tree. As Sam is getting out of the car, Ray stands up to introduce himself to her and Amanda. Sam sticks her hand out and Ray offers her a metal clamp to shake. Sam squeezes it. Feeling awkward, she stares at the ground.

Ray doesn't seem to notice Sam's embarrassment. He's too busy showing them the marks on the driveway where a car was firebombed. With obvious amusement, he tells them the former owner of the house was a drug dealer now doing time in a federal pen. The dealer's rivals blew up his car just before he was arrested. Ray and Elena bought the house at a city auction a year ago for almost nothing.

Inside the house, Elena is placing dishes of food on a harvest table scored with grooves. Younger than her husband, Elena is handsome and serious looking with long hair in a braid. She calls to her son in Spanish. A boy of about six is sitting in the living room, watching television, but the sound of his mother's voice launches him into the kitchen where he sets the table. Sam peers around their place. It has a comfortable ambience. There are shelves and shelves of books, cotton rugs and pillows in primary colours, and a forest of plants in clay pots. When she sits down to eat, she feels a gentle pressure on her feet. Under the table, she spies an orange cat slinking away. Over a bean lasagne and a salad with avocados, Ray and Francis discuss politics while Amanda and Elena chatter in Spanish. Sam entertains the kid by pretending to drive over his dinner with a Hot Wheels car left on the table. This makes her a big hit, leading Elena to cast indulgent smiles in Sam's direction.

After dinner Elena puts her son to bed while the guests bring in their stuff from the car. Francis gets the living-room couch while Sam and Amanda are sharing a cot in an upstairs room. When Sam and Amanda finish unpacking, they troop out to a cement patio in the back, where they find Ray and Francis sitting on rusty lawn chairs, drinking bottles of beer corked with lime wedges. Ray is also smoking, which, he explains, he's not allowed to do in the house. In the sky the sun is an orange fireball with a crown of white light and appears as manufactured as the rest of Motor City. Sam thinks, perhaps the sun will become obsolete. Maybe the way we pollute the environment is a form of planned obsolescence.

Amanda paces around the yard, extricating empty chip bags and gum wrappers from the untrimmed grass, amassing them into a small heap. Ray and Francis chat about ECHELON, which Sam learns is a way for the American government to eavesdrop on everyone. ECHELON is a vast global electronic dragnet that uses statistical techniques known as data mining to check for threatening patterns among everyday transactions.

Ray blows a sloppy smoke ring. "Every single person I've met who used to work for the government, who has been part of a black operation, is on disability. They all have chronic fatigue or fibromyalgia."

Amanda stops what she's doing to join the conversation. "Anyone who was part of a covert operation would never admit it. You've just met people who are mentally ill, who are suffering from chemical imbalances or have emotional problems. That's what makes them fatigued and delusional."

Francis prods his lime slice below the stem of his beer bottle. "Don't you think your explanation is a bit pat? People with Gulf War syndrome also suffer from chronic fatigue and fibromyalgia."

Amanda replies, "On the contrary, your military vets confirm my theory. Did you know there's research that shows similar clusters of symptoms have afflicted veterans of previous armed conflicts?"

Ray says, "Don't forget contactees. They're often sick as

well." He flicks his cigarette butt onto the cement with a provocative grin at Amanda. Ignoring him, she stoops to retrieve the butt. Ray likes to stir the pot, and Amanda has a coltishness that reminds Sam of Romey, except it isn't sexuality Amanda exudes but something else Sam can't put her finger on. She asks Ray what contactees are.

It is Francis who answers her. "They're people who believe they have been abducted by otherworldly visitors. If they're men, they believe marauders from another solar system have anally probed them; if they're women, they think aliens have abducted them in order to remove their uterus to initiate them against their will into an ongoing intergalactic, interspecies breeding project."

Amanda interrupts, "They're obsessives who have projected their fears of emotional and physical penetration onto medical technology." She flings herself down on the patio. Her cotton skirt is carelessly stretched above her knees. "In plain language—the walking wounded."

The wounded. Sam thinks of Romey's scar, of the gunshot that killed Chloe. Sam supposes Amanda would have a neat category for them as well: depressives. But a category isn't the same thing as an explanation. Knowing Chloe was unhappy isn't knowing why or how she died. The revelation of Omar and Romey's fling is flypostered over Sam's attempts to find out about her sister's death, yet someone sent Sam an anonymous card, leading her to Montreal and now Detroit. She is reaching for answers, but they arc away from her like an exploding star she can't break open, that she can only watch as it shatters against the earth.

The next morning, which is a Saturday, Amanda asks Sam to drive her to Dearborn. Dearborn is a suburb of Detroit, except the suburbs of Detroit are considered separate cities. Ray explains the purpose of these artificial divisions is to di-

vide municipal tax bases in order to prevent upscale neigh-
bourhoods from having to foot the bill for the poor. Downtown is a wreck due to a Darwinian economic policy.

Dearborn, or Little Arabia, turns out to have the biggest
population of Iraqi citizens outside of Iraq along with the
emigrants of many other Middle Eastern countries. Sam
drives past dollar stores, bakeries, dry cleaners, and fruit markets, all of which have signs in English and Arabic. On one
street men clad in cotton robes and woven caps hasten
through the front doors of a domed mosque. This evening
Sam will be going to a meeting of Gulf War veterans. For
both of these communities of people to share the same ge-
ography is, she thinks, a painful irony.

Sam glances at Amanda. "Can I ask you a question?"

"Sure."

"What exactly are militia organizations? I know they're
into gun ownership but so is most of America."

Amanda, who is sorting out her Canadian and American
money, dumps it back into her satchel. "Funny you should
ask. I've just been doing some research on them."

"Francis mentioned that."

"Right. Well, militia organizations are paramilitary groups
who believe the American people need armed force to defend
themselves against the federal government, which they view
as the puppet of a global socialist conspiracy. The United Nations, international bankers, and corporations are considered
part of the so-called New World Order, whose agenda is the
erasure of national and economic borders. People in the militia are horrified by what they fear will be the dilution of white
American identity, and the target of their hatred is an
'other'—Jews, Muslims, or the Arab world in general."

Sam backs the car into a small space. "Why are they so
afraid?" What made some people join militia groups while
other people took ecstasy and preached peace, love, unity,
and respect?

Amanda undoes her seat belt. "Is that a rhetorical question?"

Sam shrugs. "I don't know."

"I think people hate a particular group as a way to avoid hating themselves." A glint of metal from Amanda's eyebrow piercing blinds Sam like a camera flash.

Sam blinks. "What are we doing here in Dearborn?"

"I'm buying an outfit of Muslim women's clothing."

"Why?"

"I like disguises."

Sam regards the black vintage slip Amanda is wearing as a dress. The flimsy material is slack across her A-cup chest and pulled taut across her wide hips. A pair of chunky leather sandals from the '60s complete her retrophile look. Is she an artsy chick who listens to emo, or is her whole presentation a charade? Sam continues her scrutiny of Amanda: pleasant features, pink cheeks, high forehead, and hair like stretched taffy. A Gerber baby all grown up, except Sam senses Amanda has another skin. Francis is equally enigmatic, but Sam isn't as interested because it is always women who seize her attention. Wagging her finger, Sam says, "I think Francis's right. You're an agent."

"If I told you, I'd have to kill you."

"I'll keep an eye out for black Ford Explorers."

Getting out of the air-conditioned car is almost intolerable, even though Sam broke down just before she left Montreal and cut her black jeans into shorts. Michigan feels much worse than Montreal; the air is more humid, wet, and gummy. Beneath her knapsack, sweat sprouts across Sam's back. Within minutes, her throat is parched. She goes into a convenience store to buy bottled water. Inside the store a Middle Eastern teenager wearing cargo pants is working behind the counter. When Eminem comes on the radio, the clerk raises the volume on his boom box. As he counts out Sam's change, he swings his body to the beat, and an older woman stocking the shelves glares at him. Her head and mouth are covered by cloth, but there is no mistaking the censure in her eyes. Their interaction turns out to be a microcosm of the whole area. On the streets Middle Eastern pop competes with hip hop, burger joints vie with falafel stands, while clothing stores carry both head scarves and designer jeans. The melting pot is boiling over, hot liquid scalding everything.

When they reach a strip mall, Amanda pulls Sam into an air-conditioned Arabic emporium. Sam wanders along the aisles of merchandise, browsing her way through displays of frankincense and incense burners, brass Aladdin lamps, and tapes of belly dancing music. She fingers the hip scarves belly dancers wear, wondering how Romey would look in one. Sam picks up a crimson sash made of chiffon and dangling gold coins and brings it to the counter. If their relationship isn't over, Sam hopes Romey will like it. Just ahead of Sam, Amanda is buying a black dress, or *abaya*, as she informs Sam, along with a *hijab* Muslim women use to cover the head, and a *niqab* to cover the face. When they get outside, Amanda suggests they go next door to smoke a hookah pipe. Sam has never done that before but, as long as the place is air-conditioned, she is willing to try it.

They enter a small, dark restaurant with blue walls and wine-coloured carpets. Bronze busts of Nefertiti are propped up here and there, and a wide-screen television is showing Arabic music videos featuring beautiful women sinuously wriggling their bellies. The place is almost empty, and what few customers there are, are all men. After seating Sam and Amanda in a booth, a middle-aged man hands them paper menus, which, along with food and beverages, lists different flavours of hookah tobacco.

"What kind do you want to try?" Amanda asks.

Sam shrugs. "I don't know. I don't even smoke cigarettes."

Amanda leans over the table to read Sam's menu. "We don't want to get rose water because that's gross." She puts a finger on the first item on the list. "Let's get strawberry, it's a classic. Do you want anything to eat?"

Sam shrugs again.

"I'll decide," says Amanda. When the waiter returns, she places her order in Arabic, so Sam has no idea what to expect. What does arrive, before long, is the hookah pipe. It looks like a combination of a lamp and a teapot. The bottom, or base, is made of blue glass, and connected by a metal tube to a triangular cup. Springing from the tube is a thin, coiled-metal hose. The waiter fills the cup at the top with tobacco.

"He's packing the hookah," Amanda explains. She points to the tobacco, which the waiter is covering with tinfoil. "That's the *shisha*."

He pricks the tinfoil with a toothpick and sets tiny grey cakes of charcoal on top of the foil. An older woman arrives holding a tray containing two coffees and a plate of baklava, which the waiter takes and sets in front of them along with the coffees. He says something else to Amanda in Arabic, but she responds with a wave of her hand, sending him off.

Sam hears a gurgling sound and realizes the bottom of the hookah pipe is filled with bubbling water. Amanda takes some matches out of her satchel and lights the charcoal. After a minute, she takes the metal hose, puts her mouth on the plastic clip on the end, and breathes in for a moment, then releases a curling wisp of sweetly scented smoke.

Sam asks Amanda how she learned to speak Arabic.

"I just know a bit. I used to have a Lebanese boyfriend."

"The first girl I kissed was born in Greece, but I don't speak Greek."

Amanda explains, "I pick up people's accents, speech patterns, and languages. If you surround me with people speaking an unfamiliar language, I'll start to speak it within a few months." She picks the pipe up from the table, offering it to Sam. "Do you want to try?"

As Sam sucks in smoke, she tries to prepare herself for the harsh burn of something in her lungs. But—surprise—the smoke is smooth and cool in her chest. She inhales again, more deeply, exhales a candied vapour.

"What was your Greek girlfriend like?" Amanda asks. She stares at Sam with eyes Sam decides are grey, although the colour grey doesn't encompass their intensity.

"She wasn't gay, and she wasn't really my girlfriend. She was sexually abused by her father." Sam stops, tips her eyes down. Why is she even talking about Dyna? The smoke must be making her light-headed. Sam doesn't want to do some girlie inventory of her relationships with Amanda. For one thing, that would mean thinking about how many relationships Sam's screwed up, which means thinking about Romey. Sam hands the hose to Amanda. "How come you're asking?"

"Just making conversation. If you would prefer, I'll tell you about my ex-boyfriend."

Sam shrugs, which she's been doing a lot lately.

"Okay, boys don't interest you—I see that." Amanda corrals Sam with another stare. "Francis tells me we're in Detroit to find out about your sister, who may have killed herself or been killed."

Sam sips her coffee. "Yeah."

"What was your sister like?"

That *is* the question Sam is trying to answer, or more precisely, what was her sister capable of—suicide or getting herself killed? When Sam puts it that way, she realizes there isn't too much of a difference. She picks up the pipe and inhales more of the strawberry smoke into her lungs. Wasn't there something in *Alice in Wonderland* about smoking a hookah? Ah, yes, there was a caterpillar who smoked a hookah and kept asking Alice, who are you? Their conversation went around in circles like the smoke, which is now also swirling between Sam and Amanda. How would Sam describe Chloe? Smart, fierce, and protective, but also thoughtless and annoying. A woman who never tried to charm anyone but whom some people couldn't help but like. To the caterpillar, Alice was unable to say who she was because her body kept changing size and she couldn't see herself; that was Chloe.

Sam says, "Remember how you said you liked disguises?"

Through a mouthful of baklava, Amanda nods.

"Well, my sister lived her life like it was a series of disguises. I don't think she knew who she was."

The group of Gulf War veterans meets in the early evening in a computer repair store not far from Dearborn. The store is a mess. It is crammed with broken computers, some of which are so clunky and old Sam can't understand why they haven't been thrown away. Flavescent computer monitors line one wall, stacked on top of each other and pitching in all directions. Lying across a series of tables are open hard drives with coloured wires springing out. Sam is about to hear from men who have also been taken apart, whose experience of the Gulf War caused them to short-circuit.

A dozen or so people sit on canvas chairs in a semi-circle at the front of the store, where an attempt has been made to clear an area of the carpet. Most of the people are single men, but there are also a few straight couples. Parked in a wheelchair is a husky man who exudes an aura of authority. He is smooth-shaven with light hair nearly buzzed off. He has a plump, pink face but wary, cynical eyes. Sam can't judge his age—he reminds her of the way babies can simultaneously resemble old men. Behind the man is a white projector screen.

She sits in one of the canvas chairs and tries to remember what she knows about the Gulf War. In theory, the

United States declared war on Iraq because of the injustice of Saddam Hussein's 1990 invasion of Kuwait, but myriad dictators have committed genocide and invaded countries without being sanctioned by the United Nations Security Council. Why did Iraq face repercussions from the United States? Oil.

Sam hears one man say to another: "I heard my company First Sergeant is sick now. I'm telling you, this guy could battle a football team and win." She should mingle, but what can she say to these guys? She has nothing in common with them. Suburbanites who brag about the size of their satellite dishes. Assassins who killed for oil so they could have SUVs.

The man in the wheelchair introduces himself to everyone as Jason Weaver, a former US Marine.

"Hi Jason," everyone says, as though they were at an Alcoholics Anonymous meeting—but the similarity immediately ends.

Jason, despite being sick and disabled, speaks confidently. "America's assault on Iraq resulted in victory; one hundred thousand Iraqis died compared to less than two hundred allied forces. But a decade later, twenty-five thousand vets from the war have filed disability claims. Many of us say we have Gulf War syndrome. We won't all use the word but the memory loss, the aching joints, the fatigue, the insomnia, the headaches, they're real. They're real, but the media says we're fakers, that any scientific study we can come up with to prove we're sick doesn't have a large enough control group."

Almost as if on cue, a man at the back interrupts. "The media is just plain arrogant, people debating just for the sake of debating. When you wake up in the morning and your body has shut down, that's when you figure out something's wrong."

Jason nods. "That's exactly right. We don't know why we're sick; we're not scientists, but we know something's wrong. We know the theories: chemical and biological weapons, stress, vaccines, and oil fires. I believe my illness was caused by chemical weapons."

The guy at the back speaks up again. "I was a radio operator in the Gulf, and I remember this Iraqi Scud missile attack. As soon as the warhead landed, every chemical-agent monitoring device in the area went off. We got put onto the highest alert for twenty minutes, and then got told it was a false alarm."

"That's the military for you," Jason says. "Everything's on a need-to-know basis." He pauses to wheel himself away from the screen, then calls for volunteers to turn off the lights and to operate the slide projector.

Sam switches off the lights. This meeting doesn't seem like a support group. She expected each veteran would get a chance to talk briefly about themselves and their experiences, but clearly Jason has something else in mind. His talk seems rehearsed, as if he has given it many times before. No one is asking any questions, so she must be the only one who is out of the loop.

Slides display the flash-bang spectacle of war: convoys of tanks, oil wellheads spewing smoke, and the oil fires—toxic cascades of light in the night sky. There are also slides of guys on board the ship playing cards, waiting in line for chow, and on "liberty" in Hawaii bars. One slide shows a picture of a corpse in the sand, an Iraqi soldier dowsed in blood, flaps of his skin hanging from his body. Up until then, the slides didn't look like war so much as men training for war, playing at war. The dead soldier is the only picture of the enemy Jason has taken, and he doesn't say whether he killed the man. He does say the ground war was so "successful" it stopped one hundred hours after it began, and Sam gradually realizes that while Jason spent months in the Persian Gulf, he only did a total of a few hours of actual combat time. The Gulf War was no Vietnam; it was an accelerated music video.

Jason saw action for the first time only after the ceasefire—shooting hadn't ended in all sectors. His company was checking out a series of bunkers in a forest close to the oil fields when they began receiving small arms and automatic weapons fire from enemy soldiers. They returned fire and called in air support. "We finally got to do what we were supposed to do," Jason says, sounding relieved. Despite the Gulf War having made him sick, he is glad he had the opportunity to fight in it. Sam can't understand him. How can anyone aspire to being a killer? How can these men justify the invasion of a country far less powerful than the one in which they live? It's shooting goldfish in a bowl.

A slide appears of a dead dog lying on its side, its legs like bent sticks. Jason wheels himself in front of the screen, and the illuminated dust from the projector jets onto his chest. He says, "It was during that operation I saw what the government won't admit, evidence of chemical weapons." Near the oil fields, his company found enemy tanks and supply trucks destroyed by helicopters. They also discovered hundreds of dead animals: not just one kind, but cows, goats, dogs, chickens, birds, and cats. The animals had no bullet wounds, and insects lay dead around them as well. "That made us stop and think; was there some chemical warfare agent in the air? Should we be putting on gas masks? The head of our command called someone and, while we were waiting, I took pictures. The higher-ups insisted the area wasn't toxic, so we kept going. But a day before my ship arrived in the United States, a team of customs agents was flown on board by a Navy helicopter. Our company was told to take all our stuff and go on deck, where each Marine had his bags checked. They told us it was for weapons, but then they took everyone's rolls of film. But they missed this one—it was in my jacket pocket, and they didn't search us."

After Sam puts the lights back on, Jason reveals the purpose of his slide show: he wants to start a class action suit against the military and the government. The slide of a dead dog is his evidence he and others were harmed by chemicals. So far, over a hundred people have joined the suit. Who else wants to sign up? For the remainder of the meeting, the men discuss legal strategy, what it is Jason wants to accomplish, whether it is possible this action can be heard outside of a military court, and how much money the suit will cost.

Was there a military cover-up? Sam tries to decide. She doesn't think Jason is lying, but the whole presentation is like a sales pitch. Maybe it is because she's Canadian and not used to people turning whatever shitty thing happens to them into litigation or a talk show episode. When the meeting draws to a close, she approaches Jason Weaver.

"Hi, I'm Sam. I'm visiting from Canada."

Jason gives her a quizzical stare.

Sam continues, "I, uh, was wondering if you could tell me if you've run into a Gulf War veteran named Bernie who lives in Detroit. He's also suffering from Gulf War syndrome. I need to talk to him."

Jason peers across Sam to the next person waiting to speak to him. "I don't know a Bernie. As you've heard, there's a lot of people with Gulf War syndrome."

"He dated my sister, and they were investigating a political conspiracy to do with the Gulf War." Sam improvises. "Maybe the same one you're talking about."

This gets his attention. His face reddens. "This isn't one of those nut job conspiracy theories. This is real. This is real suffering." Jason punches his legs. Sam has uncorked his frustration, liquid nitrogen has escaped from a beaker— smoke with the power to change the temperature of the room. People are staring at them.

"I'm sorry if I offended you," Sam says. "I think you've misunderstood me."

"A lot of people think nothing happened to me, that I'm making it up," Jason says, sounding as though he feels sorry for himself.

Sam crouches down so she can look him in the eye. "My story is pretty hard to believe, too. The guy I'm trying to get a hold of—he may be involved with some kind of militia organization."

Jason seems to really see Sam for the first time. He wets his lips. "There's a bar not far from here, Pat's Place. Ask for a guy named Rick. He's always around. He can maybe help you."

Pat's Place is not so different from Le Lapin Blanc. People come to the bar to play games and not just metaphorical ones. You can rent chess sets, Monopoly and backgammon boards as well as games like Risk and Trivial Pursuit. The place is mostly full of college kids. Navel rings adorn the sloping stomachs of lithe girls, peeking above their low-rider jeans. Boys sit in knots, not bothering to move their long legs from the aisles when Sam walks by. At the back, she finds older men playing blackjack and poker. She is about to ask a bartender where she can find a guy named Rick when she hears a man behind her yelling. She turns to see a scrawny guy in fatigues jump up from the table where he is playing cards with four other guys. One of the guys looks as if he's in college while the other men are in their thirties with military-style hair, crewcuts and brush cuts.

The man in fatigues squawks, "What, aren't you glad we terminated their asses? We should have fucked them all up when we had the chance."

"Rick, we fought for the Kuwaiti people," one of his friends says.

Lazily brushing his bangs out of his eyes, the college kid puts in his two cents. "Man, you're the type of guy the military really needs to keep their eye on."

Rick shakes a fist. "We fought to make the camel jockeys

keep pumping our oil, and we should have annexed their fucking country. We should have ripped Saddam's heart out and drank his blood. If the fucking United Nations weren't running everything, American people wouldn't have had to die."

The college kid sighs in exasperation. "Dude, would you fold, already? You're just getting pissed because you're losing."

Rick glares at him. "Losing? What do you know about losing? We won the war, but then all those towel heads came over here. Some bitch practically ran me over with her car today because she couldn't see with her motherfucking sheet over her head." Turning away from his friends, Rick storms off in the direction of the bar.

The college kid folds Rick's hand over: he has nothing, no cards in numerical order, no pairs, no more than two cards in the same suit. The kid announces, "Told you. Loser."

The men return to their card game while Sam follows Rick to the bar, hoping he will reveal himself to her as easily as he did to his friends. She puts a five down on the bar in front of Rick's glass of draft. "Let me get it."

His eyes bulge. He is probably used to people just tolerating him; his green T-shirt is rimmed with dark patches of sweat and he smells funky. Lifting the beer in Sam's direction, he says, "Thanks, buddy."

He thinks she's a guy; she hopes her voice won't give her away. "You're welcome. Jason Weaver said you might be able to help me—I'm trying to find a guy named Bernie."

Rick jerks his head back. "I don't really know Bernie, but I know the CIA slut he runs with only too well. What do you want with them?"

Sam chews her lip while contemplating the options. She decides to show her hand. The truth sounds crazy but then so does he. An unforeseen advantage to dealing with the paranoid is they expect the world to be scary and irrational, to be like a Hollywood movie where the plot is strung together with special effects. "My sister died five years ago. She may have been investigating a political conspiracy, and it's possible Bernie fed her some information that led to her death."

Rick snorts. "Figures. You can find Bernie and his bitch selling their shit tomorrow at the gun show."

"What gun show would that be?"

"The one in Eldon at the arena."

As if she has some idea of where Eldon is, Sam nods. She hopes the place is nearby. "You wouldn't happen to have a phone number or address for Bernie or his friend?"

Rick chuckles. "I don't talk to my ex anymore. She's got a restraining order out on me due to my so-called anger management problems. But that's part of my Gulf War syndrome, right? Mood swings. Not to mention, Cheryl's the real psycho. It took me awhile to figure that out." Rick spins his index finger in a funnel, then picks up his beer and goes back to his buddies.

Amanda squirms in the front seat of the car and flips the visor up and down to examine herself in the mirror. She is wearing a flowered sundress she hopes will make her blend in at the gun show. Sitting beside her, Sam feels the back of her neck twitch, as if a bug is crawling across her skin, but when she brushes her neck, nothing is there. In the rear-view mirror, she can see Francis gazing out the window. By the Detroit river there is an enormous used bookstore, where he plans to spend several hours browsing before making his way back to their hosts' home on his own.

"It's just here," Francis says. "You can let me out on the street."

Sam ignores him, choosing instead to roar over a wedge of curb and race through the parking lot to the front door of the store. She turns to grin at him, but the set of his mouth is hard.

He holds up his wristwatch, tapping the face. "I expect you two to report back to me on your mission by no later than seventeen hundred hours. If I don't hear from you by then, I'll assume your mission has been compromised and take the appropriate measures."

"You want us to call you?" Sam asks.

Francis nods, then gives Sam a short salute as he gets out of the car. Amanda's shoulders shake with laughter. She is acting as if they are on an anthropological field trip while Sam *does* feel like a spy, or rather, a prowler. Looking like an obvious queer among militia types in the Midwest isn't smart so Sam is hoping she can pass for a guy. Passing is trickier in the summer when her breasts aren't hidden under a jacket. When she got dressed in the morning, she vetoed her collection of cool T-shirts in favour of once again borrowing Francis's long-sleeved white shirt. Then she bound her chest with a pair of pantyhose she bought the night before at a drug store. To complete the all-American-boy look, Amanda lent Sam a pair of baggy cargo shorts. The plan is for Sam to tell Bernie she is Chloe's brother and pray he won't remember Chloe had a sister.

Sam crosses the torsion of highway to reach the outskirts of the city. Without any buildings, the flatness of the land is more evident. She can follow the trajectory of the road with her eyes for miles and miles. They drive past fields of hay and corn shrivelling in the heat. The candescent sun, the sparseness of trees, and the lack of people walking around makes everything seem desolate. Matthew Shepard and Brandon Teena were both murdered in the American heartland. Sam thinks about their killers: men for whom killing a queer had no greater significance than crushing a cockroach.

The town of Eldon begins as small farms, two nurseries, and a kennel advertising Jack Russell puppies for sale. Then they reach a grid of residential streets with a few schools and churches and an actual Main street with a hardware store, a grocery store, a movie theatre, and a post office. Sam stops at a gas station because she doesn't know when she will get another chance to use a single-stall washroom. The gas station employee gives Amanda directions to the arena, which is just outside of town, beside a Wal-Mart.

The parking lot of the arena is full, so Sam parks on the edge of the highway. She and Amanda walk by trucks and SUVs and read bumper stickers that tell them all they need to know about the drivers. "Wife and Dog Missing, Reward for Dog." "You Can Have My Gun When You Can Pry It From My Cold, Dead Hands."

"Let me get this straight," Amanda says. "Bernie's a Gulf War vet suffering from Gulf War syndrome who dated your sister just before she died of a gunshot wound in a New York hotel room. Bernie may or may not know something about a political conspiracy she may have been investigating."

"That's right." A bead of sweat rolls into Sam's eye. The air, the heat, is as sticky and thick as cotton candy.

Across the door of the arena is a painted sheet with the words "Armageddon Expo." The homemade sign isn't so different from ones Sam has seen at Pride marches and antiglobalization demos and in a strange way, the antiestablishment sentiment is similar as well. But the cultural gulf is driven home as soon as she reaches the door. Two middle-aged bikers with leather vests and Santa Claus beards ask the man standing in front of her if they can check his weapons. The man hands them a gun. The bikers don't confiscate it, just open it up to make sure it isn't loaded before giving it back. When Sam was growing up, she loved heading east on the streetcar to Little India, where she ate curry and samosas and stared in the windows of shops, admiring the bolts of lustrous silk cloth East Indian women use to make into saris. She thought of herself as a stranger in a strange land, but she now realizes she was a confident white tourist in a Third World country. Here, she is an illegal immigrant sneaking across the border.

Sam peeps inside the door at the people milling around. There are a lot of families. The men, wearing jeans, checkered shirts, and John Deere caps, appear to be farmers. Their wives, who are clad in sundresses as Amanda correctly surmised, keep winding their heads around to hurry along their Slushie-slurping progeny. Amanda and Sam *might* be mistaken for curious college students. When one of the bikers asks Sam for an entrance fee but doesn't ask Amanda, Sam realizes she is at least passing for a guy. A sign above them announces "women and kids free."

Armageddon Expo turns out to be a trade fair for survivalists. Most of what is for sale are guns and firearm accessories. There are pistols, rifles, and shotguns, but at a few tables Sam sees machine guns and wonders if they can be sold legally. Ammunition, holsters, crossbows, scopes, and rangefinders are also available. Sam jerks her shirt out of her shorts; perspiration is plastering her clothes to her body. A hip check from Amanda makes Sam halt. The table in front of them displays Nazi flags and pamphlets. Amanda begins to leaf through various political tracts with the word "Zionism" in the title. A piece of paper taped to the table says "No Visa, American Liberty currency accepted." A stocky man with a bar code of hair crossing his scalp stands behind the table. Skinhead politics, but he looks like middle management. No shaved head, no camouflage pants—he is concealed in ordinariness.

"Can I help you, Miss?" he asks.

Amanda lifts up a newsletter entitled the "Patriot Report." "I'll take this."

"That'll be two dollars."

She hands him the money. "Do you know if Bernie's working today?"

The man points to the back of the room. "He and Cheryl are at the very end. I hear he's got some new videos.

You wouldn't be one of his actresses, would you?"

"Could be. You take care now." Her accent is Midwestern twang with a touch of honey. She rewards him with a coy smile and he looks surprised, then pleased—the power of the skinny blonde over straight men. Even Sam feels a pull of attraction to her. The hard law of desire dictates that you can want what you don't like, and like what you don't want.

Sam and Amanda race through the rest of the exhibit. At the last table they see a straight couple in their thirties who don't look like farmers. The man is quite handsome, although his appeal lies in the fact that he has no unattractive features. His blond hair is turning grey, and Sam can imagine him coaching minor-league baseball. He seems healthy, however, so perhaps he isn't Bernie. Just as Sam is trying to decide, she hears the woman say to a boy of seven or eight, who is tugging on her shorts, "You need to play now. Mommy's busy talking to Bernie."

The child picks up a toy gun and begins smashing the butt of it into the cement floor. Only after he has chipped away two inches of the gun does he realize he may have broken his toy. He hurls the gun, then himself onto the floor. Gripping his ankles, he rocks back and forth while making a high-pitched howling sound. Cheryl rushes from her chair to put her arms around her son, and coo.

When the child has quieted down to a whimper, Amanda states in a loud, cheery voice, "Boys will be boys."

"Devon's a special boy," Cheryl replies.

"Aren't they all?" Amanda simpers.

"Devon has advanced capabilities. Those idiot teachers at school think he has ADD, but he's just bored. The way his mind works, he's so far beyond what they want him to do."

Sam puts off introducing herself to Bernie. She surveys their merchandise: cassette tapes of New Country bands, survival manuals, and videos of women in bikinis firing guns and wrestling with each other. Judging by the video covers,

Cheryl stars in most of them using the name Honey Black. Bernie and Cheryl's enterprise is the extreme niche market of patriot arts and culture. Sam opens a survival manual and reads the chapter headings: sniping, explosives, dirty tricks, and counter-surveillance.

Amanda elbows Sam out of the way in order to stand in front of Bernie. "Excuse me, but your name's Bernie, right?"

He knits his eyebrows. "Yeah."

Amanda continues, "I think you may have gone out with my sister Chloe about five years ago. She was Canadian."

Sam almost drops the book she is looking at. Amanda is improvising, and Sam isn't sure her strategy will work. Sam resembles Chloe, so who is Sam supposed to be? This is Sam's mission, but Amanda is hijacking it for some reason.

Bernie says, "I used to know this girl Chloe from Canada. What's she up to these days?"

Fuck. It didn't even occur to Sam he might not know her sister is dead.

Amanda blinks several times and manages to make her lower lip quiver. The girl missed her calling. Or did she? "Chloe died in a hotel room in New York. Not long after she met you."

"What're you talking about?" Bernie stands up, unfolding his giant frame. Beyond his size, however, Sam doubts he would intimidate anyone; he speaks slowly and his gestures are executed with uncertainty. Colour is draining from his cheeks as he topples back into his chair. "I thought she got back together with her ex-boyfriend. I figured that's why I didn't hear from her. What happened?"

Amanda gulps. "We thought she shot herself, but now we're wondering. She told a friend she was investigating a political conspiracy."

Cheryl sticks her chin out. "The CIA got to her." She peeks under the table, and Sam thinks Cheryl is looking for hidden agents, but then sees she is checking up on her son.

Sitting cross-legged and tearing the pages of a newspaper into strips, he appears to have forgotten the damage he did to his gun. Catching Sam staring, Cheryl asks, "Who're you?"

Before Sam can reply, Amanda answers, "My boyfriend. We drove here together from Canada."

Her boyfriend? At this point Sam has no choice but to go along with the charade. Clearing her throat, she does her best to deepen her voice. "Hi there."

Amanda interrupts, "Can we sit down?"

"Sure, sure." Bernie goes over to the next booth and borrows a couple of wooden chairs, which he sets down for them. Amanda sits on one of the chairs while Sam opts to stand. She could be at a church bazaar but she isn't.

Folding her arms across her chest, Cheryl asks, "How'd you track us down?" She smiles with her mouth closed—her dark glossed lips remind Sam of slashed cherries. Cheryl has this undercoat of slyness. When she wrestles on her videos, Sam bets Cheryl uses the ropes.

Amanda glances over at Sam for help but she is silent. She is tempted to tell Cheryl they found her using a Global Positioning System, but since this is Amanda's show, she can invent her own lies.

With a partial truth, Amanda forges ahead. "We met this Gulf War veteran named Rick who said you'd be here."

Cheryl tosses her hair. "That butt head. He'd turn me over to the authorities even if it meant he never got to see his child again."

Amanda frowns. "If either of you can tell us anything about what my sister may have been investigating, I would appreciate it."

As if she is communicating with a mentally challenged adult, Cheryl bobs her chin up and down at Amanda. "The CIA supported Iraq in the Gulf War."

"I suppose you have evidence of this?" Amanda's tone is haughty with disbelief.

Cheryl stabs herself in the chest with her fingers. "Yeah. Me. I used to work for them. I was trained and utilized by the CIA as a deep cover operative. I was part of a covert operation to assassinate the head of the National Security Agency, who was in cahoots with the aliens that are here now. My employers thought a female would stand a better chance of getting close to the target, but what the CIA didn't count on was my being impregnated by the aliens. Then, about five years ago, I broke out of the black operations to protect my son. I've been a political prisoner ever since, persecuted by the government as part of their neutralization campaign against me for being a whistle-blower." She takes an inhaler from her pocket, shakes it, and then puffs in.

Sam takes advantage of the gap in Cheryl's conversational flow to offer sympathy since Amanda doesn't seem to grasp there is no point in being rude to crazy people. "That must be really hard for you."

Cheryl sighs. "You don't know half of it. You from Canada, too?"

"Yeah. Toronto. Lately Montreal."

"We've thought about going there, putting ourselves into a witness protection program. Or just getting the hell out of this country. For four years now, the military, the FBI, the CIA, and just about every nasty creep you can think of have been stalking and terrorizing us." Cheryl bends forward to place a hand on her son's back, but he flattens his spine so his body is out of her reach. Pretending not to notice his reaction, she withdraws her hand. "You see, all the agencies down here believe my son's an alien hybrid. He has all the characteristics of a Starchild. When it comes to technology, he's so smart, he's got advanced abilities." Crouched on the floor beside a pile of torn-up strips of newspapers, the boy seems barely capable. His eyes dart at the people passing by with the fierce yet fearful expression of a poorly trained guard dog. Sam wonders if he is suffering from fetal alcohol syndrome. Something is definitely wrong with this kid that goes beyond having crazy parents.

Amanda toys impatiently with the pleats of her sundress. "But none of this has anything to do with my sister."

"It does," Bernie says. "It does." Just as he is about to explain, a guy wanders over to leer at the videos, deciding to buy two. Cheryl cranes her neck for a last look at her picture on the box covers. She is an exhibitionist who likes to be watched, who likes to believe everyone is watching her. Paranoia, Sam decides, is another way of being the center of attention.

When the buyer leaves, Bernie continues, "Chloe and my friend Mark were looking into what the Hells Angels were doing in the Gulf War, how they made us sick."

Suddenly Sam is on the alert. Her information fits Bernie's story: her sister was involved with a bona fide member of the Hells Angels, who might just have told Chloe a thing or two about their illegal activities. Real information has emerged from lunacy. To pan reality from the silt in the mind of a paranoid and untrustworthy individual, you need corroboration. Sam has watched enough conspiracy theory movies with Chloe to know corroboration is the key.

"Can we talk to Mark?" Sam asks.

"Yeah, you guys should talk to him. My memory's been all screwed up since I got back from the Gulf."

"How do we find him?"

"He runs a tattoo shop up in Detroit. Most nights he's there late." Bernie hands Sam a business card, which is nestled amongst the survival manuals. The card says: Lone Wolf Tattoo. An address is provided along with the name of the proprietor, Mark Berringer. Also displayed is a logo of a rose with a thorny stem entwining the nose of a gun.

A gear slips in Sam's brain; aiming for second, winding up with third. "Did you give Chloe a gun?"

Bernie straightens up in his chair. "Yes, I did—for her

protection. She didn't know how to shoot but I showed her, using pop cans. Guess she wasn't a good enough shot to protect herself from the wrong guy."

"Or from herself," Sam replies tartly, forgetting to deepen her voice, which causes Amanda to whip her head around with a warning look. Sam isn't sure whether her sister's death was murder or suicide—the shimmer of one possibility immediately throws the other one into relief. Is it easier for Bernie to imagine someone killed Chloe than to consider the effect giving her a gun may have had? Dumb fuck cowboy.

"What kind of gun?" Amanda asks.

Bernie perks up. "A double-action Smith & Wesson .357 Magnum. I always recommend revolvers for women. The guns are a smaller size so the recoil is easier to handle. They also don't need much maintenance. You can just stick them in a drawer if you want."

Cheryl holds up her purse. "I got my gun in here. People who say women, kids, and guns don't mix are going to wake up one day with their bodies on the street. Then cha-ching, the big light will go on. But it'll be too late for them."

"Too late," Amanda seizes the words. "We're late. We've got to go. Nice to meet you folks." She stands up, shakes Bernie's hand, then grips the back of Sam's shirt and steers her in the direction of the door. When they are a safe distance away, Amanda mutters to Sam, "If Cheryl's a former operative, I'm an alien clone. What a waste of our time."

"You're wrong." How can Amanda always be so damn sure of herself?

Amanda halts. "What do you mean I'm wrong?"

With reluctance, Sam also stops. Both Francis and Bernie have established Chloe was investigating a political conspiracy, and Bernie's information unexpectedly connects to Omar, but Sam doesn't want to explain this to Amanda just yet. "I didn't appreciate the way you did that Lone

Ranger thing relegating me to the role of Tonto."

Amanda rolls her eyes. "I got results, didn't I?"

"That's not the point."

"So do you want to do all the talking at the tattoo parlour?"

Sam thinks about it for a moment. The unpleasant truth is Amanda is much better at detecting. "No, I guess you can. You can drive us back to Detroit, too." Sam takes out her keys, grabs Amanda's hand and puts them in her palm.

As Amanda drives along the back roads slitting the flat fields, Sam gives an abbreviated account of her time in Montreal: meeting Omar and going to a Hells Angels party where she met Romey, talking to Francis about Chloe, and discovering Omar and Romey slept together. How the Gulf War fits in Sam can't say, but maybe Bernie's friend will be able to answer that question.

Lone Wolf Tattoo is located in a small strip mall advertising itself as a discount plaza. Amanda and Sam trudge through the mall where posses of low-income families are shopping for clothing, groceries, and dollar store specials. When they walk into the tattoo parlour, Sam can see the place isn't a hole. A poster on the open door of the parlour outlines sanitation procedures, and the well-ordered interior affirms her sense of a level of professionalism. The floors and walls are painted a high-gloss white, and Pink Floyd plays on overhead speakers. Sitting behind the counter is a man in his thirties who Sam assumes must be Mark Berringer. She is used to being inked by bald, pierced hipsters who went to, or dropped out of, art school. She prefers their irony to the authenticity of working-class shops run by bikers or biker wannabes. But the owner of Lone Wolf Tattoo doesn't fit either category of skin-scratcher. He is dressed in jeans and a baggy T-shirt advertising a local marathon, and his brown hair is buzzed into a military-style crewcut. He is medium height and would be thin if it weren't for the gut poking above the belt of his jeans like the mound on the Buddha. He is reading a book, and his plastic-rimmed glasses rest on the end of his nose. His glasses have the kind of thick lenses people called "Coke bottles" before everyone got contacts or laser surgery. Mr. Lone Wolf strikes Sam as a man who doesn't have a woman in his life, not so much because of the name of his business, but because he dresses as though he buys his own clothes. Pushing his glasses up, he places his Philip K. Dick novel on the counter and waits to hear what they want.

"Are you Mark?" Amanda asks.

He nods, and she gives him the same spiel she gave Bernie about the unexplained tragedy of "her" sister's death. Mark's eyes grow wide and are magnified even further by his glasses.

While Amanda concludes her story with a description of meeting Mark's friends at the gun show, Sam checks out the blown-up Polaroids of Mark's work displayed on the wall. I'm not going to get a tattoo just because I can, she tells herself. The shop she used to go to specialized in Celtic symbols, but the closest example of tribal art Sam sees here is a picture of a dream catcher. The subjects Mark chooses are generic Americana: skulls, hearts, roses, anchors, and the heads and shoulders of pop stars. He has skill, however. His comic-book colours are crisp while the interplay of complementary shades is subtle. A panel on someone's back reveals stylish mania; eyeballs with wings guarded by dragons; Japanimation crossed with *Mad* magazine.

Sam walks back to the counter, where Mark is slouched over his computer, clicking files open, and inadvertently showing the pale crease of his ass. He prints several pages and staples them together, then sets them on the counter in front of Sam and Amanda. A banner across the top of what is clearly his zine says *Deserted Stories*. Amanda picks the zine up and thumbs through the pages while Sam reads a name that makes her heart slam: beneath the headline, "The Ecdysis Conspiracy," is a byline from the grave—"by Chloe O'Connor and Mark Berringer." Sam snatches the zine from Amanda's hands and begins to read.

According to the article, the Montreal chapter of the Hells Angels uses strippers to sell drugs and launder money. The strippers, who are also Raelians, went to Iraq shortly before the Gulf War, ostensibly to preach peace, when in fact they were working for the Hells Angels. The Angels in turn were running an errand for the Grey Wolves, who are one of their major heroin suppliers. Drug traffickers with a mission, the Grey Wolves believe Allah wants them to kill the "Jewish race," and they use their drug profits to buy weapons. The authors claimed the real purpose of the Raelian/stripper visit was the sale of chemical weapons to the Iraqi government. A more sober article photocopied from *The Montreal Gazette* confirms a group of female Raelians went on a mission to end strife in the Middle East.

Whoever sent Sam the postcard was right. Her sister *was* investigating a political conspiracy, moreover, a somewhat plausible one. There are no presidential assassinations, no aliens, just a cult who believe in them. What Chloe describes in the article is more credible to Sam than the fact that her sister dated Bernie.

Noticing Sam has finished reading, Amanda seizes the zine back to read the article for herself. Sam wants to read the article a second time but will have to wait. She paces around the room, examining the flash. She stops in front of a picture of the horror icon Pinhead, the man with pins sewn into his head. The image carries Mark's stamp of sinister caricature. Sam points to the picture. "Mark? Could you put him on my calf?"

Mark grins. "No problem." He takes down the illustration and begins to trace it onto onion skin paper. Sam tells him she wants it to be smaller, and he leaves the shop to go to a real estate office next door to use their photocopier to reduce the tracing. Amanda mimes sticking her fingers down her throat—she isn't impressed with the image.

When Mark returns, he directs Sam to a chair behind the counter, then retrieves his tattoo gun from the autoclave bag. The needle of the gun is new and shiny, Sam notes. After transferring the design onto Sam's skin, Mark sits beside her on a low stool and dips his needle into ink. As soon as Sam hears the buzz of the gun, her skin prickles with pleasure. He carves the outline into her flesh, and a line of a song about hurting so good plays in her head. The needle burns and scratches, and Sam has to keep herself from braiding her body away from the pain, yet she craves the sensation.

Amanda opens the gate in the counter that separates the front of the parlour from the back where Mark is working. She stands for a few moments, watching him unzip Sam's flesh with his gun, then asks him if he is willing to answer some more questions.

He speaks to her through gritted teeth. "What do you want to know?"

"Did you or Chloe have any evidence the Hells Angels had dealings with the Iraqis?"

Mark holds the tattoo gun away from Sam's skin in order to look at Amanda. "I put her in touch with this guy in New York, Wells, who used to work for the CIA. He said he'd been in the field when the Raelians went to Iraq, and he had a video that could prove Iraq bought the chemical weapons that made so many vets sick, you know, with Gulf War syndrome."

Amanda says, "Is that *all* you know?"

Sam, too, senses there is something more, another card to be dealt.

"Yeah, that's it. Just—Wells is a bit of a loose cannon." Mark refills his needle with ink, buzzes the gun on, and re-treats to the canvas of Sam's skin where he begins to fill in his outline. Morse code messages of pain tap Sam's spinal cord and run upwards. She tries to concentrate on what she has learned. If her sister had evidence of a chemical weapons deal, someone may have shot her. The Hells Angels? Sam remembers the last time she saw Omar, he said Chloe shot herself. But how does he know Chloe died of a gunshot wound? Sam's father had told everyone that Chloe overdosed, a lie Sam hasn't corrected in her conversations with Omar. When Sam was at the Tam Tams, she didn't really pay attention to Omar's choice of words; she was too upset about finding out he had cheated on Chloe with Romey. Now Sam wonders if Omar revealing his infidelity had been a ploy to keep her from asking him more dangerous questions. Everything keeps twisting back to him.

"I'm finished." Mark holds a small mirror up to her leg, showing Sam the tattoo from all angles. She has always avoided getting tattoos of devils and skulls, anything creepy, but she's meeting weirder and weirder people and could use a little protection, a tattoo that will act as a talisman. Chloe's death is starting to look more like murder.

Mark bandages the tattoo, for which he charges forty dollars. He throws a tube of ointment in for the price. Gesturing towards the star on Sam's leg, he says he doesn't need to tell her about aftercare, but then he does anyway, finishing with a warning to wait until her tattoo has healed before exposing it to the sun.

Amanda asks Mark if he can give her contact information for his friend Wells. Pushing the screen away from Amanda's curious eyes, Mark starts up his computer again, and Sam wonders whether he doesn't trust Amanda or has something to hide. He scribbles some words on one of his business cards. Handing it to Amanda, he says, "I'm sorry about your sister. She was really cool, a nice woman."

In the parking lot, Amanda passes the card over to Sam. Written beside the name Wells is a phone number with a

New York area code. When they are in the car, Amanda digs the zine out of her backpack and gives it to Sam as well.

Sam says, "There's one thing I don't understand. Why is it called the 'Ecdysis' conspiracy? Is that like a place in the Middle East or something?"

Amanda tries not to smile. "Ecdysis means a snake shedding its skin. Speaking of skin, did I mention that your tattoo is really ugly?"

To report on the success of their mission, Amanda calls Francis at their hosts' home, but he isn't back yet. To call, Amanda uses a little black cellphone. Sam thought Amanda would be one of those people who doesn't use a mobile phone because of concerns over the radiofrequency radiation they emit, but apparently she isn't.

When Sam and Amanda get back to Ray and Elena's place, Francis has arrived. Elena, however, is out. She has taken her son swimming at a local public pool. Amanda and Sam volunteer to cook supper, an offer Ray happily accepts. Sam chops vegetables while Amanda cooks rice to make a stir fry. They both feel pumped, hypercharged, on a high of accomplishment. They tell Ray and Francis about their day, about everything they learned, interrupting each other to add details. As Ray thumbs through the zine, Francis leads Sam backwards and forwards through the story as though he were a police officer taking a statement. The more she talks to him, the more she begins to feel uncertain. Ever since she started trying to find out what happened to her sister, Sam has felt as if there is an inverse proportion between what she learns and what she understands.

Sam says, "Maybe if I see the evidence this guy Wells has, the videotape, I'll be able to decide whether the Ecdysis Conspiracy is real or whether Chloe got taken in."

Francis says, "You'll never see a videotape."

"What do you mean?"

Glancing up from the zine with a smile, Ray explains, "If the Ecdysis Conspiracy is genuine, then any hard evidence was destroyed the moment it surfaced, and any witness was discredited or killed before they could raise an alarm. If this story is a hoax, there will be no evidence to see." He chuckles, causing his dreads to swing back and forth.

Sam asks, "How often are conspiracy theories proved to be correct?"

Ray abruptly stops laughing while Amanda swoops her eyes in Francis's direction as if he is her attorney, and she is wondering if she should answer the question or take the Fifth. Without a word, Francis draws out his wallet. Flipping it open, he places it on the table in front of Sam. Beside his identification cards is a tiny colour snapshot sealed in plastic: a black man and woman holding hands as they stand in front of the iron gates at McGill University. The picture appears to have been taken in the summer: there is lots of light, and the couple are dressed in lightweight clothing. The man is wearing long navy shorts with a tan shirt while the woman is clad in a sleeveless yellow and orange frock with a flared skirt. They both have straightened hair and could have stepped off of an early Motown album cover. Their arms are slung around each other and their smiles are confident, hopeful. Francis turns the photo over so Sam can read the inscription on the back: "Frank and Cecelia, 1960."

"My parents," Francis says. "Upwardly mobile, middle-class blacks who believed in meritocracy. They thought their pursuit of higher education and their hard work would reward them. My mother was just finishing a nursing program while my father was at medical school. My mother was pregnant with me when my father began to experience some spasticity in his limbs. He thought it was due to playing sports, but, being a medical student, he wanted to rule out neurological damage. He wound up at the Allan Memorial Institute, where he was experimented on. He was given injections of LSD, intensive electroshocks, and forced to listen to tape-recorded messages. Then he was put to sleep for a week. He wasn't told that he was being experimented on; no one obtained his consent." Francis pauses to take a breath. "Sounds insane? Yes, except it actually happened. What was insane was the reason: McGill University was carrying out research funded by the CIA on covert brainwashing techniques."

Sam remembers hearing about this on CBC; there was an investigative report on the *Fifth Estate*. The CIA approved the program with the caveat that it was to operate outside the usual administrative channels, an objective that was fulfilled by operating in a clandestine manner in Canada. Decades later one of the victims, who married a man who became a Member of Parliament, managed to file a lawsuit and start an investigation. Personal credibility, especially when established by money and power, is crucial when determining the reality of a conspiracy theory. By their nature, conspiracy theories are unbelievable.

Francis seems to read Sam's mind. "Paranoia's a paradox. The narratives of people who are clinically paranoid are indistinguishable from the narrative of someone who has undergone a government experiment."

Sam swallows. "What happened? I mean, to your father?"

"He never recovered." Francis puts his head in his hands. Mourning, as Sam knows, is so harsh and unrelenting. Getting up, Amanda puts her arm around his shoulders while Sam notes the vulnerability of his ears, shorn of extra flesh. She closes Francis's wallet, sets it close to his elbows. Now she understands why he agreed to help her find out about Chloe, why he didn't dismiss out of hand a conspiracy theory and the possibility of murder. Truth is stranger than fiction because it doesn't have to convince anyone.

When Sam steps outside, she discovers the temperature has finally cooled. It is almost dark; the sun in the horizon is an orange smear. Pollution cloaks the stars. She feels like a race car driver rushing towards a finish line. She can't see the finishing line, but she's in motion—that's what's important. She can't even see the lines demarcating the racetrack. She is smashing into pylons but doesn't care. She wants to hit more of them.

Sam drives to a techno club with Amanda. In Toronto, when Sam had the use of her father's car, she always took the subway if she was going out so she was free to drink as much as she wanted. But the subway system in Detroit is a single line leading the commuters from the suburbs to downtown. You can't get around the sprawl of the city without a car, and Sam wonders if the motor industry played a role in keeping public transport from developing. If you examine the possible relationships between facts, conspiracy theories are ubiquitous. Spotting a cover-up is similar to tracing a pattern in the night sky; once you locate the geometric configuration, individual stars are transformed into constellations.

The club is in a converted garage. Exposed pipes are left intact to weave across the ceiling. Youth in phat pants and long skirts jam the dance floor, fluorescent T-shirts and tongue piercings twinkling under the laser lights. Sam and Amanda duck into a chill-out grotto at the back, where they sit on chairs covered in purple shag carpet. Amanda takes off. When she comes back, she takes out two little white tablets. Rather than getting them drinks, she scored some ecstasy. Good, Sam thinks.

They swallow the drugs and wait for them to take effect. An effluxion of chilled beats washes over them—bossa nova remade into electronica with muffled horns and a swagger of synthesizers. The kitsch samba beat wraps around Sam, smooth enough to soothe, but with a steady bass keeping her alert.

Sam says, "After your performance this afternoon, I'm

convinced you're an agent."

"What if I told you I was? Would you believe me?"

"Show me a pay stub from the government." Sam isn't really sure who Amanda is, why she came along for the ride. But perhaps the answer isn't that complicated, perhaps she likes Sam.

Sam says, "You know, being gay is kind of like being an agent. You're always wondering if people can tell, if you're safe." What Sam is really wondering is whether Amanda likes girls.

"I'm bi. Does that make me a double agent or a mole?"

Ah ha. Sam gets something right for a change. "I'm not sure. Have you been activated yet? Or are you a sleeper agent?"

"Actually, I'm an anarchist. Not politically, but when it comes to sex I'm all about insurrection and throwing bombs. Whoever's the last possible person I should want, that's who I'm doing."

This is something Sam can relate to. And when you're queer, you can't help wanting to protect desire from words like "shouldn't."

Amanda flicks her tongue over the edge of her teeth. "I guess you're not one of those lesbians who hate bisexual women."

Sexual politics, in Sam's opinion, are often counter-productive to getting laid. "There are only two reasons for a lesbian to be threatened by you: either she's afraid she's bi, or she wants to fuck you but is afraid you don't want her."

"And you're not threatened by me?"

Sam shakes her head.

A sly smile forms on Amanda's lips. "So does that mean you *don't* want to fuck me?"

Sam laughs. "It means I'm not afraid."

"Great answer!" Amanda takes Sam's hand, tugging her forward. "Let's dance." Sam allows herself to be pulled upright but says she doesn't dance.

"Why not?"

Sam points to her leg. "War wound."

"You sound like someone's uncle."

Sam laughs again. She feels nervous but also a little detached. She's excited by Amanda, but that is all. "Does that make you my bratty niece?"

"Bratty? That makes me sound as though I'm eleven. Why don't you call me your wayward niece?"

Sam is adamant about not dancing. While Amanda grooves to the music, Sam stands nearby, watching. A silly grin appears on her face as her body absorbs the ecstasy. In accompaniment to the hypnotizing thud of the beat, Amanda twirls an imaginary orb over her body. Her pink sleeveless shirt is cut tight around small, firm breasts, and Sam can't stop staring at them. Pleasure gushes through her brain. She goes to the bar, buys a bottle of water and drinks about a third of it. Then she seeks out Amanda to give it to her. As Amanda gulps down the water, Sam watches the eager thrust of Amanda's throat. Her greed, her urgency, is sexy. When Amanda finishes drinking, Sam takes the bottle from Amanda's hands, sets it on a speaker and leads them both off the dance floor and into the women's bathroom. It is still early, so there isn't a lineup. They go into a stall that is none-too-clean and tagged with graffiti about blow jobs. The setting is seamy, but Sam likes it that way. She kicks the door shut, twists the lock, and pushes Amanda up against the wall, tattooing her neck with bruises

When Amanda groans, Sam puts a hand over her mouth. "Want to get us thrown out?"

Amanda shakes her head, and Sam releases her hand. Puts it under Amanda's shirt, over her breasts, which aren't bound by a bra. Lifts up Amanda's shirt, licks pink nipples into tight points, then touches her lower down. Beneath the band of her underwear, Amanda is soaked. Something about her makes Sam think of pools, chlorine, languid blondes splayed out on towels. Sam slowly spins Amanda around, un-wrapping her cotton skirt and discovers Amanda hasn't bothered with underwear. Taking a bit of time so as to tease them both, Sam fussily folds the skirt and sets it on the toilet tank before entering Amanda with a muscular hand. Fingers travel along a liquid path to reach into ridges and corners, then head upwards to a pearl, guarded by flesh. As Sam strokes her, Amanda gasps, clutches Sam, and says, "Oh, God, just like that." Seizing Sam's hips, Amanda thrusts her-self against Sam's hand.

"Get me off," Amanda commands, "Now."

Sam stops moving her fingers altogether. At the moment, Miss Smarty-Pants is not in charge. "If you ask a little nicer."

Amanda sighs but then capitulates by managing to say in a polite and quiet tone: "Please, Sam. Please make me come."

"Tell me how."

While Sam fingers her, Amanda lists a surprising number of acts. She's one of those women who can come a whole bunch of different ways, which is helpful for the present sit-uation. Taking her hand out of Amanda, Sam spits on it a few times. Then she squeezes her fingers into a fist and uses her knuckles to fuck Amanda. "Penetration is the trickiest," Amanda says, reaching her own fingers down to touch her-self. But Sam brushes away this offer of assistance, and keeps grinding the hard edges of her fingers against warm, wet muscle. And come Amanda does—"Oh, yes, God, yes"—the hot core of her fastening around Sam's hand.

When Amanda's breathing returns to normal, she asks, "Do you want me to do you?"

"Nah." If Sam doesn't come, it won't count. That's Sam's rationalization and she's sticking to it. If she com-partmentalizes what she does with Romey from what she just did with Amanda, the leak can be contained.

"I knew you'd say that."

"Then why'd you ask?" Even though Amanda is still

straightening out her skirt, Sam unlocks the door of the cage they are in. Two teenagers shoot them dirty looks. Sam ignores them.

When Sam wakes up, she feels the low that too often follows a lovely high. On top of that, it's Monday morning and she has to drive back to Montreal. Words twang in her head: "Why don't you call me your wayward niece?" Sam has an instinct for the dirty ones. She rolls over on the cot, tucks the sheet over Amanda's bare back, as if that can cover up what happened between them. Why did she do it? Sam's in love with Romey. Was Sam just keeping her options open, the way she usually did? No, the answer was simpler and more pathetic. She invited drama into her life to lick her pain. The law of probabilities dictates Romey could have done the same thing, may have gone to a tacky bar in the Village and picked someone up. At this very moment, she might be getting her brains fucked out. Sam's hands clench into fists. She could drive herself crazy with jealousy, she really could. A clock radio tells her it's six o'clock in the morning, not quite time to get up, but she's wide awake. She needs a distraction.

She takes the biography of Sid and Nancy out of her knapsack. On the back cover, Sam reads favourable quotes from dubious magazines on the "compelling veracity" of the story. As she opens the first page, a card and a photograph fall out. The picture is Sam as a kid, seven years old, wearing a one-piece bathing suit, standing on the shore of the ocean. Sun is shooting all over the water. The photo was taken during a summer holiday in Nova Scotia, a vacation with mostly but not entirely good memories. Sam shoves the picture back into the knapsack and takes a look at the card. It has a picture of Paddington Bear on the front. He's wearing his famous battered hat and duffle coat with the note pinned on that says "Please look after this bear." Who had given this to Chloe?

Opening the card, Sam reads the words: "To my little bear—I promise to take care of you." At the bottom of the page is a signature: "Omar." Sam's mouth drops open. At any other time she would be amused by such raw sentiment, especially coming from Omar. But this morning it makes her sad. A splatter of tears comes into Sam's eyes, which she wipes away with a fist. These were the items Chloe chose to keep, and the items she chose to leave behind in Romey's apartment. We hurt her, Sam thinks, and is surprised to find herself using the word "we" in conjunction with Omar. But she and Omar have something in common; they both found themselves in a triangle where Chloe's love was concerned, Sam with her father, Omar with Romey. Tossing the book and card back into her bag, Sam returns to the cot. She's rigid with anger but doesn't know who to blame.

Amanda crawls along the cot and ripples her fingers in Sam's face. "Good morning."

Sam doesn't reply.

Amanda tries to hug Sam, who pulls away from her, and stands up. After briskly retrieving shorts and a T-shirt from her knapsack, Sam starts to get dressed. She keeps her boxers on from the night before because she doesn't want to be naked in front of Amanda.

In a cool voice, Amanda says, "Let me guess—you have a girlfriend."

Sam doesn't answer, lets her eyes zip to an unattractive mole on Amanda's cheek.

Amanda's eyes narrow. "Of course. The stripper who slept with your sister's boyfriend. Is that what this is about? Payback?"

"Fuck you." Sam twists around to button up her black jean shorts.

Amanda sighs. "You're transferring your hostility to me. Who are you actually mad at?"

Sam refuses to meet her eyes. "You started it."

Amanda wraps the sheet around her pale limbs. "Fair enough. I baited you because you're so absent, so distant after last night." Her cadence is dreamy, lingering, as if an invitation is forthcoming.

Sam slices the air with her hands. "We're never going to have a relationship, okay?"

Amanda's tone mutates to crisp: "I don't recall proposing that we have one. In fact, I have a lover." Checking first to make sure the sheet is squeezed tightly around her, she leans over to scoop a dress out of her bag. She tugs the dress on over her head, plucking the sheet away only after the hem has fallen into place.

Sam sits down on the cot. She knows she is being an asshole, or, as Amanda might say, Sam is projecting. Amanda is smart, not to mention sexy, and Sam bellowed that she didn't want to have a relationship because she is afraid of what she might start to feel. And seeing the picture Chloe kept makes Sam feel guilty. There is *so* much for which Sam feels guilty.

While Amanda is primping, Sam gets up and stands in front of the closed door. She stretches her arms out, resting her forearms on either side of the door frame. Amanda tucks away a hairbrush and moves towards her.

Sam says, "I'm sorry. I was a total jerk."

Amanda slowly nods her head up and down. "Yeah, you were. Now can you get of my way?"

Sam takes a sideways step. "Sorry."

"You said that already."

The trip back to Montreal is uneventful. Ray is still sleeping when they leave Detroit; Elena is yawning and gives them each a distracted hug while her son yelps in English and Spanish of a calamity involving cornflakes. As soon as the border is crossed, Amanda and Francis fall asleep. Sam is relieved not to be obliged to make conversation with either of them but she, too, is struggling to stay awake. She stops at a drive-through and orders an extra large coffee. As she waits in line, she rereads Chloe and Mark's article. The Ecdysis Conspiracy is a rather strangle tangle of alliances and enlightened self-interest in the carrying out of criminal enterprises. If Sam takes Deep Throat's advice to Bob Woodward to "follow the money," the story is pretty simple. The Grey Wolves did a joint venture with the Hells Angels that helped the Iraqi government; the Hells Angels used the Raelians to carry out some dirty business while the cult made money and promoted itself in the mass media. The only people who didn't seem to benefit were the women, the nude dancers, who were used by everyone. Is this story something Romey can confirm? Sam's thoughts have a way of looping back to Romey.

The caffeine does its thing. Sam keeps driving, weaving past big transport trucks with swinging plastic dice wrapped around the stems of their rear-view mirrors. She knows she's at least twenty klicks over the speed limit but doesn't care— she wants to get to her next destination; she wants answers. How did Chloe get mixed up with criminals, terrorists, and cult members? Thinking about these different groups, Sam realizes they have a few things in common: they are all cloistered communities with charismatic leaders and stockpiles of weapons. In other words, they're all armed and dangerous and unlikely to tell her a damn thing. How will she be able to find out whether the conspiracy is real or a hoax?

On the other hand, does it matter whether the conspiracy is genuine? To some extent the truth of the conspiracy is irrelevant. No one knows whether Gulf War syndrome was caused by exposure to chemical weapons or by the guilt, horror, and fear of the soldiers, but when a large enough group of people believe in something, it can take on a life of its own. She can try to investigate the facts, but the conspiracy theory is like the process of ecdysis—another skin has already formed underneath, that of myth. Myth is as powerful as truth. People are just as invested in it. A conspiracy freak who read Chloe's article might have sent Sam the postcard—with all the information floating around on the web and in news databases, someone could have mined the different pieces, soldered them together. A conspiracy freak could even have killed Chloe if he or she thought Chloe was part of some plot.

When they get to Montreal, Amanda gives her phone number to Sam. "We should grab a coffee sometime."

"Sure," Sam lies.

CHAPTER SIXTEEN

When Sam tried to get Chloe and Tory to play a game or to go outside and build a fort or something, they just rolled their eyes. Since they had turned thirteen, all they liked to do was talk. What they talked about was so boring: which girls in their class were goodie-goodies, which girls in their class were sluts, which boys in their class were cute, and which boys in their class were losers. When they had these stupid conversations, they pretended Sam wasn't in the room, didn't answer when she tried to butt in. They acted as though she couldn't hear them, but she could. Once in awhile, the girls talked about other things.

Tory: My mom gave me riding lessons for Christmas. What'd you get?

Chloe: Nothing. I don't have a mother.

Tory: My dad doesn't live with me any more either, but he still gave me a present for Christmas. Doesn't your mother give you stuff?

Chloe: I'm not allowed to see her.

Tory: Why?

Chloe: She tried to murder herself.

CHAPTER SEVENTEEN

Sam sits on her balcony in Verdun swilling a bottle of beer, breathing in the stink of tar. The building across the street is having its roof redone. Sam watches a skinny old guy drive by on a bicycle with a battered wooden cart attached to the back. He is delivering beer and cigarettes from a *depanneur*. On the next balcony over, Sam hears two guys debate how much pot to buy. They speak French with the rough rhythm and catenation of English and use enough English words that Sam understands them: *beaucoup de* pot, *c'est* full cool. In Verdun, you can also get weed delivered to your door.

Sam swallows the last of her beer and goes inside to call Romey. Even though she doesn't work on Monday nights, she isn't home or isn't answering her phone. She's not answering her cellphone either. As Sam opens her fridge to take out another bottle of beer, she imagines a tearful reunion with Romey, each of them protesting they were the unwitting cause of their separation. But Sam's fantasy gets stuck in neutral, and she can't seem to imagine a happy ending. She puts the beer back into the fridge, unopened and covered in wet patches from her sweaty hands.

Sam decides to drive over to Romey's apartment. If it is all over between them, Sam wants to know. Romey doesn't answer the doorbell, but the front door, which is usually closed, opens in Sam's palm. She goes up a flight of stairs and knocks on the inside door. When she hears someone groan, she steps inside to find Romey lying on her couch with her legs propped up on pillows. A hot water bottle peeks out from under her back. She is wearing white shorts and a pink blouse. She looks like a nice Italian girl; the pall of sex and glamour that has entranced Sam is gone. She is still attracted but feels as if she is seeing Romey's ordinariness for the first time. When Sam reaches down to put her arms around Romey, she gasps and pushes Sam away.

"Careful. I put my back out at work."

"Is there anything I can do to help?"

Romey makes a face. "I'll be fine in a couple days—it's just a muscle spasm. I have some Tylenol with codeine."

Sam takes out the sash she bought in Dearborn and gives it to Romey, who barely glances at it. She doesn't seem to care one way or another that Sam is here, which is shattering, worse than fighting. Sam wants to ask, Don't you like the sash? But instead she says nothing. Taking her cue from Romey, Sam acts as if everything between them is cool, nothing special but nothing terrible. Kneeling on the floor beside the couch, she recounts her weekend in Detroit. While being careful to minimize Amanda's presence and role in the adventures, Sam describes the meeting with Cheryl and Bernie at the gun show and the encounter with Mark. Then Sam unbends her leg and peels off the bandage to display the tattoo of Pinhead.

"Hellraiser," Romey murmurs. "Scared the pants off me the first time I saw it."

A tiny fissure of friendliness, of the-way-they-were. Has Romey forgot how, aside from sex, they just plain like each other? Sam tapes the bandage back in place. "So, do you know anything about Raelian strippers selling chemical weapons to Iraq on behalf of the Hells Angels?"

"No. Sounds kind of out of the Angels' league if you ask me. The only thing I can tell you is it's true the Raelians encourage their female members to bring in money by working in the sex trade and by selling dope. And selling drugs pretty much means getting involved with the Angels. Hey! Is it called the Ecdysis Conspiracy because of the Raelian dancers?"

Romey has lost Sam. "Huh?"

"Strippers used to be called 'ecdysiasts.' You know, because they shed their clothes."

Sam asks, "Am I the only person who has never heard of the word 'ecdysis'?"

Romey smiles, biting her lip. "I read it in a history of stripping."

"Oh. Do you think Omar knows anything?"

Her smile dissolves. "He knows better than to talk about the Angels. He's not stupid. He would never have hurt Chloe that way." She lifts her hand into the air as if to block Sam. "He's a good guy, he means well. If he thought it was going to be such a big deal, Omar never would have slept with me." Romey's faint Italian accent asserts itself. When she is tired, she can't sound out a soft "th" without dropping the "h."

Sam sighs. Why is it that when someone says a person means well, it is always in conjunction with disaster? People who don't mean to harm anyone often inflict the worst damage because of what they rouse in others: sympathy, loyalty, and rescue missions that are compromised before they begin. What would it take to make Romey see how dangerous her best friend was?

Sam says, "Omar knew a gun killed my sister. My father told everyone she died of a drug overdose. I only found out recently how she died, and I didn't tell him, and I didn't tell you."

Romey waves this off with a hand. "What is this? You think Omar shot Chloe because he's Arab? Everyone *knows* what violent, dangerous terrorists *they* are. Kind of like I'm Italian Mafiosi?"

Sam's mouth drops open. How can Romey have so much faith in him and so little faith in her? "For God's sake Romey, Omar *is* a fucking criminal."

Romey picks up the hot water bottle and throws it across

the room. Not at Sam but not too far from her either. "Are you trying to get me to tell you to fuck off for good?"

Sam is stunned. "No."

With her hand, Romey gestures for Sam to come close. Sam stands up hesitantly—she isn't sure if Romey wants to whisper in her ear or slap her face. Romey continues to urge Sam, who reluctantly bends down her head. Romey reaches up and grips Sam's chin the way Italian mothers do. All five of Romey's nails are long enough for Sam to feel them as they dig into her face.

Romey says, "I've loved Omar for a long time; I haven't loved you for very long." She lets go of Sam whose skin continues to tingle.

Sam says, "I guess you want me to leave now."

Small shake of Romey's head. "I'd like you to make me some dinner. Sam, did anyone ever tell you that you take yourself way too seriously?"

The next morning Sam collects a final paycheque from Le Lapin Blanc and makes arrangements to keep the rental car for another week. She and Romey spent the night in the same bed but didn't fool around. Romey's back rendered sex out of the question, but Sam isn't sure anything would have happened if physical discomfort wasn't the issue. They didn't discuss the status of their relationship, retreating to what felt more like a truce than a reconciliation. Over coffee the next morning, Sam said she was going back to Toronto and then to New York to try and find out more about what Chloe was doing just before she died. Romey said, "This feels very déjà vu. You know, before Chloe took off, she was talking about seeing her mom in Toronto." Sam nearly spit out her coffee. Their mother? Sam hasn't seen her mother since she abandoned her family.

Sam drives west, leaving the island of Montreal. She puts

the radio on, listens to traffic reports and inane chatter about sports, but her attention strays. Her mom. A woman Sam can barely recall, although she remembers missing her. When Sam walked the three blocks home from elementary school, she was always careful to step over the splinters in the concrete. Step on a crack, break your mother's back. A mother Sam wanted to protect for some reason. She remembers sitting on the couch with an afghan wrapped around her, watching cartoons on television while, beside her, her mother smoked. Sam felt not so much safe as marooned. She tries to visualize her mother but can't. Memory is like a card deck in which someone has stolen all the face cards. But then another memory is dealt to Sam, a memory which was always there, but which she didn't understand earlier: Chloe saying their mother tried to murder herself. Mom—the family cover-up. When Sam considers her family, her sister's obsession with political conspiracy and assassination makes a strange kind of sense.

When Sam arrives at her father's house in Toronto, she discovers he and Steven aren't home. She hasn't told them she is coming. She doesn't have a key to the house, so she climbs over a fence in the back lane and breaks into the garden. She is carrying a case of imported beer, which is a gift for her father, but she drinks one because she is thirsty. A second bottle tamps down emotions Sam can no longer sort into discrete classifications; her feelings are bunched together like clumps of wet laundry.

She walks along the stone path through a garden drowning in greenery: a viridian, bat-like tamarack tree; lumpy chartreuse fruit dangling from a paw-paw tree; the dull sage of a mound of moss. The only contravention in colour are the lemon chrysanthemums with their heavy scent of earth and burning incense. Sam was raised in this nice middle-class home and has returned to discover the tabloid talk show episodes to which her family was not immune. They were just careful not to make a spectacle of themselves—that is, everyone except for Chloe. She displayed her emotions in the same offhand manner Romey exposes her body.

The Japanese garden in the backyard, which favours serenity and containment over colour, was recently designed by Sam's father. Kenneth O'Connor loves the formality, the austerity, and the rules involved in the creation of a Zen garden, which is intended to be a microcosm of the natural world: the pool sparkling with koi is a lake, the raked sand in front of Sam is an ocean, while the rock she sits on is a mountain. She swigs the last of a third beer and chucks the bottle onto the sand. Then she leans over to carve a message with her finger: "Sam was here."

Wind chimes clamour and a breeze tickles the back of Sam's scalp. She stands up, takes a step onto grass trimmed in the same style she has barbers cut the sides of her hair: immaculate and down to the stubble. Hair as tidy as this bloody garden. She's her father's daughter but doesn't want to be. Reaching down, she yanks out a stone and props it at a different angle, vertical rather than horizontal. She extracts another stone, shifts its position. Around the garden she goes, rearranging the rocks like pawns on a chessboard, checkmate to her father the implacable queen.

"Samantha." Draped in dusk Sam's father watches her. A light goes on in the back window, and Sam sees Steven moving about in the kitchen. "What are you doing?"

Sam waits for her father to yell about the garden but he doesn't say a word. She aligns her mouth into a sneer. "Destroying your Feng Shui."

Sam's father raises an eyebrow, a gesture Sam realizes she imitates. "If you meet the Buddha on the road, you must kill him."

"What's that supposed to mean?"

Her father gives Sam a faint superior smile. "It's a Zen koan. It means 'do not cling blindly to the rules.' Context always needs to be taken into account." He sits down on a bamboo chair and pats its mate. "Why don't you sit down and explain the context in which you're getting soused and making my garden inharmonious?"

Before joining him in the other chair, Sam grabs another beer from the case, opens it and drinks half of it. She says, "I'm sick of your need-to-know-basis. How come Mom took off? What happened?"

Her father bends down to root out a dandelion from between a crack in the stones. The dandelion has gone to seed, and her father blows on the silky cobwebs, an unexpectedly whimsical gesture for him. He leans back in his chair. "Okay. Where do you want me to start?"

"Why did you get married if you're gay?"

Her father sighs. "I got married because I didn't want to be a homosexual—I wanted to be a father, a husband."

So Stonewall hadn't had an immediate impact on his life. Well, she knew that. "How did you meet?"

A look somewhere between a grin and a grimace crosses her father's face. He says, "I met Della at a gay bar actually. I was in my first year of university, and she was working under the table as a shampoo girl at a downtown hair salon. She liked to go dancing at the clubs with the hairdressers she worked with. I suppose you would call her a 'fag hag.' She was good fun then, and she seemed to accept me. She was on a visa from England, and she had this terrific accent. I sometimes wonder if I hadn't been such an Anglophile, would we have ever gotten together? Our class differences would have been more apparent to me if she had been from around here." He pauses to allow Sam to digest the information. None of it is surprising, but it is the first time her father has talked to her about being gay, rather than simply alluding to it. He doesn't go to Pride, he's never joined a gay choir or gay fathers' group, and he's never discussed her lesbianism. The only thing gay about her father, other than the Danish furniture and the garden, is Steven.

Her father takes a beer from the case Sam left on the ground, and uses a handful of his sweater to open the bottle. After he takes a sip, he continues his story. "What can I say? The marriage was a disaster. After Chloe was born, Della quit working. I was pretty absorbed with my dissertation so I didn't realize at first she was depressed. She pulled herself out of it, but after you were born, she had another postpartum depression that just flattened her. I came home one day to find an ambulance in front of the house we were renting. Chloe was at a friend's house, and Della had locked you into a bedroom, gone into the bathroom, and slit her wrists. She probably would have succeeded in what she was attempting if you hadn't been screaming at the top of your lungs through an open window, which attracted the attention of a neighbour."

Does Sam know this? While she can't remember what he is describing, it isn't shocking to her. On some level, she does remember—the same way Dyna knew her father raped her without remembering the details. Knowledge and memory are often entwined in a conspiracy, where pain is covered up and plausible deniability is always an option. Sam doesn't realize she's crying until she wipes her nose on her arm, and her father reaches into the pocket of his Bermuda shorts and hands her a tissue. She wipes her eyes, blows her nose, and tells him she's sorry she messed up his garden.

Her father nods. "It's okay." He studies the label of his beer bottle for a moment before meeting her eyes. "The hospital treating your mother alerted Children's Aid who opened a case file on us. I think Della expected me to be sympathetic, but I was furious. For years, I had been trying to complete a Ph.D. while doing most of the work of looking after you two. I basically sent her packing by threatening to have her committed. She hadn't worked in some years, or been much of a mother, so off she went. When Chloe died, I began to doubt what I did. You see, I never questioned why your mother was willing to marry a man she knew to be gay or why she didn't seem to mind that we rarely had sex. In a profound way, I never knew Della. I was just grateful to her for marrying me because it permitted me to hide from my sexuality. Then I stopped being grateful. I used her suicide attempt to get rid of her, although I didn't see it that way at the time, or even later, when Chloe was in Montreal and accused me of having deprived her of a mother. Now I understand, and I feel guilty. But I'm used to guilt. It's a legacy of homosexuality, or at any rate, it used to be."

Sam covers her face with her hands. She, too, feels guilty—it is stitched into her skin, a permanent tattoo, but her reasons are different from her father's. Bad things happened to Chloe, so it is only fair they happen to Sam. Something bad is waiting for her because it is only fair that everything between two sisters be shared, be equal. Their father's love for instance. Peeking through her fingers at her father, Sam asks, "Did you love Chloe?"

Her father gazes at a spot in front of him as if Chloe's ghost were floating in the air. "While there were times I didn't like her, I always loved her. I loved her very, very much."

Sam is relieved to hear this. She wanted to believe her father loved Chloe, but, in the face of Chloe's disbelief, Sam was never sure. "Chloe had a way of pissing people off. I think someone might have killed her."

"I just told you that your mother had depression and tried to commit suicide. What makes you think Chloe didn't do the same thing, with the difference being you weren't around to scream?"

Sam doesn't argue—her father will never believe Chloe's death was anything but suicide. He can't see it is equally possible Della's suicide attempt was a reason for Chloe not to kill herself. She was eight years old when her mother went away, old enough to remember her, to miss her, to understand the impact of what Della had almost done. There is also the promise Chloe made Sam, the time Chloe said, "Don't you know I'd never leave you?"

Sam says, "Just before she died, Chloe talked about seeing our mother."

Her father sips his beer. "Yes, I know. Chloe did go to see her. I suppose you'd like to meet her, too? I'm still in touch with Della."

In the outside world, crickets hum, neighbourhood kids splash in a backyard pool, and bass thumps from car speakers. Sam hears it all, yet it feels so far away. Her mother, a woman who didn't even bother going to her daughter's funeral. But Sam will go see her because Chloe did. Sam is trying on her sister's life, wearing it like another skin. A skin which, like a snake's, is too tight, isn't malleable. But Sam can't slide out of it.

The next day Sam takes the streetcar to the east end to see her mother. Her father turns out to know quite a lot about her mother's life. She remarried a man whose wife died in a car accident, leaving behind two sons whom Della adopted and raised. As a result of the same accident, Della's husband is on disability. Working as a waitress at an east end diner, Della supports her new family.

Rain spatters the windows of the streetcar, but the shower ends by the time Sam reaches the restaurant where Della works. The diner is old-fashioned but not retro. A counter with stools runs along one wall of the long, narrow interior while booths upholstered in Naugahyde line the other three sides. The walls are decorated with sports pennants, framed black and white photographs of Lake Ontario in the

'40s, and, oddly, Christmas tinsel. Sam takes a careful look around; her father thought Della worked a regular Monday-to-Friday schedule, but shifts often change in the restaurant business. Fortunately the waitresses have little plaques with their names pinned to their white uniform, so she is able to identify Della, who doesn't look anything like her daughters. She could have been an incubator for Dad, creating offspring marked with his genetic traits. It is hard to believe she is the same age as Sam's father. His youthful appeal can be glimpsed through the creases on his face, but the rough lines jerking from Della's nose to the corners of her mouth offer no such tunnel in time. Short, broad, and chesty, she reminds Sam of a maidenhead on the prow of a ship. Only her hair and makeup evoke the young woman Sam's father described as a "fag hag." Even though it is daytime, she is wearing three shades of eyeshadow, and her hair is trimmed into a short, chic tulip shape. Perhaps she still hangs out with the same hairdressers.

Sam leaves the counter to sit in a booth in Della's section. When Sam's father spoke about Della, Sam was nervous about the prospect of meeting her mother, but her jitters are being replaced by altogether more volatile emotions. How dare her mother *not* be dead, in jail, or in a mental institution! How can her mother just exist? How could she take up an entirely new life, discarding her kids the way, well, the way a snake does its skin? A translucent sheath left on the ground—that was what Sam was to her mother.

Sam eavesdrops on Della's conversations. She doesn't talk so much as exchange a sparkly patter of quips. Even after all these years, she has retained her British accent. An accent Sam hasn't heard on television, a softer, flatter tone than the extremes of plummy period drama or Cockney tart. When she collects Sam's order, Della jokes about Sam's tattoos, which are visible since she is wearing a tank top.

Della says, "At my age, love, that girl on your arm is

going to be hanging off you." With a rectangular, leopard-spotted nail, she points to Sam's tattoo of Bettie Page.

Sam is stunned. Della is staring directly at her daughter with no idea they are related. At least Della immediately recognized Sam as female.

Della holds her pen up to her notepad. "So what'll it be?"

"Coffee?" Ordering food is not why Sam is here. "Uh, coconut cream pie?"

When Della brings over the coffee and pie, Sam feels her heart box with her chest. She wants to say something to her mother but instead sips the weak coffee and spoons mounds of custard into her mouth. When Della comes by a second time with a metal pitcher of ice water, Sam tries again. She opens her mouth, but nothing comes out. Finally, in desperation, she reaches out and touches Della's wrist.

Della pauses, a questioning look on her face.

Sam takes a deep breath. "I'm Samantha. Your daughter."

The water being poured in Sam's glass overflows, spills onto the paper mat and the napkin Sam didn't bother to put in her lap. Before she can point out what is happening, Della jerks the water jug away.

"You should have called first," Della says. With a squeak of her black rubber sneakers, she pivots away from Sam.

Sam watches her walk to the back to take a cigarette break. Della doesn't return, not even when Sam has finished her food and goes up to the counter to pay the bill. Leaving a two dollar tip, Sam saunters out of the diner as if it is all the same to her that her mother, whom she hasn't seen since she was a little kid, won't talk to her.

Just as Sam is about to hop onto a streetcar, she sees Della jogging towards her. Sam steps back from the swarm of people crowding onto the car and allows Della to lead them to a nearby bench. It's a little damp from the rain, but they sit down anyway. Della smells like a combination of hamburgers and hairspray. When she lights a cigarette, she extends her pack to Sam, who refuses with a wave of her hand.

Della says, "You don't smoke. Smart girl." In the restaurant, her starched, white uniform and perhaps a girdle reigned in her chunky frame, and she looked, if not smart, pulled together. Now her uniform is covered in wrinkles, her face is flushed, and rings of sweat have bloomed beneath her arms. The air around them is humid, taut with moisture as if the rain never happened.

Della peers at Sam. "Christ, you look like your father. I don't know why I didn't see it right away."

Sam pokes the ground with her foot. "I'm sorry I didn't call."

"No, you're not."

Sam's mouth flops open.

Della swings her legs, which are crossed at the ankle. "Your sister did the same thing to me. I've seen it on enough talk shows, people springing themselves on their biological mother. But your sister wasn't interested in me. Didn't want to meet her brothers. 'I have all the family I can take,' is what she told me. She just wanted to dig up dirt on your father." Della takes a long drag of her cigarette. "So what do you want?"

To hear more about that chat you had with Chloe, Sam thinks. Her family is a closed loop, which doesn't include her mother, but that's not Sam's fault. "You never even went to my sister's funeral."

A wariness comes into Della's eyes. "I was out of the country with my boys. Went back to England for the first time since I left."

Standing up, Sam begins to pace back and forth in front of her mother. Sam wants to put her mother on the stand, wants to cross-examine her. Excuse me, but why wasn't this information brought to the attention of the jury earlier? Excuse me, but are you aware that your actions speak louder than your words? Her mother dumped her kids because her bastard husband made her. She was unable to get an earlier flight back to Toronto to go to Chloe's funeral. Yeah, right.

Sam says, "Inconvenient isn't the same as impossible."

Della scowls, but Sam sees something else in her eyes—uncertainty. Della covers it with bluster. "For crying out loud. You came all the way out here to ask me five years after the fact why I didn't go to your sister's funeral?"

"Uh huh."

"Who would I be going to the funeral for?"

Sam stops in her tracks. It isn't the answer she expects.

Della grunts, and Sam sits down again. They don't speak. Across the street a backhoe is excavating a vacant lot, and a billboard displays pictures of the future townhouse units. Beyond the foundations of the houses lies murky, polluted Lake Ontario. Sam can't see where the water ends. She can wade into the surf, chase the rendezvous point of sky and water, but she will never be able to reach it.

Della uses her cigarette to point to the billboard. "People are paying up to half a million dollars to live in those because they're by the water. They're also next to a sewage treatment plant. On a windy day, no one's going to be sitting on their terrace, that's for sure." She wrinkles her nose.

Sam says, "You could have said goodbye to Chloe, hello to me." Her mother is a disappointment, or perhaps Sam is just disappointed because she feels so little—she can't tell.

Della says, "I was too brassed off at your father. After I left I once asked him about seeing you girls, and he talked me out of it, said I wouldn't be doing you any favours. He's a convincing man, you know. But after I heard what Chloe done to herself, well, it didn't sound as if he was in the running for parent-of-the-year. Mind, he would say your sister did what she did due to my genes; I'm the crazy one, after all. But there's decent meds these days."

Sam wouldn't know. The sound of a streetcar grinding as it changes direction makes them both glance up. Has she been a bit self-centered, getting into this stuff with her mother after all these years? Maybe, but she can't bring herself to apologize. She settles for ratcheting down the drama. "You're right, I do want something from you. I want to know about your conversation with my sister before she died; I think you owe me that at least. Did Chloe say anything to you about a political conspiracy she was investigating that had to do with the Gulf War?"

The skin on Della's forehead puckers as she takes a moment to think about the question. "No, nothing like that. She just asked me about your dad. I asked her what she was doing with herself, and she told me she dropped out of university." Curiousity appears in Della's eyes, which Sam notices are hazel. "Guess I should ask you the same question."

Her interest acts like a switch for Sam whose resentment and apathy is replaced by longing. But, with practiced nonchalance, Sam shrugs her shoulders. "I work in a restaurant. Same as you." Since she plans to get another job in a restaurant as soon she gets back to Montreal, she doesn't see any point in explaining she is currently unemployed. "I'm thinking about becoming a chef." Even though she is saying this to impress Della, Sam realizes, as she says it, that it's true. Working in a kitchen is the first job Sam has liked.

"Your father must be pleased."

Although she wants to say, "Aren't you?", Sam holds her tongue. Della accepted her abdication of her role as a parent a long time ago. What Sam does with her life is not Della's concern. The person who is having a hard time with this is Sam. She wants her mother to feel responsible for her or, failing that, to at least like her. Sam wants so much for Della to like her—Sam always wants women to like her. Even though she isn't sure whether she wants to have a relationship with her mother, she asks Della if she can see her again.

"If we don't talk about the past," Della says. "I've never been one for fussing over the past. I made my mistakes and your father made his. But what's done is done." With her cigarette butt, she chars the wood of the bench. The butt falls from her hand onto the ground, rolls until it stops amidst gum wrappers and empty chip bags. Sam feels like picking up the butt with gloved hands and putting it into an evidence bag, something to prove Della was here.

When Sam gets back from meeting her mother, her father doesn't ask her about it. For once, Sam is glad of his discretion. As she lounges around the living room, reading magazines, she decides to stay at her father's house for another day or two. She wants to regress, to be taken care of, to be a child again in spite of the sorrow sewn into her childhood like a hidden pocket.

Steven brings a tray of biscuits into the dining room and Sam sniffs the air. The biscuits have a peppery smell she can't place. She asks, "What are they made of?"

"Cheddar and caraway." Steven peers at her over the square frames of the microsized glasses he has begun wearing instead of contact lenses due to a small cataract in his left eye. "Be careful. They're hot." He lifts the biscuits onto a plate with a spatula.

Sam says, "Did I tell you guys I'm thinking of becoming a chef?"

Her father glances up from the paper. "You are? Really?"

"Really."

"If you learn French working in Montreal, you could go to France. The best culinary schools are in Paris," Steven says.

Sam grabs a biscuit, scalding her fingers. Ignoring the disapproving jiggle of Steven's head, Sam drops the biscuit back onto the plate. If Sam studies cooking at a community college, Steven and her father will make her feel fourth-rate. Her interest in a career, her excitement about food, is irrelevant if she isn't willing to strive to be at the top of her field. Sam wants to stomp out of the room as if she were a kid, which is how Steven treats her. Their roles are mechanical, a key fitting into a lock. When Chloe died, Sam stopped trying to be friends with Steven. She emerged from the theatre wings, an understudy who took up her sister's role of punishing him, but Sam no longer knows why she bothers. She doesn't need his or her father's approval to do what she wants with her life. While she isn't sure about Steven, Sam knows her father loves her.

The next day Sam goes to see Tory's mother who still lives around the corner. Sam wants to get Tory's phone number. Scrambling for insights, Sam has decided to call her sister's one-time best friend and ask her for her opinion as to whether Chloe's death could have been murder or suicide.

Walking across Mrs. Sharp's lawn, Sam's feet are suddenly wet. She didn't notice the sprinklers, which she guesses go on automatically. While Mrs. Sharp's neighbours have adopted an eco-friendly ethos and are allowing their lawns to brown, Tory's mom keeps hers the colour of fresh limes.

Mrs. Sharp is a tiny woman in her late fifties with a face like a wrinkled apple—a granny doll in the making. She was always rather proper, but when she opens her front door she is wearing a lavender jogging suit with Top-Siders. She must be retired, Sam thinks. Like Sam's father and Steven, she taught for a living. Working in the public school system, she made her way up to the position of high-school principal. She married and divorced twice. Tory is one of several siblings, the product of a "blended" family that Sam and Chloe once envied. Television shows about big families such as the *Brady Bunch* and *Eight Is Enough*, which glossed over the economic realities of hand-me-down clothing and after-school jobs, convinced Sam and Chloe they were missing out by just having each other.

Leading Sam to the den, Mrs. Sharp says, "I'll just go get us some snacks." Sam sits down on a plush, pink loveseat, which faces a widescreen television. Mrs. Sharp is watching the show where friends and neighbours take turns redecorating each other's spare rooms. What is it called? *Invading Spaces?* As far as Sam can tell, the show isn't about picking up interior decorating tips; it is about the voyeuristic *schadenfreude* of watching someone try not to freak out after they have been publicly humiliated.

Mrs. Sharp reappears carrying a platter, which she sets on the large glass coffee table that is crammed between the loveseat and the television. The platter holds chips, blocks of cheese, carrot sticks, and dip. Mrs. Sharp sits down beside Sam, who moves the food so it is positioned between them.

"Oh no, hon, I'm on a diet," Mrs. Sharp says with a delicate shudder. Clicking the television off with a remote, she asks Sam what she is doing with herself these days.

"Living in Montreal."

There is a pause as Mrs. Sharp waits, face quivering expectantly, for Sam to add details about a great job or internship or graduate school. Sam can hardly say she just quit a minimum-wage job as a dishwasher to pursue an ongoing obsession with her sister's death, so she blurts out the purpose of her visit. "I want to get in touch with Tory."

Mrs. Sharp squints as if the sun is in her eyes, but all light has been banished from the room by drawn beige drapes stretching from ceiling to floor. "Tory's married now, although she's kept her own name. She has a daughter. She lives on a farm about an hour and a half outside of the city. She and her husband aren't Amish, but they live like it. They don't use pesticides."

"You mean they're organic farmers?"

Mrs. Sharp grips the television remote, her eyes spraying disapproval like a shower of metal sparks. "They use horses to plough the fields and even travel sometimes by horse and buggy. They plan to home-school their daughter. But can you guess what the great irony of their lives is?"

Like the teacher she was, Mrs. Sharp awaits Sam's response.

"No, Mrs. Sharp, I can't."

"They're economically dependant on the world of technology they oppose. Tory went to school to study dance but wound up taking computer courses. Now she works as a freelance web designer. She does her grocery shopping by horse and carriage, but she has all the latest, fancy-dancy computer equipment. Can you imagine that?" Mrs. Sharp rises from the loveseat, leaving the room in a quick tempo of steps. She soon returns with a pink piece of floral-scented paper, which has Tory's name, address, and phone number scribbled on it. Sam thanks her, then sticks around to eat some of the snack food. The tension produced by bringing up Tory gradually lessens, and Sam leaves with chips and cookies wrapped in tinfoil. She always gets along with people's mothers, makes an extra effort in the hope they might be a mother to her, rub maternal care onto her like moisturizer on dry skin.

On Friday morning Sam drives to the country, exiting off the highway onto a back road where a row of townhouses have sprung up in a field. Last night she called Tory and told her she wanted to talk about Chloe. Tory insisted they meet in person the next day. As if a visit was Sam's idea, Tory added, "Your timing's good. My husband's buying some equipment tomorrow." When Sam was younger, she was bossed around by Tory, who acts as if their relationship is the same. Driving to the farm, Sam wonders why Tory refused to talk about Chloe over the phone. When Sam told her father where she was going, he forgot she had a rental car and offered to let her borrow his and Steven's car, a red Neon with a sunroof and all the right accessories—air conditioning and a compact disc player with more bass than they will ever use. The two of them can afford a larger vehicle, but Sam's father likes to buy new cars. If there is a mechanical failure, he wants the problem to be covered by a warranty. Her father is a control freak. The only reason he lets Sam use his car is because he taught her how to drive. He tried to teach Chloe to drive, but the lessons were so fraught she paid for a driving course. Dad wouldn't let Chloe do more than put her feet on the pedals while he steered and operated the gearshift. Was there any activity Dad and Chloe enjoyed doing together? Ah, yes. The two of them liked buying antiques. On Sunday afternoons, they went to garage sales and flea markets to paw through old furniture. He coached her on periods and styles, taught her how to recognize different types of wood and assess the value of a piece. Sam thinks of the antique furniture she inherited from Chloe, her expensive taste. Romey and Omar both thought Chloe would have clawed her way back to the middle class, and they may be right. Does Romey have these concerns about Sam? She has no idea because Romey never shares her insecurities. Their relationship is passion squared while knowledge and understanding of each other are a smaller quantity, a square root.

Sam checks her directions—she's almost at the farm. An old tobacco-curing shed with worn and broken boards stands in the middle of a field. This was once tobacco country, but most of the current crops are soybeans. Farming is so anachronistic, yet the business is rife with change. Finding the correct address, Sam steers the car up a long and bumpy driveway. A flock of giant birds with cable-thin legs and stomachs the size of bowling balls run alongside her car. Sam wonders what they are until she notices a handmade wooden sign nailed to a tree advertising "Emus for Sale." A field on the other side of the road is filled with tiny spruce and pine trees being grown for the Christmas season. Tory and her husband run a rather eclectic agricultural enterprise—an impression exacerbated when Sam gets out of the car, and Tory hands her a bucket.

"You're late," she says. "You can pick blueberries with us." Tory shared with Chloe a brusqueness, which is unvarnished by time. Tory's goth style, however, has mutated to hippy: her frizzy hair is no longer a testing ground for Manic Panic hair dye but is back to her original shade of well-brewed tea. Her scarves have been discarded, and her droopy, black clothing has been exchanged for a droopy, red skirt and a white T-shirt with the logo "No Logo" printed on the front. She is still thin but two vertical lines indent her forehead, just above each of her eyebrows. A slender girl of about three or four stands at her side. Tory attempts to flatten a stray curl of hair springing from the girl's head. "This is my daughter, Pagan."

"Nice to meet you," Sam says.

Pagan captures her mother's T-shirt with both of her hands and buries her face into the cloth so she doesn't have to look at Sam. How does Pagan manage with her peers?

Tory seems to read Sam's thoughts. "She doesn't meet many new people. I'm planning to home-school her."

"Are you and your partner religious?" Sam spies a spider in her bucket and tips it over, shaking the insect out.

Pagan sticks her head out. "Yuck."

Tory prods her daughter's shoulder. "Spiders are good. They eat other insects that feed on the leaves of our garden." Shifting her attention back to Sam, Tory says, "My husband and I aren't part of a church if that's what you mean. We just try to be as self-sufficient as we can. We heat our house with wood, grow our own vegetables, and generally unplug ourselves from consumer culture."

Behind Tory's yellow brick house lies a narrow, weed-filled path that runs parallel to the lake. The path is bordered by a fence, and, as the three of them walk in single file, Sam hears what sounds like the pounding of hooves. She looks up to see the emus bouncing towards her. They bob and strain their necks through holes in the fence, shaking their shawls of ratty feathers and making rattling noises. Tory and Pagan ignore them so Sam does the same. The path ends in a large patch of earth, which has been planted with cultivated blueberry bushes. When Sam touches the berries, they fall into her hand. Choosing a spot a few feet away from Sam, Tory gathers the berries in a systematic manner from the top of a bush to the bottom. Her daughter picks berries more haphazardly, eating rather than collecting them. When she sticks out a purple tongue, her mother suggests she go off to play. Pagan wanders up the path a few yards.

Tory says, "Judging from your hair, or lack of it, I guess you're a lesbian."

How can Tory just say that to Sam with no preamble whatsoever? People watch too many talk shows. "You guess right."

"Chloe thought you might be."

"Did that bother her?" She was afraid to come out to Chloe, to confront her about what she said about Dyna. Chloe tended to shoot first and ask questions later: what if Chloe said something Sam couldn't forgive?

"Your sister thought you being a lesbian would be one more thing you had in common with your father, one more reason for him to favour you."

Wrong, Sam thinks. Her father was, probably still is, so uptight about being a fag that Sam being queer doesn't work in her favour. Not being queer, Chloe wouldn't understand this. But she obviously worked out that their father was gay long before Sam did.

Tory continues, "I don't think Chloe would have cared you were a lesbian. I know her politics were all over the map, but she was never a prude. Besides, she loved you more than anyone. In the long run, it wouldn't have mattered."

"Yeah?" Sam supposes Tory is right, that Chloe would have accepted Sam bringing a woman home—except maybe if the woman was Romey. Holding onto Tory's words, Sam feels a new and shiny freedom. The mid-morning sun radiating her back is pleasant, not too hot for a change. The bottom of her bucket is now covered in berries, although filling it will take hours. A few of the berries she plucks still cling to the bush. Turning over one such berry, she sees it has a pale green underside. Not quite ripe yet.

Tory says, "So why did you come to talk to me about Chloe? Why now, after all this time?"

Good question. "I got this anonymous postcard suggesting Chloe was killed because she was investigating a political conspiracy. Turns out she *was* investigating a political conspiracy. Something involving a lot of dangerous people."

"About a month before she died, Chloe called me. We hadn't spoken for years. She told me if anything were to happen to her, not to believe it was an accident."

Goosebumps scale Sam's arms despite the heat. Chloe told Francis the same thing. According to him, coincidences in a conspiracy theory are revelations. But Sam is an agnostic, and for her, coincidence is more like a fortune cookie: when you snap open the shell to withdraw the ribbon within, the result can range from banality to profundity. But which does Sam have? She asks Tory if she thinks Chloe could have been murdered.

Tory sets her bucket down and stretches her neck like one of her emus, checking to see what her daughter is up to. Pagan is sitting cross-legged in the middle of the path constructing a tiny hut using sticks and grass; she's an astonishingly well-behaved child. Perhaps she's just cowed by her mother, who waves at her daughter before turning back to Sam. "People like to create conspiracy theories around charismatic figures like Princess Di or Kurt Cobain. I think maybe Chloe thought she deserved a conspiracy theory."

Sam is not sure what Tory is getting at, but it sounds as if she didn't like Chloe very much. "Why did you guys stop being friends anyway?"

Shielding her eyes with her hand, Tory squints up at Sam. "Chloe and James had this fight. They kind of broke up, and I slept with him. Chloe was furious. She told him I had herpes when I didn't. He believed her, or at least that's what I thought at the time. Maybe… maybe he just pretended to." Tory's cheeks, neck, and ears glow pink.

Sam puts a berry into her mouth, tastes wood. Chloe was betrayed in the same way by her two closest girlfriends. She found herself in one triangle of love after another. Even as she changed her life, it had a strange way of repeating itself.

Feeling thirsty, Sam asks Tory where to get water. Tory holds her bucket in the direction of the house. "The door's unlocked. Just go into the kitchen and pour yourself a glass. If you could bring back a pitcher for me and Pagan, that would be great."

Sam walks back along the path. The emus don't pay as much attention to her this time. When she reaches the house, she stares longingly at her car. She wants to get in and drive away but doesn't. It would be rude to leave Tory's place without saying goodbye, and Sam was brought up in a home where good manners are expected.

Sam lies awake in bed. The more people she talks to who were close to Chloe, the more Sam is reminded of the Agatha Christie novel, *Murder on the Orient Express*, where everyone on the train took a turn stabbing the victim. Everyone is the perp, everyone is guilty. Except the people who were part of Chloe's life weren't guilty of murder; they were guilty of hurting her. The knives they stuck into Chloe were metaphorical—*Suicide on the Orient Express*. But then there's the Ecdysis Conspiracy and the postcard and the Hells Angels and Omar. Thinking about all of it is like looking into a kaleidoscope—it keeps shifting, disintegrating into itself. Now you see it, now you don't, now you see something else altogether. Was Chloe killed or did she kill herself? Sam still doesn't know. But she's getting closer. She just needs to unpeel another layer.

PART FOUR
ANSWERS

CHAPTER EIGHTEEN

Summer vacation in Nova Scotia. Snap of the screen door as Chloe and Sam busted out of the rented cabin each morning to race down to the beach. Their father read books and commented on the peacefulness of their surroundings, but for seven-year-old Sam the place was full of adventure. Looking out at the horizon, it seemed to her as if the sky was zooming straight into the ocean. Water shimmered with sunlight she could never seem to touch. She leapt into waves strong enough to hold her aloft and push her to shore. On the shore she found treasures buried beneath the sand: shards of glass bleached and softened by the tides, scrambling crabs, blue-black mussels, and prickly green orbs that turned out to be sea urchins. The wind rising from the water carried the smell of salt, which was cut with the sweetness of the wild roses growing everywhere.

Chloe, at thirteen tottering into adolescence, had another interest: a local boy. His name was Jess and he repaired boats. Every day the girls saw him scraping old paint from a yacht. He was wild-animal beautiful with long tawny hair and golden skin covered only by faded, paint-speckled cut-offs. "He's got such a hot bod," Chloe said. When they walked by, he always waved. Sam waved back, but Chloe pretended not to notice him. Down on the shore Sam searched under rocks in tide pools for tiny crabs while Chloe lay on a towel, tanning, reading romances, and discreetly ogling Jess.

During the month they were there, Chloe left notes for Jess signed "your secret admirer." He usually quit work by mid-afternoon, but Chloe waited for nightfall before creeping onto the boat and searching out places where she could cram her notes. To hold them in place against the breeze blowing off the water, Chloe used rocks and shells. Sam usually came with her sister to keep a lookout. She felt like a spy or how she imagined spies felt: exhilarated, part of a pipeline of something greater than she could ever be on her own. She scanned the harbour as if she were expecting German U-boats rather than what she actually saw: the raw red sun falling into the sea.

Chloe's notes were short, piquant: "I think you're cute," "I would like you to take me out on your boat," and once, "You look good in those shorts." She could have spent her days talking to Jess, but instead she preferred to watch him, to imagine having conversations with him. As she walked with Sam along unpaved roads to the corner store to buy Popsicles, Chloe constructed an entire world of her and Jess, his love and tenderness. She would point out some small shingled house painted a crazy colour, pink or green with yellow trim, and say, "We'll live there. We'll get a dog. I'll work in the city while he fixes boats. At night, he'll hold me in front of the fireplace."

The plan was for Chloe to reveal herself to Jess as the "secret admirer" shortly before they left. She fretted over his being several years older than her; how could she make herself look older? Makeup? High heels? A wig? Where could she get these items? She asked Dad to take her and Sam into the nearest town so they could shop. Their father dumped them off on the largest street with strict instructions to meet him in two hours at the library. They wandered up and down but couldn't find a wig store. Didn't all cities have wig stores? They asked some women who worked at a hair salon and were directed to a Frenchy's, the local equivalent of Goodwill. Bingo. There they found a second-hand blonde wig for ten dollars along with some previously used, grimy green eyeshadow, and a pair of backless spike heels.

Chloe left her last note for Jess. "It is time for me to un-
veil myself to you. If you can meet me here tomorrow at
seven o'clock, take these rocks and spell the word 'yes' beside
the boat." She left him a pile of white stones rubbed smooth
by the tides. The next day she hid inside the rented cabin,
too shy to see him, too scared his response might be laughter, a merciless kick of the stones across the sand. While
being careful not to stare at Jess, Sam went about her usual
activities. She didn't find many crabs, but on the sand she
found a baby jellyfish, a tiny transparent globe too young to
have grown a purple stinger. The sun could dry up the jellyfish, kill it. She waded out into the water with it. Holding the
jellyfish in her cupped hands, she let the waves slosh it away.
The defencelessness of the jellyfish reminded her of her sister. Sam thought, Jess knows it's Chloe. After all, who else
could his admirer be? None of the other tourists were
teenage girls. But Sam also understood Chloe truly believed
he didn't know; her inner world was so powerful she convinced herself it was real.

As soon as she was sure he was gone for the day, Sam
ran down to the boat Jess worked on. He had taken a stick
and carved the letters Y, E, and S into the sand. Huge, jagged
letters like skywriting. Letters everyone could see, letters no
one could miss. The rocks Chloe left were dropped into the
grooves of the letters.

Back inside the cabin, Chloe had locked herself in the
bathroom.

Sam banged on the door. "He said 'yes,' he said 'yes.'"

Chloe opened the door, then went back to viewing herself in the mirror. She was dressed in her cut-offs, a white
blouse with embroidery, and the spike heels. Her freckled
eyelids were smeared with a line of light green. Sam didn't
think her sister looked older or more sophisticated, just like
herself, only with strange footwear.

"Where's the wig?" Sam asked. Surely the wig would transform Chloe, would disguise her. Then Sam glimpsed the wig curled in a ball like a dead thing on top of the closed toilet seat.

Chloe pulled the wig on, shoving her long red hair under it as best she could. The wig was short, and even Sam could see it looked fake. The hair on it was like fishing line, only beige. Chloe was wearing a Halloween costume.

"I'm Jodie Foster in *Taxi Driver*," Chloe said.

"That's good, isn't it?"

Chloe shook her head furiously. "No! She was a child prostitute." She ripped the wig off and flung it onto the floor. "This is totally not going to work. I'm not going."

"But you have to," Sam said.

Chloe balled up some toilet paper and started rubbing off the eyeshadow. "No, I don't." She shut the door in her sister's face.

After supper, Sam asked Dad if she could go out.

He looked up in surprise. "It's started raining."

Right. Sam could hear it patter down. Could see the sequins of rain sticking to the windowpane. But she needed to know if Jess was there. "I left something on the beach. I won't be long."

When Sam got outside, she checked her watch: quarter after seven. She was running late for her mission, which was to prove something to Chloe, but Sam couldn't say what exactly. She crept along the edge of the road, trying to stand in the shadows, but the short fir trees didn't cast very long ones and besides, it was too dark. She should have brought a flashlight. When she got to the part of the embankment leading to the shore, the foghorn blasted, startling her so much she almost fell down. Below, she could make out Jess in the moonlight. He was standing huddled by the boat, trying not to get soaked from the rain. He was wearing jeans and a windbreaker and drinking a beer. There was an opened six-pack beside him. When he finished gulping down his beer, he lifted the bottle over his head and sent it hurtling towards the sea. The bottle smashed on a rock, didn't quite make it into the water, although the tides would tug it in eventually. Sam's father was always tut-tutting about smashed glass. "You kids could get hurt." Jess didn't care about that or about the environment. He was pissed off.

Sam went back to the cabin to tell Chloe Jess showed up. "Guess that's the end of our relationship," Chloe said. She wasn't being sarcastic. In her mind, if not in Sam's, Chloe and Jess had been involved and now it was over. The knowledge that he was interested in her was enough. She would go back to Toronto and tell Tory all about her cute boyfriend. Except it didn't work out that way. Jess didn't follow the scripts of the romances Chloe read, romances she was growing tired of. The next day she didn't read a book but went swimming with Sam. It wasn't a good day for swimming; summer was coming to an end, and the temperature of the air felt cool. The water was still warm from the daily sun, but when they emerged after the first plunge, the breeze chilled their skin. Afterwards, they trudged up to the road and found Jess waiting for them. He was sitting in his parked car, a beat-up Ford Mustang with a rusted underside.

"Chloe," he called. "Want a ride to the store?"

"All right," she said. She looked a little flustered but got into the front seat and gestured to Sam to get into the back.

"No," Jess said. "Just you."

Sam stopped. He was older, so she was afraid to contradict him, even though she felt nervous about Chloe going off with him. Dad always said to never get into the car of a stranger, except Jess wasn't a stranger. They knew him. They watched him every day like their favourite television show.

When Chloe came back from the drive, her face was clenched so tight Sam wondered if her sister had been electrocuted or something. Was she mad, sad, or just stunned? Hard to say. Had Jess known Chloe was the secret admirer? Yes, as soon as she got into the car, he had said, "I know it's you."

Chloe began to cry, silently, so their father wouldn't hear. Her skinny shoulders heaved. "It was just a game, just a game," she sobbed. He believed her notes more than she meant him to. He thought she was in love with him, but she wasn't, she wasn't at all. In fact, when he had said she was, she thought, what an idiot. Doesn't he know I'm too young? But he didn't seem to care about her age. He was big and muscular, he smelled of beer and cigarettes, and he tried to get her to make out with him. He put his hands inside her bikini, inside her. When she started crying, he called her "stuck-up bitch." But he let her out of his car. Made her walk home from the lighthouse where he had taken her.

CHAPTER NINETEEN

Sam has a reservation at the Chelsea Hote,l where her sister died. As Sam is walking into the Chelsea, a man in an undershirt and jogging pants tries to sell her a pamphlet listing all the famous people who have stayed at the hotel. Sam is about to brush past him when she thinks, why not? Why not find out everything she can about the place? After all, it's why she's spent all day driving from Toronto to New York. Digging through her pockets, she finds a crumpled American dollar bill and hands it to the man.

The hotel room is stuffy, so Sam opens a window. She is in New York. She is as close as she can get to her sister's death. Sam paces around, surveying the room as if some crucial piece of evidence will turn up inside a drawer of one of the pieces of chic teak furniture or clinging to the orange carpet fibres. But being here feels as empty as visiting any popular tourist monument.

She picks up the pamphlet. As she begins to read, she realizes why, when she booked the room, a clerk said so chirpily, "You're in luck. We just had a cancellation!" Practically every room has been anointed with celebrity, dating back to Mark Twain. A veritable Who's Who of bohemians have stayed here: Bob Dylan, Jimi Hendrix, and Edie Sedgwick. Andy Warhol and Nico made a film about the Chelsea. Leonard Cohen wrote a song about having a fling here with Janis Joplin. Sid and Nancy were also guests.

Oh my God. Is it possible? Sam digs through her knapsack until she finds the biography of Sid and Nancy. The book is too trashy to have an index, but Sam's suspicions are confirmed when she checks the pictures in the middle. According to a caption beneath a photograph of the hotel she is staying in, Sid stabbed Nancy to death in room one hundred.

Sam spends the next hour skimming the biography, trying to understand the significance this punk confidential had for her sister. A few months after Nancy's death, Sid overdosed. A suicide note was found in his pocket claiming Nancy had asked him to kill her. The pair were so young, almost teenagers, when they died: she was twenty, he was twenty-one. Through a curious mixture of circumstance and desire, they were losers who became celebrities. Sid the famous bass player who could not play bass. Famous for *not* being able to play, for being the embodiment of punk rock. Nancy Spungen, like Edie Sedgwick, like so many women, an icon because of who she fucked, because of what happened to her, rather than for what she achieved. Sid and Nancy's story is a perversion of Romeo and Juliet; they killed each other not because they couldn't be together, but because they *were* together. They are completely unsympathetic. Reading about them, Sam feels ill. For her, there is no romance in death and destruction. She enjoys the irreverence of punk without taking either the movement or music seriously. When she once read that the lead singer of a band called Joy Division hanged himself, she found it ironic, darkly amusing. But Chloe, who died in the Chelsea, would have empathized with singer Ian Curtis rather than distanced herself with humour or anger or disgust. Her stay here wasn't about fandom or melodramatic posturing, or at least that's not all it was. Staying at the Chelsea, Sam thinks, was her sister's suicide note. That is, if someone didn't kill her. But if she invited someone to kill her, as Sid alleged Nancy did, was it suicide or murder?

Everyone around Sam strides with fierce intention while she just drifts, soaking up the city. She's too tired from the drive the day before to start investigating Chloe's last days. Plus it's Sunday; there's not much she can do, so she walks around. She hears a man in front of her refer to a guy who interviewed him for a job as a "bimbo." She sees a kid use a cellphone to yell to another kid half a block away. As the afternoon slips into the evening, she passes bars full of boisterous, energetic people drinking and laughing. If they aren't enjoying themselves, they make a successful hologram of fun.

She takes the subway down to the Lower East Side. Just off St. Mark's Place, she sees a raver boy twirl a glow stick in his fingers as he chats to a slightly older, bald guy who has one foot planted on a skateboard. Their opposing styles, not to mention the calculation that has gone into them, tell Sam they're family. Behind them is a bar, and she wanders in. The space is cute if a little cramped. Exposed brick walls on the sides lead to a small riser at the back where a trio of classically trained musicians are performing disco covers on a cello, a violin, and a flute. Cute girls, who have a gritty, kitsch style Sam likes, hand her flyers for their upcoming events: a drag king show, a burlesque show, and a graphic novel launch. Everyone wants to be an underground star. An evening out holds the promise of better ones—like Russian nesting dolls. Sam orders a beer but leaves before finishing it.

Back at the hotel, she decides to call Romey. Sam last saw Romey on Tuesday morning, only five days ago, but it feels longer, as if a hole has been torn into their time apart. The voice mail on Romey's cell isn't accepting messages. Sam tries her at home. No answer, but her airy greeting, which can be understood by both French and English callers, clicks on: blah, blah, blah, la, la, la. After leaving a gentle sigh, Sam hangs up. She checks the voice mail on her Montreal phone to see if Romey called. She didn't, but there is a message from Amanda proposing a drink. Where is Romey? Gathering a pillow into her hands, Sam considers the possibilities. Romey's back is better so she's picking up shifts to make up for ones lost? She's hanging out with Omar? Romey's friend or not, Sam is going to confront him. But she needs to be prepared, to have all her facts straight, before she puts it to him: what did you do to my sister? Sam strangles the pillow into a tight tube.

CHAPTER TWENTY

After their father took Chloe and Sam to see *Cats* in New York, he critiqued the production, tallying up failures in the direction, the costumes, and the acting. Why, he had seen a better performance in Toronto! To Sam, his incredulity was belied by the smugness glimpsed in the curl of his mouth. He was enjoying himself in his own way. He was asserting the superiority of the city he lived in, proving that a visit to New York was an unnecessary expense. Her father had excellent taste but liked a bargain.

Chloe banged one of her pointy new wave shoes against the sidewalk. "Why do you have to ruin everything? Sam and I enjoyed the show and now you've destroyed it for us."

Sam felt like protesting but didn't want to make Chloe any angrier than she was.

Dad asked, "Why should how I respond to the show affect the pleasure you took in it?" He sounded genuinely baffled.

Chloe marched ahead without answering.

Sam explained, "You made her feel stupid for liking the show." How come she could understand her father and her sister better than they understood each other? She was only ten years old while Chloe was a teenager and Dad was grown up. Weren't people supposed to get smarter as they got older?

"I see," Dad said. He and Sam tailed Chloe discreetly for a block, waiting for her to calm down. At the corner stoplight, Dad put his hand on Chloe's shoulder and asked her what he could do to make her feel better.

She said, "I don't want to go to a restaurant that you've read about in some guidebook. I want to walk in anywhere and let whatever happens, happen." Her proclaimed desire for spontaneity seemed like a prepared speech. She draped her right hand over her eyes and performed a pirouette with her left hand flung into the air. Her black skirt spun out like a cartwheel. When she stopped, her arm was pointed to a restaurant with a sign advertising "Portuguese Home Cooking." She said, "I want to go there."

The restaurant was empty. A house band seared their ears with melancholy songs, which Sam's erudite father identified as Fado music long before it became popular. The smoked sausages tasted and looked as though they had been dug out of the bottom of a fire. Only Chloe finished her plate, but the set of her mouth told Sam her sister hadn't enjoyed it. When Chloe was in the bathroom, Sam muttered, "This place sucks."

Dad winked at Sam. "Don't mention it."

"Why can't we make her happy?" Sam asked. Usually she bonded with Chloe against their father, viewed him as omnipotent, as always having the upper hand in his interactions with his daughters. But at this moment, Sam and her father were united in their supplication to Chloe, were mutually held hostage to her sense of being wronged.

Dad set his chin in his hand, the corners of his mouth sloping. "I don't know, Sam. I just don't know."

CHAPTER TWENTY-ONE

First thing Monday morning Sam calls the New York City police department to ask how she can get a copy of the report on her sister's death. Before Sam left Toronto, she asked her father if he kept the police report. He said, "Are you out of your mind?" The New York police department puts Sam on hold, and then bounces her from one municipal functionary to another, all of whom inform her the request cannot be met; the report was archived, and the protocol for retrieving a copy can take months. One clerk, who seems to take pity on her, suggests Sam try a third-party information provider. Can he recommend a particular company? He can. Sam calls them. For two hundred dollars American, the police report will be faxed to her hotel within twenty-four hours. Thank God for credit cards. Hers has a streaky, worn look to it these days.

Sam calls the Lone Wolf Tattoo guy's friend Wells, who may or may not have been the last person to see her sister alive. Wells isn't surprised by her call—apparently Mark emailed him about her. Wells won't talk about the Ecdysis Conspiracy over the phone but invites her to visit him at his apartment in Brooklyn later in the afternoon. Sam counters by suggesting they meet at a bar. He pauses, then gives her an address in Brooklyn.

"Can you bring the videotape you showed Chloe?" Sam asks.

"The videotape?" He talks as if he has sand in his mouth. Sam isn't sure if it is his Brooklyn accent or a speech impediment.

"Mark said you had a video proving Iraq bought chemical weapons from the Hells Angels." Sam is convinced the video is the one item that will indicate to her whether what her sister was investigating was real or a hoax. People can tell stories, but faking a videotape is too elaborate a ruse for the average paranoid person.

Wells doesn't answer at first. Then he says, "No one's supposed to know about that." He hangs up.

Sam takes the subway to Brooklyn. On her way through the tunnel, she gets déjà vu, which usually gives her a thrill but doesn't this time. She feels as if she is forgetting something important.

The address Wells gives her leads Sam more than a dozen blocks from the subway. Located beneath the on-ramp to the Brooklyn Bridge, she finds a flophouse. It's a three-storey brick building advertising furnished rooms and rooms by the hour. The bottom floor has a bar. Entering it, Sam is blinded by the shift from daylight to twilight created by windows boarded up with Styrofoam. When she can see again, she glances around but doesn't notice anyone waiting for her. Older men, clad in thrift store specials, drink by themselves and in groups, although the men seem solitary even when they sit together. Sam can imagine them in their rooms upstairs, heating up canned food and watching game shows on crappy television sets. Buzzing around the men are two women—fruit flies drawn to softened bananas. One woman is white while the other is Asian, but they have the same torn-up look in their eyes. They guffaw one minute, yell the next, and are dressed in clothes they could have borrowed from teenage daughters. The Asian woman leads a stumbling man out the door, dragging him by the hand as though he were a kid.

Sam wanders to the back of the bar, where she settles on a bar stool and watches the middle-aged bartenders pour foamy pitchers of beer and ring up tabs on an old-fashioned brass cash register. A ceiling fan stirs soupy air smelling of beer, tobacco, and sweat.

"Sam?"

She spins around on her stool. "Yes?"

A pear-shaped man in late middle age stands before her rubbing his hands as if there's a bar of soap between them. His scalp is a salmon dome topped with white bristles, and he's dressed conservatively—grey flannel pants and a navy golf shirt. He is as out of place in the bar as she is. He points to a small table. "I got us seats. What can I get you to drink?"

Sam shrugs. "Whatever's on tap is fine."

He goes over to the bartender while she sits down at the table he indicated. After bumping her foot into something solid, she swings her head under the table and spies a black briefcase. She hopes it contains the videotape.

Wells returns with a glass of water for himself and a half pint of beer for her. He reaches over to pick up a piece of plastic wrap discarded from a cigarette package and accidentally tips her beer. Before all the liquid spills out she manages to grab the glass. He leaps up and insists on retrieving a fresh beer. After getting a wet cloth from the bar, he furiously scrubs the table.

"I'm sorry, I'm sorry, I'm so sorry," he says.

Sam wipes her beer-sloshed hands on her shorts, feeling uncomfortable. He is acting nervous, as if they are on a date. It never crossed her mind when making plans with him that flirtation would be on the menu. She knows she's young, slim, and wearing shorts and a tank top, but her butchness generally renders her either invisible or unappealing to straight men.

Wells raises his glass. "Cheers."

"Cheers." Sam clinks her glass against his, takes a sip.

Without taking a drink, Wells sets down his glass of water. He peers around the bar. "I hope you don't mind the bums and the whores." He rolls the word "whores" in his mouth like a hard candy. He continues, "This bar does a million dollars worth of business in drugs every year. It's owned by the Irish mob."

"Really."

"Yes, really." Wells mocks her tone. His nervousness has dried up. He sticks his face up to hers. His eyes are glass shards, the colour rubbed and indeterminate. "Who are you?"

Sam coerces her lips into a smile. "No one really—an unemployed dishwasher. Who're you?"

Wells draws his head back and places his hands on the edge of the table as if he is planning to push it over. "I'm what they call a spook defector. I was forced out of the agency. Everyone has their secrets, and the agency ferreted out mine to prevent me from spilling theirs. I had hoped your sister would reveal the story behind the Gulf War. I thought she could be the credible whistle-blower that I can't be. Of course, I knew it was dangerous for her. The government and the military don't want citizens to know what a bungle they made of things. When I didn't hear from her, I assumed she had decided not to take the risk. Now I know—the agency killed her."

Sam thinks: everyone who believes my sister was murdered is crazy. Does that make me crazy? But then she remembers what happened to Francis's father. Francis said it is impossible to tell the difference between someone who is paranoid and someone whom the government experimented on. When an unbelievable event occurs, something extending beyond the boundaries of the everyday world, how does a person tell if it is real?

Sam asks, "So what is the story behind the Gulf War?"

In a serious tone, Wells replies, "The president was manipulated by a cabal of businessmen out to protect their own economic interests."

Duh, Sam thinks. "And you believe the CIA killed my sister because she wrote about the Hells Angels selling chemical weapons to Iraq?"

Tapping his index and forefinger on Sam's side of the table, Wells says, "The Angels may have their finger in every narcotics pie in the country but chemical weapons?" He pauses for rhetorical flourish. "Getting the defence industry to sell weapons to organized crime isn't exactly one, two, three. In the former Soviet Union, sure, but in North America? No, what happened is the CIA set everyone up. Cults are an ideal way to incubate ideas and irrational belief systems. They're the perfect cover for foreign spies. The CIA infiltrated the Raelians. A so-called Raelian convert contacted the Angels, claiming to be a former defence industry contractor and offered them access to chemical weapons."

Sam places her elbows on the table like an attentive student in the vain hope she might be able to sort out what he is saying. "Why would the CIA sell weapons to Iraq?"

"Because that's what the shadow CIA wants, the Tergum Corporation. Whenever the CIA conducts an operation it doesn't want Congress to know about, they call Tergum. They're a private security company who protect nuclear facilities, the Alaskan Oil Pipeline, and also carry out the FBI's and CIA's dirty work. A third of Tergum's billions of dollars of annual revenue comes from federal contracts. They're an arm of the government, but they're also war profiteers."

To Sam, his answer makes everything murkier. "Do you have evidence of what you're describing?"

"I have the videotape your sister gave me."

"Wait—I thought it was your videotape?"

"No, it was hers."

"Can I see it?"

"Sure. We can go to my place and you can see it. I live

a few blocks from here."

Sam takes a deep breath. "I would feel more comfortable if I could just borrow it and watch it in my hotel."

Wells stands up. "No problem. We'll go pick it up."

Sam remains in her seat. "If this videotape caused my sister's death, am I in danger?"

"Isn't it a bit late for you to be asking that question?" His lips stretch like loose rubber into a simulation of a smile. He reaches under the table to pick up the black briefcase.

Sam follows Wells along a main street. As he walks, he swings his arms. His stride is fast and rough; he pummels past people while she steps aside. The part of Brooklyn they are in isn't cool or trendy. A laundromat is just a place to do your laundry; you can't buy espresso there or surf the web. They pass Polish delicatessens, bars, liquor stores. It is just after six, so some of the businesses are pulling steel shutters over their display windows. It is as if the store owners have to put their entire operation into a safety deposit box.

Sam almost trips over a teenage girl and boy draped along the sidewalk. She stops to apologize, but the boy waves his hand in slow motion, "Forget about it." His eyes are black rings: he's a junkie with smack shimmying through his veins. He is so young, much younger than Sam. She hurries to catch up to Wells.

Wells is unlocking the front door of a walk-up. She is surprised—she expected him to live somewhere nicer. He holds the door open for her, and she climbs up a steep flight of stairs, then steps back to let him unlock the door. She tells herself she isn't going to go inside. She stands in the doorway while he disappears from her sight. Sam peeks in. There is hardly any furniture, and what is there is mismatched and looks as if it was dragged in from the street. There are a couple of chairs, a table, and a white laminate bookcase. The floors are covered in two distinctly different carpet remnants. Nests of cracks have formed in the plaster walls. Either Wells doesn't actually live here or he is more low-rent than he presents himself. From the back of the apartment, Sam hears him grunt as if he is in pain. Is he being sick? She steps inside and peers down the hall—she can't see him. She calls, "Are you all right?"

There is no answer. She is reluctant to enter, so she examines the books crammed into the bookshelf beside the door. Her unease is increased by the titles she reads on the spines. Wells has a collection of paperbacks on the occult and true crime. There are also how-to books on magic, hypnosis, and the manipulation of people.

At the sound of footsteps, she glances up. Wells is back, wearing black leather gloves. In his left hand he holds an electric kettle with steam pouring from the spout.

"Would you like tea?" he asks. His tone is gracious and unruffled as if everything is normal.

Sam lunges towards the door but pain halts her movement. She twists around and watches in astonishment as the skin on the back of her bare legs peels open as if she has been shot. In fact, she has been burned—Wells dashed boiling water from the kettle onto her skin. Blood rises to the surface of her wounds. She reaches for the door again, but Wells throws the kettle down and tackles her, pitching her onto the floor. He rolls her onto her back; his arms are wires holding her in place. She struggles but is no match for him. He shoves his gloved hand into her mouth.

"If you make noise, I'm going to get a knife from the kitchen, cut you into little pieces, and put you out with the garbage."

His calm tone frightens Sam more than the threat. He can control who witnesses the storm in his head. Horror whistles through her body. She feels dumb. This man is going to kill her, and it's her fault for coming into his lair.

He takes his hand out of her mouth and pats the cavities of her armpits, her belly, and her thighs. "Just tell me who you really are, who you work for," he croons.

"I told you. My name is Sam. I don't work for anyone. I used to wash dishes at a restaurant in Montreal."

"You think you're so smart. Sam has long blonde hair." Tugging the short hair above Sam's right ear, Wells bends Sam's head sideways like a doll. "Did you think I wasn't going to ask Mark what you looked like? I'm nobody's fool."

Sam tries to think. Maybe he won't hurt her. Is he just afraid she wants to harm him? Her body doesn't believe it. She tries to speak but is out of breath because she's hyperventilating. She squeaks, "Check my wallet. There's my ID. Mark got me confused with a friend of mine."

Wells sucks on his lips as if he is considering her explanation. Then he unclips her wallet from the chain she is wearing and studies her identification. As he tosses her wallet onto the floor, her credit card slides out. "Could be a clever forgery."

Sam is fucked. He is going to kill her. "Did you kill my sister?"

"No, that bitch pulled a revolver on me. But I was smarter with you, I made sure you didn't have a gun." He hits her cheek, then backhands the other.

Ripple of pain in her jaw. She swallows. She can't overpower him so her mind runs through other programs: make him talk, figure out what he wants, try and give it to him. "Why did my sister pull a gun on you?"

"Because she was a terrorist under command of her Arab boyfriend. She was no patriot; she was a stateless nomad helping him get rich. Filthy rich. Her boyfriend brokered the deal with Iraq for the Hells Angels. They're clannish; they only deal with their own. But you know all about that, don't you?"

"Chloe broke up with her boyfriend." If Sam enters into his fantasy, can she get him to believe her?

He runs his gloved hand over her scalp. "She was tricky. She did everything he said. She was like all Muslim women, obedient. She did his bidding, just like I'm going to make you do mine." He reaches into his pocket to take out a lighter, and Sam stops thinking. He holds the flame from the lighter under her chin the way a person might hold a butter-cup. She can feel the heat and her skin tingles. He lets the flame climb upwards. At first she feels nothing, then agony. Wells leans over and blows air on her face. "Fire is a chemical reaction that needs three ingredients for it to occur. Do you know what they are?"

Sam gulps. Knowledge from a high-school chemistry class floods into her head. Oxygen, the air she is struggling to breathe. Heat, which is created by friction—a spark will do. Fuel, which is anything combustible: wood, paper, her. She smells singed flesh. Hers. She remembers to scream, and he jams his hand back into her mouth. She gags. Being afraid of what will come next is worse than the pain. Being bent to another's will is the worst of all. Some part of her disappears, leaving behind a rind of rage and fear and shame. She has never felt so many things so thickly. She holds up her hands to make him stop, and he takes his knuckles out of her mouth.

"There's no video," she says. She touches her chin, and her fingers come away dotted with blood.

"It's in a safe place," he replies.

Liar. Bastard. Psycho.

His lower body anchors her in place while he manoeu-vres sideways to get at his briefcase. At the sound of a snap, she twists her head around. The briefcase has been popped open, revealing a blowtorch. He picks it up, raises it over her head as if he is going to hit her with it, then lowers it so it is level with her eyes. The torch is shaped like a gun with a brass tube, a metal handle, and a trigger. He is going to weld her, braze her, melt her skin away.

"It's a gas torch." His breath on her face inflames her burned chin. "It uses pure oxygen instead of air to create a higher temperature flame. I can make you tell me the truth." He stares at her with his tongue poking between his lips as if he can barely contain it in his mouth. Beneath his pants, his penis twitches against her crotch. He might rape her. Rape happens to lots of women—guess it's her turn. After all, she gripped her sister's dangerous life. Sam realizes she holds two contradictory beliefs wound together like an Ouroboros: she will never be harmed and she deserves to be harmed.

He lifts the strap of her tank top, and she wrenches herself away from him. She kicks her leg against his bookshelf, and books collide onto the floor, falling on them. His grasp loosens, and she slides out from under him. The torch rolls from his hand onto the floor. Picking up the torch, Sam throws it at a front window. Glass cracks, shatters onto the floor.

"Bitch," he screams and dashes over to the window.

Before he can turn and catch her, Sam kicks books out of her way and opens the door. He runs back, breathing hard, and grabs at her. She whirls around and punches the door closed against his hand, and then bolts down the stairs. When she hits the street, she looks over her shoulder. He's jogging after her.

Screaming for help, she enters a corner store. Around her people's mouths move like goldfish nuzzling the glass of an aquarium. She ignores them and heads to the back of the store. Wells doesn't follow her inside. Instead he stands in front of the window looking at her. She paces back and forth in front of the fridge, dodging out of the way of patrons taking out cartons of milk and bottles of beer. An Asian man working at the counter stares at her for a moment before turning back to serve the line of customers. After a little while, Sam walks up to him and asks if she can use the phone.

He squints. "What for?"

She's not sure. Should she ask him to dial 911? But she doesn't require an ambulance and might have to pay for emergency services. "I need to call a cab."

He flaps his hand in the direction of the door. "Go outside."

She swallows. Stares out the window. Notices Wells has disappeared. But what if she sees him? Her mind repeats her fear like a chorus: what if I see him?

She follows a group of young men out of the store. Tucks herself beside the door so she can get back inside if she needs to. A customer entering the store blasts his annoyance at her while she looks around. Where has Wells gone? Not seeing him, wondering if he's preparing a trap for her, is almost as frightening as having him chase her. Cabs amble by and her hand lifts. One slows down to double-park in front of the store. As Sam dashes over to the vehicle, Wells's face flits through her peripheral vision. Turning her head, she sees him standing at the entrance of his apartment, watching her. She bangs into the open door of the cab, nearly falling, but manages to climb into the back seat. Through a glass partition, she gives the driver the coordinates of her hotel. He nods but doesn't seem to be paying attention. As he speeds past other cars and turns down streets without bothering to signal, he carries on hostile dialogues with the other drivers, even going so far as to invent their responses. Mental illness is everywhere.

As the cab crosses the Brooklyn Bridge, Sam wonders if she should tell the driver to take her to a police station. But what would she tell the police? She went into the house of a strange man she just met who claimed to be a former employee of the CIA? They would lock her in a psych ward. Blaming her burns on aliens would be easier—at least that way, she could join a support group. She laughs but feels a spasm of tears swelling beneath her mirth. She wants to go home.

Shit. Wells has her wallet. She has no money. She has money in her bank account, of course, but her debit card is gone.

She knocks on the window behind the driver's neck. When he stops at the next light, he slides the glass open.

"I'm sorry, but I have no money. Someone stole my wallet."

The cab balks. While cars whiz around them honking their horns, the cab driver gets out in the middle of the street and opens her door. He spits on the ground. "Get the fuck out of here."

The cab driver has dumped Sam in Manhattan. She asks a woman who looks like a college student for a subway token. The woman's face constricts. Reluctantly, she draws out a token. Sam looks down and sees her leg is bleeding.

When she gets to her hotel room, she discovers someone has slipped a manila envelope under the door of her room. She picks the envelope up from the floor and sets it on the night table. Then she opens the mini-bar and takes out a bottle of whisky. Retrieving a glass from the bathroom, she pours herself some of the whisky, then leaves her room to collect ice from the machine down the hall. Dropping some of the ice into her drink, she gulps it down. She doesn't want to get drunk; she just wants to feel less scared.

She goes into the bathroom to clean her burns as best as she can. Wrapping up the remaining ice into a T-shirt, she gets into bed and places the compress under her legs. Then she opens the envelope and reads the contents of the fax she ordered. The cubes in her drink snap and crackle.

The first paragraph of the police report is euphemistic. The decedent was observed unresponsive inside room 211 of the Chelsea Hotel on 222 West Twenty-Third Street on a date almost exactly five years earlier. Chloe was found dressed in brown corduroy pants and a black T-shirt. Her clothes were wet with blood. Wet—meaning liquid in enough quantity to dye clothes. Sam hobbles to her feet and runs to the toilet. She retches but nothing comes up.

She leaves the bathroom. Picks the report up from the floor and tears it in half with shaking hands. What is she trying to prove? She doesn't know anything about science or forensics. She can't argue that the trajectory of the bullet makes a finding of suicide impossible. Standing over a trash can, she rips the pages into smaller and smaller pieces. For reasons she can't explain, she doesn't want anyone else to see the report. When she finishes tearing it up, she sits on the edge of the bed and dials Romey's cell. Still no answer. Sam hangs up. What is she going to do? She has no way of paying for the hotel. She doesn't want to call her father. She has too much pride, and he will blame her. Sam already feels like what happened is her fault, which is more than enough for her. Lying back on the bed, she starts to bawl. Her nose runs, but she doesn't bother to get a tissue. Tears pool into her earlobes.

Someone bangs against the wall, yelling, "Shut up in there."

She stops wailing, breathes from her stomach the way some earth muffin once taught her. When she is a little calmer, she remembers her passport is in the glove compartment of the car—she will be able to get through the border. She goes through the pockets of all of her clothes and manages to find a twenty dollar American bill and a Canadian ten. Gas money. After stuffing her clothes into her knapsack, she retrieves her hair gel and toothbrush from the bathroom. She calls Romey again, this time at home. When her voice mail finishes playing, Sam leaves a message. "Hi Romey, this is Sam. I'm in New York, but I'm leaving for Montreal tonight. I'm not doing too well. Some guy tried to kill me this afternoon. I'm not trying to get you to feel for sorry for me. I just had to tell someone. I really don't want you to feel sorry for me."

She hauls her knapsack onto her back and leaves the hotel. Getting into the car, she drives away as fast as she can. Wells has her wallet, but worse he has taken the Ecdysis Conspiracy away from her and the possibility for heroics it gave her. Is he the one who sent her the postcard? He and Mark seem to have the greatest investment in the conspiracy, except how would they have known about Sam's existence? How did they track her down? Of course one can find a lot of information on the Internet, but, if that's the case, the note could just as equally be random, sent by a conspiracy buff who wound facts, data, and speculation into a narrative. Who knows? Does she care? Not really. Caring is beyond her. She isn't angry or depressed, or at least not as she has ever experienced it. She is empty, a chant breathed out of someone else's mouth.

Around dawn, after Sam passes the border into Canada, she stops at one of the gas stations designed for truckers, parks the car, and sleeps for what winds up being ten hours. Her burns throb, waking her at intervals, so she is conscious of her dreams. She is a snake. She slithers through a desert, a place where heat offers no comfort, light administers no clarity, and stillness provides no peace. The desolation doesn't matter; she is just a snake. A predator, except suddenly she is prey. Something is after her. Something with holes in its face, light and dust where there should be eyes. She tries to run but has no legs. All she has to get away is the movement of her flesh.

When she wakes up, her fear diminishes only to be replaced by more fear. Some guy tried to kill her. While trying to find out what happened to Chloe, Sam almost died. She touches the back of her leg, feels a crust of skin and blood. She remembers reading that one of the Boston Strangler's victims answered the door by saying, "How do I know you're not the Boston Strangler?" Going into Well's apartment was so fucking stupid. But all along Sam has been stupid. Only now has she stitched enough information together to answer the question of how her sister died. The Ecdysis Conspiracy is real—it just isn't what Sam thought it was. Chloe's Ecdysis Conspiracy is "fuck you" and "pay attention to me." The only question Sam has left is: who was in on it?

Around mid-afternoon Sam arrives in Montreal, drives over to St. Laurent Boulevard, and parks half a block away from the entrance to Omar's escort agency. She is going to make Omar tell her once and for all what he has been hiding. The problem is he doesn't think he owes Sam shit. She has no moves left but settles for what worked in her first meeting with him: ambush.

She doesn't want to be blocked from his office by his receptionist, so she decides to wait for him to leave the building. Anxiety has cannibalized her hunger, but she wishes she could get a coffee. Unfortunately, her money was spent on gas. Would Romey give Sam a loan until she gets another bank card? Maybe. If Sam can find her.

The sun swims through the windshield, heating up the black upholstery covering the front seats. Afternoon merges into evening. Sam listens to the radio, flipping the dial, stopping frequently at McGill University's radio station. A show comes on in which a man insists the CIA were involved in the Gulf War on the side of Iraq while his female partner scoffs—Scully and Mulder decking it out.

He says, "This is real. It was reported in mainstream magazines like *Forbes* and *The New York Times*. A bank in the United States gave five billion dollars to Iraq during the Gulf War. The government blamed it on rogue operators, who were later prosecuted, but the media and Federal Reserve officials claimed the government was lying because it wouldn't be possible for a bank to do a transaction of that size to a foreign government in the Middle East without government knowledge. The CIA had to have authorized the loan."

The coincidence of this news item with the recent events in Sam's life is odd, but she doesn't care. She is so over the Gulf War.

Just as rush hour is ending, Omar strolls down the stairs of his building accompanied by a mannequin wearing a spandex dress barely covering her ass. He chivalrously opens the passenger door of his car for his escort, then walks around and gets into the driver's seat. Not bothering to gear up gradually, he roars onto a main boulevard.

Sam tails them. Yesterday she was the quarry, today she is the hunter. This morning she was on the run; now she is chasing someone. She likes the feeling. I'm in control, she whispers. She is lying. She has never been so out of control.

Because she is being careful not to be seen by him, she almost misses Omar's turn off onto a highway. But he's tooling around in his chrome car, so she spots him. Surveillance of the image-conscious is not too difficult. Sam wonders if he watches gangster movies. Probably. After all, she watches movies straight people make about lesbians.

She tries to keep behind Omar by about four cars, but the perilous driving style of commuters keeps dumping her further away from him. After ten minutes of being convinced she will lose him, she tracks him off an exit onto another major street. A red light allows her to tag him again, and she follows him up another street, where he drives into a motel parking lot. By ducking into a gas station, she manages to wheel around and double back while he is parking his car. She parks the rental car just outside the lobby, even though she could get towed or get a ticket. But, compared to her reckless plan, such concerns are minor. She gets out of the car and surveys the motel, a line of grim, grey bunkers with a solitary front door and no back patio. The dwellings wind in a C-shape along a slope overlooking a snarl of highways. There are no neon signs boasting pools or luxury rooms or even colour televisions. Everything about the place is temporary, a means to an end.

Sam jogs to the back of the motel. At the end of the lot she finds Omar's vehicle parked sideways in front of a Harley-Davidson motorcycle. He and the escort must be visiting a biker, an Angel. Sam's plan is unfolding like destiny. She is scared, which makes her hyper alert, although the volume on all of her senses has been punched up. Whatever common sense she has is overridden by her ragged need to put an end to her investigation into her sister's life and death. She walks up to the door of the last motel room and bangs on it. There is a sound of scrambling feet, but no one opens the door. She pounds again.

The door stretches the length of a gold chain lock. The escort pokes a wigged blonde head out. "*C'est qui ça?*"

Sam stands on her tiptoes, trying to peer over the woman. Standing behind her is an enormous white man wearing wraparound sunglasses. Huge muscles squish out of his tattooed arms. The front and top of his head are bald, but a ginger braid hangs down his chest like a tail. He is holding a gun, not pointing it at Sam exactly, but letting her know he has it.

Her mouth goes dry. She tries and fails to gather spit. She calls out to Omar. "It's Sam. I need to talk to you."

"Shit." Omar squeezes past the biker and the escort to undo the chain lock. "What the fuck are you doing here? We thought you were *les flics* or worse."

"You bragged to Chloe about the Hells Angels. You told her..."

Omar grabs Sam, puts her in a headlock, and starts to drag her away from the motel room. She bites his hand like a girl, like a sissy. Omar has a high pain threshold; he doesn't move his palm an inch. To the biker, he says, "This drama is personal." After the man closes the door of the motel room, Omar moves his hand from Sam's mouth.

He says, "I did that to protect you, you know. What the hell were you doing, pulling up my file in front of that guy?"

Sam rubs her mouth. "I want you to talk to me."

Omar snorts. "You're licked. Romey says I should apologize to you, but you're not making it easy. Do you know that?" He begins to walk away from Sam. "C'mon, get into my car."

She stumbles after him. The city is sprawled below them. She can see the river and churches and duplexes and triplexes. She can hear cars and trucks rumble by on the highways. Omar opens the door of his car for her and she climbs in. He glances at his watch, and she wonders if he has to be somewhere soon.

He waves his arm in an expansive gesture. "Okay, talk to me." Taking a pack of cigarettes out of his front pocket, he lights one.

Sam feels her heart pop, then freeze. "I think you told my sister some stuff about the Hells Angels, and she told some other people. I don't know whether or not the Hells Angels brokered a deal with Iraq to buy chemical weapons from the American government, and I don't really care."

Smoke steals out from between Omar's lips. "I never told her any fucked up shit about a conspiracy theory, but I told her more about the brotherhood than I should have. I've learned since then to keep secrets from the people I care about. I don't do anyone a favour by telling the truth, do you understand?"

Looking into his eyes, Sam says, "Yeah, I do. But can you tell me the truth about one thing? My father told everyone Chloe died of an overdose, but you knew there was a gun involved."

Omar's smile dissolves, water poured over sugar. "That's what this is all about?"

"Didn't Romey tell you?"

He shakes his head.

Sam feels glad. It would be nice to think loyalty and consideration for her kept Romey from saying anything to Omar. Sam continues, "You see, I've been wondering just how far my sister was prepared to go to make her death into, well, something larger than life. Did she talk you into a suicide pact, into shooting her?"

His eyes on hers are a whorl of fire and pain. "I didn't pull the trigger. I didn't put her in the boneyard that way. But she called me from New York. On the day she died I got two messages from her on my pager. When I called her back a few hours later, the clerk who answered the phone told me that the woman I wanted to talk to had shot herself. I don't know if she called to say goodbye. I don't know if I could have talked her out of it. Believe me, I've asked myself that question more times than I can count. But mostly I think, if her death had a message for me, it was 'fuck you, I can kill myself better than you can.'" Omar takes a last drag on his cigarette before pinching it out with his fingers. "Is that real enough for you?"

Sam slowly nods. Adrenaline streams from her body. "You're right, Omar. My sister's suicide was a fuck you. I think the conspiracy theory was more of a fantasy than anything else. Chloe was pretty good at creating fantasy worlds. She wanted people to remember her, to wonder what happened to her, so she told her friends who believed in conspiracy theories not to believe her death was an accident. She created her own myth just like her teenage heroines, Sid and Nancy. She was mad at everyone: you, Romey, my parents, my father's boyfriend Steven, her used-to-be best friend Tory, not to mention a creep named Wells, whom she threatened with a gun. I was probably the one person she wasn't mad at. But she didn't leave a note because the way she staged her death was the last word."

Omar rubs his eyes with his fists. Sam realizes he is wiping away tears.

He says, "She was the opposite of me, but underneath we were alike. Neither of us wanted the life we were living. I never had the guts to do what she did, so I tried to find someone else to do it for me. A guy I'm friends with now once waved a gun in my face, and I laughed. I was a reckless son of a bitch because I had no feelings for me or for anyone. It was like there was this big hole inside of me. I couldn't fight, steal, bang enough dope to fill it. Chloe was empty the same way. Except, she made me not feel so empty—until she left me."

"She left me, too," Sam says. All the anger and hate she felt towards him disappears, as they sit together sharing their grief. Suddenly everything Sam feels about Chloe's death seems to shrink into smaller, more manageable feelings.

Omar says, "Romey wants to get back together with you."

Sam says, "She does?"

EPILOGUE

Sam hurries along the cobblestone streets of Old Montreal. A horse-drawn carriage holding middle-aged tourists swathed in blankets rattles by. The sky is a grey, streaky colour prophesying snow: this will be her first winter in Montreal. She takes out her new cell, pushes a button.

Romey answers on the first ring. "Hey babe. Are you coming home soon?"

"Yeah, now. The wine tasting lecture took a little longer than I expected." The lecture was an extracurricular event, recommended but not mandatory for the program Sam is currently enrolled in at a culinary institute. She takes classes five hours a day, five days a week. Her classes are in French, which is difficult, but a few things help. Her teachers are mostly from France, and their enunciation is easier to follow. There are also a lot of physical demonstrations, so she has a context from which to pick out words. Besides French, she is learning to master the distinctions between braising, grilling, sautéeing, and roasting. She dislikes having to cook meat, but it is a necessary compromise. Her pastry class, where she transforms dough into bread and brioches, is preferable. She has a natural flair for artful presentation.

Romey says, "I can't wait. I hardly get to see you any-more." Weekends, Sam works at Le Lapin Blanc, where they were happy to hire her back.

Romey continues, "By the way, I think we should call the dog 'Felony.' He stole some Gorgonzola cheese from the counter today."

Sam laughs. She and Romey have just adopted a half-starved, wretched-looking dog from the Humane Society. He has short little legs and a huge head. Romey thinks he might be a Chihuahua mixed with a Labrador retriever. Not an obvious combination, but then neither is Sam and Romey.

A beeping sound comes on the line, and Romey says, "I think that's my uncle. I got to talk to him. We're looking at a property tomorrow." She has this plan that she and Sam are going to buy a triplex. Romey keeps having meetings with her various male relatives to discuss mutual funds, tax breaks, and what types of buildings are good investments.

"See you soon," Sam says. "I love you." She grins into the phone. She is, as they say, *bien dans sa peau*.

The streets of Old Montreal are glutted with expensive restaurants, and Sam stops in front of one a teacher has praised; the food here is "*exotique*," by which he means novel, exciting. Sam reads the menu shielded in glass beside the door: there is smoked duck with apples, curried tempura prawns, grapefruit Pernod sorbet. Interesting selections, but there are no vegetarian options and nothing is organic. Inside the darkened window, Sam catches sight of two patrons whose faces, illuminated by a flicker of candlelight, she recognizes.

She draws closer to the window. Omar is more dressed up than she has ever seen him as is his beautiful date—Amanda. She is clad in a slinky dress with spaghetti straps. Her blonde hair is pinned into a chignon, and her neck is bent to the side as if to indicate a vulnerability she does not, as far as Sam knows, possess. As the waiter sets down two elaborately designed plates of food, Amanda's fingers lift from Omar's arm. Before gliding off, the waiter tops up their glasses of wine. Sam ducks back from the window as it dawns on her how dangerous it could be if they see her.

Fuck, Sam thinks. Sometimes there is no such thing as a coincidence, and this is one of those times. When he guessed

Amanda's life was a cover, Francis was right, even if he didn't know what she is, even if Sam still isn't sure who or what Amanda is. Omar's lover, obviously. But is she also investigating Omar? Sam remembers Amanda saying, "Whoever's the last possible person I should want, that's who I'm doing." As Sam struggles to piece the information together, she remembers something else. The anonymous postcard about Chloe was postmarked from Mexico, and Amanda's passport was stamped Mexico. At the time, Sam didn't think of the fact as a coincidence. She didn't think anything of the fact. But now she realizes Amanda sent the postcard, sent Sam on her mission. *How often do women kill themselves with a gun?* It would take a woman, or a cop, or both, to notice that detail.

As she walks away from the restaurant, the wind from the nearby river tears at her face. Did Amanda kill Chloe? Or did she, like Sam, just want to find out what happened? That's more likely. But Sam isn't sure she wants to know what Amanda was up to, why she, like Sam, borrowed Chloe's life. This is a game of hide-and-seek best abandoned.

Wondering about the name of the conspiracy, Sam read up on the process of ecdysis. Somehow she was sure Chloe came up with the name; she was always good at that sort of thing. Sam discovered that, along with skin, the snake discards its protective eye covering. When a snake loses its skin, its eyes turn milky and it becomes almost blind.

Acknowledgements: I would like to thank my agent, Margaret Hart, my official editor, Gillian Rodgerson, and my unofficial editor, Claude Lalumière. For comments on an earlier draft, I would like to thank Angel Beyde; for assistance with proofreading, I would like to thank Neil Smith, Elise Moser, Fred Holtz, and Susan Holtz.